Richard Madeley was born in 1956. He worked on local newspapers before moving to the BBC. He met Judy Finnigan when they both presented a news programme on Granada TV. Their eponymous TV show ran for seven years and was an enormous success. His first book, *Fathers & Sons*, is a moving account of three generations of the Madeley family. Richard has four children and lives in London and Cornwall.

THE WAY YOU LOOK TONIGHT

Not until she was sixteen did Stella Arnold learn the full truth about her father — how handsome, charming James turned out to be a cold-blooded extortionist, racketeer . . . and killer. Knowing now what he was capable of, and fascinated by the dark backwaters of the human psyche, Stella pursues a degree in psychology. A doctorate at a top American university beckons: the chance to delve further into the mind of a psychopath — and to ascertain if such tendencies can be inherited . . . So in the late summer of 1962, Stella takes a plane to Boston. Bright, beautiful and fashionably English, she dazzles everyone she meets, including the Kennedy brothers. But far away, in the sweltering Florida Keys, a scene of terror is unfolding — and Stella is drawn to investigate a murderer even more ruthless than her own father . . .

Books by Richard Madeley
Published by Ulverscroft:

FATHERS & SONS
SOME DAY I'LL FIND YOU

RICHARD MADELEY

THE WAY YOU LOOK TONIGHT

Complete and Unabridged

CHARNWOOD
Leicester

First published in Great Britain in 2014 by
Simon & Schuster UK Ltd
A CBS Company
London

First Charnwood Edition
published 2016
by arrangement with
Simon & Schuster UK Ltd
A CBS Company
London

A catalogue record for this book is available
from the British Library.

ISBN 978–1–4448–2706–4

Published by
F. A. Thorpe (Publishing)
Anstey, Leicestershire

Set by Words & Graphics Ltd.
Anstey, Leicestershire
Printed and bound in Great Britain by
T. J. International Ltd., Padstow, Cornwall

This book is printed on acid-free paper

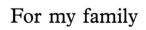

For my family

And after all her furious sound
The stillness of her face
The quiet of her sleep, tonight

Prologue

He looked out across the velvet darkness of the Gulf, the tiny breakers that had begun as confident waves a thousand miles to the west off the coast of Mexico now dying exhaustedly at his feet. Without a hurricane to resurrect them, they were as good as finished once they reached the shallows of the Florida Keys. But to give them their due, he thought, there was more life in these pathetic ripples than in the girl whose body moved slowly back and forward in their gentle sway.

He reproached himself on only two counts. One was that she had died so quickly; much more quickly than he had intended. He put it down to nerves. She was his first, after all.

The other — and this surprised him more than anything — was that despite his meticulous planning, the rehearsals and preparations for unexpected outcomes and interruptions, he had overlooked one of the most basic questions of all.

What to do with the knife afterwards.

He squatted patiently for a while, considering the matter, humming to himself and untroubled by concern about discovery. No one came out to the mangroves at this, the darkest hour of the night.

The solution, when it presented itself, was so obvious that he wondered why it hadn't occurred to him before.

He gripped the bone handle of the knife as tightly as he could and thrust its long blade vertically into one of the girl's eye-sockets. It was seemingly a random choice, but he noted that he had instinctively favoured the left one.

He washed the blood from his hands in the warm lapping waters of the Gulf and nodded to the dead girl as he stood, ready to leave, her song sung.

Her last gift to him had been to reveal what his signature would be.

PART ONE

PART ONE

1

She couldn't believe it. Her plane had taken off forty minutes earlier but only now did she realise she'd left her cigarettes behind in London Airport's first-class lounge. Her gold lighter, too, a twenty-first birthday present from her grandfather.

She turned towards the window to her left and deliberately knocked her forehead against it in frustration. She was seated ahead of the airliner's wings but if she craned her neck and looked behind her she could see two of its massive propellers whirling in shining arcs. They, and their twins on the other side of the plane, were carrying her towards Massachusetts at an impressive 350 mph, but it would still be at least eleven hours before they landed in Boston. She simply *had* to get hold of some cigarettes before then; she was tense enough as it was. She'd never flown before.

'Is everything all right, madam?' It was a BOAC stewardess, very young and all lipstick, high heels, nylons, dark-blue uniform and a hat that the girl looking at her decided was somewhere between sweet and silly. She supposed it was a sort of forage cap, an echo of the post-war military-style uniforms the airline had only recently and belatedly moved away from. You could hardly expect the poor girls to carry on dressing up as if they were in the RAF.

All four of the stewardesses on board wore them, perched above navy tunics, white blouses and pencil skirts. She thought the overall effect rather chic, despite the eccentric headwear.

'No, not really,' she said. 'I've gone and left my cigarettes behind. I'm gasping for one.'

The stewardess nodded sympathetically. 'I'll bet. I just put one out. Couldn't do this job without my twenty little friends.' She reached into her shoulder bag and pulled out a freshly opened packet. 'Here, have some of mine.' She shook out a few. 'They're menthol — I hope that's all right.'

The other woman gratefully accepted the cigarettes and jammed one of them between her lips. 'Forgot my lighter, too,' she said, indistinctly.

The stewardess laughed. 'Something tells me this is your first time in the air.' She produced a petrol lighter and flicked the top back, holding the wavering flame to the cigarette.

'Thanks . . . got it . . . yes, it is my first time. How can you tell?'

'From your face during take-off, mostly. You couldn't decide if you were thrilled or terrified.'

The stewardess sank into the empty aisle-seat beside her. 'These awful stilettos. I forgot my low heels and my feet are killing me already. I'll have ankles like balloons by the time we get to Boston.'

She lit a fresh cigarette for herself. 'I shouldn't, really. We're only supposed to smoke in our breaks but there's hardly anyone in first class today.' She waved at the rows of wide, mostly empty seats around them. 'Only a couple of others and they're asleep already with their eye-masks on. Just little you for us to take care of. You'll be feeling like the Queen by the time we're landing. Now, I know from the passenger manifest that you're Miss S. Arnold. What does the 'S' stand for?'

'Stella.'

'Ah . . . and I'm Cassandra.' She extended a slim hand. 'How d'you do?'

'How do you do yourself . . . Cassandra. Wasn't she the Greek goddess who knew everything?'

'Sort of. She wasn't a goddess, she was a prophet, but yes, all her predictions were spot-on. She even predicted the fall of Troy but her curse was that no one ever believed a thing she said. She went mad in the end.'

'You'd better not tell me we're on our way to America, then — I won't believe you and you'll go barmy.'

The two of them laughed, and smoked side by side in silence for a while. Stella turned to look out of the window at the Welsh valleys slowly rolling underneath them. Up ahead beyond the nose-cone, she thought she could catch a glint of sea.

'You were right — about take-off, I mean,' she said eventually. 'What threw me off a bit was all the noise. These planes make an awful racket getting into the air, don't they?'

The stewardess nodded. 'It's because they're prop-planes. Funnily enough, the new jets are supposed to be much quieter, as well as a lot

7

faster. Not that I'd know. Not been in one yet.'
She turned to face Stella. 'So, you're flying
alone, then. What are you up to in Boston?'

'Nothing,' Stella replied. 'Not in Boston, I
mean. I'm not staying there. I'm going on to
Northampton. It's an hour or so by car.'

'Northampton? They do love their English
names over there, don't they? I hope it's nicer
than our Northampton. I went there once to see
a boyfriend. Never again. Complete dump.
What's the Massachusetts version got to offer?'

Stella smiled. 'An education. I'm taking my
PhD there. At Smith College.'

The stewardess's eyes widened. 'Wow. I've
heard of Smith, all right. You must be terrifically
bright, Stella. Smith is one of the top women's
universities in America, isn't it?'

'Well, yes, it is,' Stella admitted, 'along with
places like Bryn Mawr in Pennsylvania, and
Vassar down in New York State. But I really
wanted to go to Smith; we had an exchange
student from there at my university who roomed
with me for a term. She made it sound
absolutely wonderful. I was incredibly lucky to
get in.'

Cassandra eyed her closely as she drew on her
cigarette. 'Oxbridge girl, are you?'

'Yes, Cambridge; same college as my mother
went to. Girton. Actually, she's Professor of
Modern Politics there now. Girton's rather like
Smith — it's an all-woman stronghold.'

'Where you got a first, I'll bet.'

Stella looked slightly embarrassed. 'Well . . . a
double-first, actually. In Psychology.'

8

Cassandra threw her hands in the air in mock alarm. 'Heavens, I should stop talking to you at once, then. You probably know far too much about me already; all my secrets, all my vices. You psychologists can read anyone like a book, can't you?'

Stella laughed. 'No! It's not like that, honestly! And I'm not a psychologist. I only have a degree in the subject.'

'Hmm . . . yes, well. I shall be on my guard all the same, all the way to Boston.' She took another draw on her cigarette and looked curiously at the girl next to her.

'So what's your PhD going to be in, then? Something exciting, I hope. Mad people? Murderers? You know, like that chap in *Psycho*. The film, a couple of years ago. What was his name?'

'Norman Bates.'

'That's it!' Cassandra clapped her hands and ash sprinkled onto the front of her blouse. '*Dammit* . . . So,' she continued, carefully flicking the debris away, 'are you studying the kind of stuff that was in that film?'

Stella nodded reluctantly. 'Sort of. Well, yes, I suppose. I want to focus on psychopathy. But most psychopaths aren't anything like Norman Bates, you know, and anyway he had split personality disorder as well. All very muddled. But psychopaths hardly ever kill anyone. They're defined by . . . ' Stella paused. 'Sorry, I don't want to get all technical.'

Cassandra smiled thinly at her. 'Don't worry. I may be a trolley-dolly but I'm quite bright myself, actually.'

9

Stella flushed. 'Sorry,' she said again. 'Well . . . psychopaths generally find it impossible to empathise — you know, connect with other people, put themselves in their shoes. That's why they can often seem unfeeling, even cruel.'

'Perhaps that's because they are unfeeling and cruel,' Cassandra said drily. 'Sounds a pretty good description of Norman Bates to me. But how did you get interested in this kind of stuff?'

The thick grey curtain separating the first-class compartment from the rest of the cabin was drawn briskly aside and another stewardess pushed through. She was older than her colleague and looked at her beadily.

'Oh. So you're in here, Cassandra,' she said crisply. 'You're needed in the galley. The captain says we should try and get dinner served as soon as possible this evening; he's had reports of turbulence a couple of hours ahead of us.'

Stella's eyes widened slightly but the woman smiled down at her and shook her head. 'Nothing to worry about, madam. Turbulence is perfectly normal. Think of it as a patch of choppy sea. We just don't want our passengers spilling their gravy all over themselves.'

Stella's new friend had already discreetly stubbed out her cigarette in the ashtray that was built into the seat's arm-rest, and now she stood up. 'Duty calls. Would you like a drink before dinner, madam?' A touch of formality had returned now a colleague was present. The woman was clearly Cassandra's senior.

'Definitely. And if it's going to be a bumpy night on my first flight, you can make it a *very* large gin and tonic.'

'Certainly, madam.' Stella thought she caught the ghost of a wink from Cassandra.

As the two stewardesses left, Stella turned to look back out of the window.

They were moving out across the sea now.

★   ★   ★

She slept after dinner and when she woke again the plane was far out over the Atlantic. It seemed to her to be chasing a setting sun that was almost motionless, a dull-red disc loitering lazily just above the horizon, going down in its own good time and refusing to be hurried. It was the most reluctant sunset she had ever seen.

So far there was no sign of the predicted turbulence.

The only other first-class passengers — a middle-aged American businessman with a crew-cut and wearing a loud checked suit, sitting across the aisle from an elderly woman wearing wing-tipped glasses and a hat with artificial cherries pinned to it — were awake now, both writing busily on light-blue airmail paper that, to save weight, was almost transparently thin. Stella reached into her bag and pulled out the last such letter she had received from Boston, only three days before.

Dearest Stella
  We are so looking forward to meeting
you in person on Thursday. We feel we
almost know you already from your letters!

11

Naturally your mother told us a great deal about you when she stayed with us during her attachment to Smith last year. She showed us photos of you, of course — you look so alike, you could be sisters!

Everyone here is very excited about having an English student in our midst and we have so much planned for you after you've had a few days to recover from your flight. Jeb says when he last flew back from London his plane had to land in Iceland to refuel because of the headwinds. He says you must be flying on a DC7 or suchlike to be able to make it across the pond in one hop. I told him I wouldn't know my DC7 from my H2O!

Anyway, we have a week or two before you start your first semester at Smith. You must stay with us at the house for as long as you want before moving into your rooms on campus. As you'll discover, our place in Bancroft Road is just a stone's throw from the college grounds — it's right across from Elm, not more than two minutes' walk from our front porch. Maybe you'll decide to stay with us here permanently. You'd be very welcome.

I know you want to do some studying before term and that's fine but you must have some fun too, Stella! Jeb and I kissed our professorships goodbye for the summer weeks ago and have no intention of going anywhere near our departments again until the last possible minute. Jeb keeps saying

*'Smith's STILL out for summer' and it is,
even though it's September now. We and
Sylvia, who is only a year younger than
you, are going to just LOVE showing you
round Massachusetts and Maine, and New
England generally. We're holding back the
fall, just for you!*

*In fact, this Sunday we plan to drive
down to Martha's Vineyard, which remains
full of folks clinging on to their vacation.
We've all been invited to a barbecue on
the beach — a private beach, of course —
and I'm told on good authority that among
the guests will be —*

For what seemed like the hundredth time since
receiving the letter, Stella read the names that
followed. Her head swam slightly. The idea that
she might see, shake hands with, perhaps even
speak to the family her generous hostess in
Northampton so casually mentioned here
. . . the mere thought made her more nervous
and excited than she had been during take-off
earlier.

Cassandra materialised in the seat next to her.
'Enjoy your dinner? What did you have?'

'The Beef Stroganoff. Yes, it was delicious,
thank you.'

The stewardess nodded towards the blue
airmail letter.

'Writing or reading?'

'Reading. It's from the family I'll be staying
with to begin with, the Rockfairs. They both
lecture at Smith. My mother stayed with them

13

last year when she was a visiting professor there.'

Stella gestured to the letter. 'This is telling me about their plans for the weekend.' She hesitated before continuing. 'It seems we're going to a private beach barbecue in Martha's Vineyard this Sunday.'

Cassandra's mouth fell open. 'Martha's Vineyard? My goodness, you'll be mixing with America's *crème de la crème*, my dear. Martha's Vineyard is where anyone who's anyone goes for the summer. It's a millionaires' playground. Lucky you! Do you know who else is going? Anyone I might have read about in the newspapers?'

Stella nodded. 'Yes, actually, I do know who will be there. In fact you generally see something or other about them in the papers every other day.'

The stewardess's mouth opened wider before she prompted: 'Go on then! Who? Who is it?'

Stella took a deep breath.

'I probably shouldn't be telling you this but . . . well . . . it's the Kennedys. Bobby Kennedy and his wife Ethel and their children, and according to this — ' The thin sheet of paper crackled as Stella waved it in the air — 'Bobby's brother JFK might actually be there too. The President! With Jackie! I don't know who I'll be more terrified of meeting — him, or her.'

Cassandra gaped at her. The stewardess seemed to be struggling for words, before she finally managed:

'Well, you can fly me to Timbuktu!'

2

Stella was disappointed that she hadn't had the chance to explain to Cassandra why she had chosen to study psychopathy. For some reason she would have been comfortable confiding in the young stewardess.

Most people were curious to know why she had chosen to follow such a challenging path, especially as a woman. Psychology and psychiatry were still overwhelmingly a male preserve. But things were slowly changing, and anyway the science of the mind was becoming increasingly fashionable. Reflex suspicion of 'trick cyclists' was fading as the bright new decade got underway. Many were willing to accept and even embrace a discipline that their parents had dismissed as being little more than witchcraft.

It was true that Hitchcock's 1960 film *Psycho* had a lot to do with changed perceptions. When it was released two years earlier, Stella was one of the first in the queue to see it at the cinema in Cambridge.

She had thought it crude and rather silly in its jumbled, sensationalised depiction of certain clinically recognised mental conditions. But, she reflected, as her plane droned on through the gathering Atlantic darkness, Hitchcock had certainly put psychopathy on the map.

Her own private interest in this extreme

15

corner of the human zoo was anything but modish. Stella had been fascinated by the dark backwaters of the human psyche for years; ever since she was ten, in fact.

Because long before Hitchcock's fictional motel-owner had become a byword for murderous depravity, she had encountered a real-life psychopath of her own.

He was, like Bates, superficially charming, persuasive, and credible.

Like Bates, he was extraordinarily dangerous.

He was Stella's father.

★   ★   ★

'Three hours to go!'

Stella jumped as the air stewardess flopped back down into the seat next to her.

'Sorry, dear. Did I startle you?'

'A bit,' Stella admitted. 'I was miles away.'

'Penny for them?'

Stella hesitated. She'd read about this syndrome somewhere recently; the compulsion to unburden oneself to a fellow passenger, a complete stranger, on a long flight — particularly at night. Cassandra wasn't a passenger but she was a girl of about Stella's age and she was bright and friendly. Her uniform gave her a touch of authority, too, and even her name added a certain distinction. Suddenly Stella laughed to herself.

'Seer and instant therapist,' she muttered under her breath.

'Come again?'

'Instant therapist,' she repeated, more distinctly. 'I read an article the other day saying that strangers tell each other all sorts of private things on aeroplanes. It's something to do with a journey into the unknown, and the fact that when you're up here, you're sort of . . . well, nowhere. I think the headline was 'Instant In-Flight Therapy', something like that, and I was just thinking — '

'That I'm your therapist! How funny, considering, you know, what *your* degree is in . . . but it's true, people do tend to open up between continents at twenty thousand feet.'

Cassandra leaned her head conspiratorially towards Stella's. 'We see all sorts of heart-to-hearts going on between passengers who've only just met. The other night coming back from New York I found myself virtually taking confession from a man who told me he'd been cheating on his wife.'

Stella laughed. 'Oh, I don't have any admissions like that,' she replied. 'I don't even have a boyfriend to cheat on.'

'Watch out for JFK at the barbecue on Sunday, then.' They both laughed.

The stewardess lit two cigarettes and handed one to the girl next to her. 'So what is it you want to tell me? Don't worry. I'm good at keeping secrets. Anyway, no one believes what I tell them. I'm Cassandra, remember?' She smiled.

Stella paused. She didn't *have* to do this . . . suddenly, she made her decision.

'All right,' she said. 'It's just that, before, you

17

were asking how I became interested in the human mind ... but we were interrupted by your boss — she *is* your boss, isn't she?'

'The Wicked Witch of the West? Oh yes. She's been on my back all night. Says I forgot my comfy shoes on purpose so I could swank about in heels. As if! I'll be hobbling for days ... anyway, go on. I think you're the first woman psychologist or psychiatrist or whatever you are that I've ever met.'

Stella sighed. 'I told you, I'm neither ... well, not yet, anyway. I just study the field. But as to why I chose to do that ... the honest truth, I suppose, is that I was scared into it.'

The air stewardess tucked her legs comfortably underneath her. 'Really? Who by?'

'My father. Or rather, what he was ... what he did.' Stella hesitated again. Maybe this wasn't such a good idea.

But Cassandra's next remark could have been no clearer sign for her to continue. 'I never knew mine — my father, I mean. He was killed in the war. Went to sea to sink German submarines before I was born but they sank him first.'

Stella stared at her. 'How extraordinary! My father died in the war before I was born, too. He was a fighter pilot. He was shot down and killed over France.'

Cassandra arched her perfectly pencilled eyebrows. 'Then how could he have scared you into anything? I don't understand.'

'Because he wasn't killed at all. He certainly vanished — but the RAF jumped to completely the wrong conclusion: missing, presumed dead.

18

'In fact he bailed out of his aircraft just before it crashed, and promptly deserted — spirited himself down to the south of France and was never heard of again. Well, not for ages, that is. My mother eventually remarried and, as fate would have it, we went to live with my stepfather near Nice.'

The air stewardess gave a knowing nod. 'Oh, don't tell me. One day out of the blue you — '

'Bumped into my father. Yes. Or rather, my mother did first. She . . . well . . . she had an affair with him, to be honest, a very brief one, before she discovered he was a gangster — a killer, too. He ran a really vicious protection racket in Nice.'

'Wow. This is one hell of a story, Stella. You should write the book.'

'Maybe one day I will. Anyway, to cut a long story short, my father tried to extort money from my mother. When she wouldn't play ball, he tracked me down. I knew him the moment I set eyes on him.'

'How? You'd never met him!' Cassandra suddenly put a finger to her lips and got to her feet. 'Hang on, Stella: don't answer that question before I fetch us both a drink. This is so fascinating that I reckon we're in gin and tonic territory now for sure.'

She vanished to her galley and returned with two brimming glasses.

'Cheers. Right. Continue.'

Stella sipped her drink. 'I recognised him from the photo I'd kept on my bedside table since I was tiny. Obviously my mother put it there so I'd know who my father was, what he looked like. He was so handsome, Cassandra, in his RAF uniform. The picture was taken about a month before he was shot down but when I saw him in the flesh ten years later, he'd barely changed.'

The stewardess stared at her. 'My God. You must have thought you were seeing a ghost.'

Stella gave a short laugh. 'Some ghost. The bastard kidnapped me — his own daughter. I was held for two days in a grotty flat before my grandfather, my mother's father, flew down from London with the ransom. Then we went straight back home to England and I never saw my father again.'

Stella looked out of her window at the blackness outside and for a while neither of them spoke. Eventually Cassandra ventured: 'That's an incredible story, Stella, but forgive me . . . I can't quite make out how this awful man forced you to study psychology.'

Stella turned to face her new friend. 'He didn't, not directly. But a few years later, when I was sixteen, my mother sat me down and told me everything she knew about him. How before the war he'd seduced her and manipulated her and lied to get her to fall for him and marry him . . . then in Nice years later he admitted to her that he was only ever interested in her father's money . . . and she told me the terrible things he'd done on the Riviera, about the people he'd killed, or had had killed . . . he was an absolute monster. A true psychopath. Charming on the outside, empty and cold as ice on the inside. And as dangerous as they come. That was my father.'

20

Stella closed her eyes. 'The thing is, Cassandra, I began to become fixated on the idea that psychopathy might be passed on in some way. That I might have inherited it from my father . . . even my grandfather. A psychological ambush from both sides of the family, as it were.'

Cassandra blinked. 'Your father, yes, I can sort of understand that. But your *grandf*ather? Why? Is he psychopathic too?'

Stella shook her head quickly. 'God no. He's a wonderful man. Kind and generous and funny. But he has certain . . . capabilities. Something frightful happened the night the ransom was paid, and we left Nice at dawn the next morning. But I can't say any more.'

For the first time, the air stewardess reached for Stella's hand, and squeezed it reassuringly. 'Of course not. Families must keep their secrets. You've told me a packet already. But I don't understand your fears for yourself.' She smiled. 'You're obviously not crackers, Stella.'

The other smiled thinly in return. 'Really? How can you be sure? Psychopaths like my father can be very good at concealing their true natures. For all you know, I'm a charming killer, like him.'

'Rot. But finish your story. Why did you decide to study psychology?'

Stella took a long swallow of her drink before answering.

'Know thine enemy,' she said at last. 'I realised the best way of laying my fears to rest was to confront them. And what's that old Greek

21

proverb? 'Know thyself.' The more I learned about psychology and the human mind, the more I gradually became reassured that I was within the bounds of what might be loosely described as normal. Of course I'm not a psychopath. But I'll tell you this, Cassandra — I've become *fascinated* by them.'

Stella gently stirred her gin with the silver swizzle-stick Cassandra had put in it along with ice and lemon. 'They're nothing like you and me, you know,' she continued after a pause, 'nothing at all. They're like creatures from a parallel world; human, yet not in the least human. When I get to Smith, my project will be to research if people are born psychopaths, or if they become so as they grow up. You know, the nature-versus-nurture thing.'

Cassandra slowly finished her own drink before speaking again. 'And what's your current assessment of the question? Your best guess, as it were?'

Stella shook her head. 'There's no place for gut instinct in science. But if I allowed myself that luxury, I'd say . . . ' She turned back to the now total darkness outside the window. When she spoke again, it was with her face still averted. 'I'd say they come straight from Hell.'

3

The battered Ford pickup most probably belonged to her boyfriend, he decided. Miami Dolphins bumper stickers and a tangle of fishing gear in the back made it obvious that she was using a guy's car.

He'd been parked up all morning outside one of the brand-new Kmarts, keeping an eye open for the peaches — he'd thought of them as peaches as long as he could remember — when he saw her pull in to one of the green-shaded parking lots kept back for employees, and jump down from the cabin.

She looked exactly like a college girl should, he thought — high-top sneakers, blue pleated skirt, short-sleeved white cotton blouse. Bubble-gum lipstick and long blonde hair pulled back in a ponytail.

Likely enough, Kmart had given her a summer vacation job. And, when he strolled into the supermarket ten minutes behind her, there she was sitting at one of the checkouts, smiling at a customer as she gave change.

He'd tracked her easily since then. She lived with her parents and brother in a pink-and-white clapboard one-storey conch house. It was on a quiet street just off the Overseas Highway, the road that ran all the way down from Miami and across arching bridges linking the islands of the Keys, right down to Southernmost Point on the

23

last one in the chain, Key West.

Gumbo Limbo Drive lay on the Atlantic side of Key Largo, and as he drove past the house, he caught glimpses of sparkling ocean between palms and bougainvillea-covered porches.

Now he figured it was the brother's car she drove to work each day. There didn't seem to be any special guy hanging around; he'd followed her on her dates and all of them turned out to be with girlfriends.

He was ready.

★   ★   ★

That afternoon he had deliberately queued at her aisle in the store, so she could be the one to sell him the knife he'd just picked out especially for her. He thought that was pretty neat. He almost laughed when she smiled up at him and asked if he would be using it for fishing or hunting, but he managed to hold it together. Jesus, it was fucking funny though.

Things had gone much better this, his second time. She'd lasted twice as long as the first one and she'd made some really exciting noises, pretty loud ones, too. He was far enough down the little-used salt creek for that not to matter and anyway the skiff he'd stolen was fairly high-sided, so most of her racket was diverted straight up into the night sky. The noise of the drumming of her heels against the deck had transferred straight down into the water. No one but him was any the wiser.

And when it was over, only he could hear her

special song, the verse he would always sing to them when it was done.

He was annoyed that the newspapers hadn't reported his personal sign-off after the first one, but to be fair to them the cops had probably held it back. Some dumb cat-and-mouse game or other. But he had the feeling that this time they'd want everyone to know about his signature. It showed that he was no random killer and the cops would get that now, however stupid they were. The papers, too; they loved that kind of angle.

And you had to admit it — as signatures went, this one looked pretty damn cool, even if it was going to cost him a fortune in knives. He bought only the best; he felt he owed them that.

He took one last look at her as he prepared to slip out of the boat and begin wading back up the channel. But he knew that the image, striking though it was, would begin to fade soon enough.

Next time he'd make sure to bring a camera.

4

'That's not a car, Professor Rockfair. That's a big boat on wheels.'

The woman standing beside Stella in Logan Airport's passenger pick-up zone laughed.

'It's a Lincoln Continental Convertible, my dear, Jeb's pride and joy, especially since he heard that President Kennedy took delivery of exactly the same model last month for his official motorcades. With the top down like that it *does* have the look of a motor-launch, I agree. But it's such a lovely day we thought you'd like the sun on your face and the wind in your hair on the drive back home.'

Jeb Rockfair was carefully nosing the gleaming silver open-topped sedan into the parking bay. Once he was satisfied, he looked up and gave them both the A-OK circle of forefinger and thumb.

'Welcome to New England, Stella,' he called to her. 'Hop in! I know it's a bit of a squeeze, but we'll manage somehow.'

Stella giggled. 'I've never seen a car as big as this in my whole life. Oh my goodness! The doors are on backwards!'

Jeb had opened the rear door closest to the kerb. 'Yup. The back doors swing open towards the front. Neat, huh? Just like the old stagecoaches. Let me get your bags for you.'

'Thank you, Professor.'

Jeb Rockfair glanced meaningfully towards his wife as he swung Stella's two suitcases into the trunk. 'She been calling you that too?'

'She certainly has, ever since the arrivals hall.'

'Right.' He ushered Stella into the back of the car and got behind the wheel, his wife sliding onto the leather-covered bench seat beside him.

'Now see here, Stella,' he said, once he'd started the engine and pulled out onto the airport's exit lane. 'Dorothy and I don't have many Rockfair rules but here's one you'll break again at your peril. No 'professor' this or 'professor' that from here on in, OK? It's Jeb and Dorothy, period. I mean, Jeez, were you planning on calling our daughter 'Miss Sylvia'?'

Stella gave a passable imitation of the Queen. 'Neow, it was going to be Miss Rockfair, eactually,' she said in a nasal, clipped tone. Her hosts roared with laughter.

'You're a chip off the old block — that's just the kind of stunt your mother might pull!' Jeb said when he'd caught his breath. 'You're quite the mimic, Stella . . . Dottie, we're in the presence of royalty! The Queen of England is in the back of our sedan! How'd you learn to do that, honey?'

'Oh, almost anybody can do the Queen,' Stella said, beginning to enjoy herself. 'It's easy, I'll show you. What do you breathe?'

'Huh?'

'Come on, it's simple. What do you breathe?

'OK . . . air,' they replied together.

'And what's on top of your head?'

'Hair.' Dorothy started to laugh. 'I think I can

27

see where this is going, but then I do lecture in linguistics.'

'One more,' said Stella. 'A fox hides in its . . . ?'

'Lair!' Jeb shouted after a moment, as he signalled right onto the freeway out of town.

'Right. Put them all together and what do you get? One, two, three . . . '

'Air-hair-lair!'

'Which is how the Queen says: 'Oh, hello',' Stella finished. 'See? I told you it was easy.'

Dorothy Rockfair clapped her hands and looked over her shoulder at Stella, her eyes sparkling.

'You know what, honey? Sylvia is going to just *love* you.'

★　★　★

Stella was surprised at how comfortable she felt with her hosts, so soon after meeting them. Of course, she'd heard this about Americans. Everyone knew they had a God-given talent for relaxed, easy friendliness. But she hadn't expected things to go quite so swimmingly from the start; the Rockfairs were, she knew, a sophisticated, intellectual couple. She was a senior member of the faculty at Smith and he was a respected historian, author of weighty but best-selling books on nineteenth-century America. Jeb was considered an expert on slavery, the American Civil War, and President Lincoln.

They were utterly unlike the professors she'd

28

known at Cambridge. Her glamorous and beautiful mother was the exception that proved the rule: most of the dons and academics they knew shared the same dusty, desiccated air, along with the dusty and desiccated clothes that they affected to wear. And how ponderously they carried their academic titles and their learning! Some of her lecturers at Girton were incapable of holding a conversation about anything outside their narrow fields of expertise.

'Walking, talking cobwebs,' was her mother's usual description.

The Rockfairs could hardly be more different. For a start, they had undeniable glamour. Dorothy wasn't exactly what you might call beautiful, Stella decided, but she certainly drew the eye. When Stella had passed from the baggage hall into the arrivals terminal earlier, she had spotted her hostess at once: tall and slim, with beautifully cut auburn hair feathered close to her face, and wearing black slacks pushed into ski-boots. She held a dark green ski jacket draped over one shoulder. Stella thought Dorothy Rockfair looked like a secret agent in a Hollywood spy thriller.

For some reason, her husband reminded Stella of what she imagined a newspaper editor might look like. Strong jaw, already darkened by four o'clock shadow (it was barely past midday), glossy black hair oiled back in a classic short-back-and-sides, and wearing a crisp, white tailored shirt tucked into well-pressed silver-grey trousers. The matching jacket — he'd called it a 'coat' when he slipped it off earlier while they

29

had stopped at a red light — was now neatly folded on the back seat next to Stella, and it looked suspiciously like pure silk to her. Jeb had rolled his shirtsleeves back to the elbows. Muscles in tanned forearms flexed as he steered the car towards Northampton. She decided he played a lot of tennis.

Stella suddenly remembered her mother telling her that, when she was staying with her hosts the year before, Jeb had been invited at short notice on to one of the USA's most popular entertainment television programmes, *The Ed Sullivan Show*.

'It's basically a variety programme, Stella,' Diana explained. 'Not at all the place you'd expect to see a distinguished Professor of History pop up. Anyway, they were doing a daft musical number based on Abraham Lincoln and afterwards Ed Sullivan did a jokey interview with Jeb, as a leading expert on Lincoln's life. He — Jeb, I mean — was *hilarious*. Extremely dry and witty. Dorothy and I watched it from home; we were so nervous for him we were drinking neat bourbon, but we needn't have worried. We raised our glasses to the TV when it was over and cheered. I remember telling her you'd *never* get Jeb's British equivalent to do something like that here. Can you imagine Dr Woodman from Girton going on *Sunday Night at the London Palladium* and larking about with Bruce Forsyth? You could hardly conceive of a more bizarre, unlikely scenario, could you? It doesn't bear thinking about.'

The Lincoln suddenly dipped into a deep

30

pothole. There was a sharp thump and groaning of suspension, and Stella gave a faint yelp of surprise.

'Hey, all right in the back there?'

'Yes, fine thanks — sorry, I was just startled out of a daydream. Where are we?'

Dorothy waved expansively at the rolling farmland and woods on either side of the road.

'God's own land — the sweetest countryside in the whole of America. I was born on a farm here so I should know.'

'You're right, it's lovely,' agreed Stella. 'I've been thinking how pretty and prosperous-looking it all is since we got out of Boston. Sort of like a patchwork quilt, lots of different-sized fields and meadows and beautiful old trees everywhere. It reminds me of that film, *A Connecticut Yankee in King Arthur's Court*. I hadn't expected America to look so . . . well, quaint and old-fashioned. What kind of farm did you grow up on, Dorothy?'

'You can take your pick around here — we've got all sorts in Massachusetts. Horse ranches, cattle farms, fruit orchards . . . but I was brought up on one of those.' She pointed to a green meadow where what appeared to be a red-painted barn on wheels was slowly scything down vast swathes of long grass.

'My dad made hay; made hay while the sun shone, you could say, on glorious days just like this . . . I used to sit on the back of his combine harvester like that one over there and read my books. He'd look round at me and say: 'Little girl, don't you get enough of those at school?'

31

and I'd smile back at him. I knew he knew I'd never be a farmer's wife, not that he cared either way. He just wanted me to be happy. So God knows how I ended up with this long drink of charged water here.' She poked her husband affectionately in the ribs.

'Hey, don't dig the driver! Anyway, she asked where we are, not where you come from.'

Jeb spoke over his shoulder to Stella. 'We're about three-quarters of the way there — it's only a hundred miles or so from Boston to Northampton, and Smith. This is Interstate 90, the Massachusetts Turnpike. See that bridge up ahead? That takes us over the Connecticut River. It used to be called the Great River — flows all the way down from Quebec up north and if you jumped on a raft here, you'd eventually be spat out into Long Island Sound. One way to get to see New York, huh?' He slowed down as they approached a toll station, fumbling inside an ashtray.

'Damn! Where's my change?'

Dorothy looked slightly hunted. 'Er . . . I took it for cigarettes at the airport, Jeb. I left my purse at home again.'

'Great. You *always* do this.' He turned as they pulled up at the barrier and looked round sheepishly at Stella.

'Sorry to ask for a cash loan, so soon after making your acquaintance, but I don't suppose you have any quarters on you, do you, honey?'

Stella nodded, enjoying his discomfiture. For some reason she felt an irresistible urge to tease him.

'Yes, actually, I do. My mother found some in a drawer yesterday and gave them to me just before I left.' She pursed her lips, making an elaborate show of considering the matter. 'But you'll have to sing for them first.'

'What the — you're *kidding*. What exactly do I have to sing?'

' 'Buddy, Can You Spare a Dime', please. Any verse will do.'

Jeb stared at her a moment and then turned gloomily to his wife. 'Can you imagine what she'll be like when she teams up with Sylvia? My life won't be worth a damn. Can't we just drop her off at the YWCA?'

The driver behind them honked his horn and Stella jingled the coins in one hand.

'Do you want these quarters or don't you?'

Jeb cleared his throat.

5

He had to drive north all the way up Route 1, as far as Coral Gables, to get the one he wanted.

It was the 900 series. They'd only been in the stores for a year or so. None of the photographic outlets in the Keys had them yet and he didn't want any of the outdated models the salesmen there had done their best to foist on him.

Like the knives he chose, only the best would do for his peaches.

He would have gone the day before, but Thursdays were his college nights and there wouldn't be time between finishing work and his class to get to Coral Gables and back. He could have skipped that week's lecture but they were studying Paradise Lost this term and he fucking loved Milton and his take on Lucifer and Adam and Eve. Fucking loved it. Others in his class were moaning that it was too obscure and boring but he didn't know what the hell they were talking about. He'd read the whole thing in under a week and was now reading it for the second time. He'd already started writing his 3,000 word review of it and planned to ask his tutor if he could go over by maybe 500 words or so. There was just so much to say. The thing was a goddamned masterpiece.

The Polaroid came with a free pack of film but he bought two more to be on the safe side. As soon as he got back to the parking lot he took the camera out of its cardboard box and inserted the double roll of film — one for recording the images, the other for instantly starting to develop them. He'd never held a Polaroid before. It was much heavier than a regular camera. He still couldn't quite believe that it would simultaneously take and develop pictures.

He wasn't sure what to photograph for the test shots but in the end he snapped off some frames of his '61 Dodge Dart. God, he loved that car, with its concave aluminium grill and fabulous elongated fins at the back above the huge rear fender. No wonder Miami-Dade police had chosen the new Dodges for their fleet of highway patrol cars. The sedans looked pretty cool in their official black-and-white county livery but he preferred the dark-red paint job on his limited-issue Dart Phoenix, with the long tapering gold-and-cream flashes down the sides that he had carefully sprayed on himself. They were meant to suggest the Florida sky at sunset.

A few minutes later he was inspecting his photographs with a kind of wonder: he'd never been dumb enough to believe in miracles, not like his mother with her holy water and rosary and Hail Marys. None of that crap had stopped his father from running out on her when she'd been pregnant with the only kid she'd ever have. Her prayers hadn't brought the bastard back, either.

But the near-instant images he was holding in his hands seemed to him to be possessed by a kind of magic. He knew it was down to basic, classroom chemistry but all the same he felt an

35

almost primitive superstition pricking his blood as he gazed at pictures he had conjured up moments earlier out of thin air. And when he suddenly remembered what the next subject in his viewfinder would be, that very night, his hands trembled slightly and there was a metallic dryness in his mouth. The prospect of being able to review his achievements, immediately, any time he liked, made him briefly dizzy with excitement.

But there was another reason for buying the camera. The papers had AGAIN failed to mention his signature on the second girl, just like there'd been no description of the first. The cops HAD to be holding out on the press; the news guys wouldn't be able to resist a juicy titbit like that. The headline would write itself, for Chrissakes. The words practically danced in front of him now:

'EYE-SOCKET SLAYINGS.'

Screw the cops, tonight he'd take two pictures — one for him, and one for the funnies. He'd send the photo to the Keys Courier. They'd be most likely to run it — they were in deadly competition with the more cautious Miami Herald. The Courier wouldn't be able to resist such a shocking exclusive, and they'd wire-syndicate it across the country for a small fortune once they'd broken the story for themselves first.

In forty-eight hours from now he'd be a fucking star from coast to coast.

He tossed the camera and photos onto the passenger seat and got behind the wheel. As he fired the Dodge up, he began to laugh softly. He'd just thought of another headline, perfect for the Courier:

'LOCAL BOY MAKES GOOD.'

6

Dear mother,

Isn't Bancroft Road gorgeous? What a house. I love the hardwood floors with rugs strewn everywhere, and that big sea-chest taking pride of place in what they call 'the great room', with those tall windows letting all the light in, and that huge open fireplace sunk into the centre of the floor. (I know it's corny, but so much of what I see here reminds me of American films, and the living room with its split-level floors and sunken fireplace reminds me of the ski lodge in 'White Christmas'. You know, where Bing Crosby kisses Rosemary Clooney in front of the fire and sings 'Counting Your Blessings'!)

Did you know that this house is known as a Colonial Revival Home? I had to look it up in the library here (imagine having a house big enough for your own private library) and apparently no sooner did the New Englanders get their independence than they began harking back to the days they were a British colony. This kind of white-painted wood-framed house with its screened porch and shuttered storm windows is a throwback to those days. The streets are full of them.

Stella tossed her pen aside. She could finish her letter home later, when she got back from the barbecue. She climbed off her bed and went into her bathroom. Time to inspect the damage from yesterday.

Stella looked balefully at her reflection in the bathroom mirror. She was furious with herself. She'd spent *far* too long on the porch the previous afternoon, gossiping with Sylvia and writing letters home, and had scarcely noticed that the Massachusetts sun had swung clear of the balcony above her to shine fully on her unprotected face. By the time she woke up this morning, her cheeks and forehead were radiant with heat and sore to the touch.

'I look like a boiled lobster,' she muttered to herself. 'I can't go to the barbecue like this.'

Sylvia, who had come into the adjoining bedroom to borrow a belt for her new Levi's, poked her head around the bathroom door.

'Good *God*, Stella,' she exploded in laughter. 'You look like you've observed an H-bomb test at close range! What *happened?*'

'You should bloody know,' Stella snapped. 'You were on the porch yesterday too. Why didn't you warn me? Why don't *you* look like this? Look at you! You're brown as a berry. Oh God . . . '

'That's because I'm a Massachusetts girl,' Sylvia replied, choking back her laughter. 'I start getting acclimatised from April when the sun comes back.'

'Bully for you. What on earth am I going to do? I can't meet the Kennedys looking like this. I can't meet *anyone* like this.'

'Don't worry — I've just the thing.' Sylvia vanished back down the hall towards her bedroom.

Stella liked Sylvia. Physically, they were similar — both on the tall side, with curly shoulder-length hair cut to a fringe. But Stella's blue eyes — her father's eyes — played to Sylvia's brown, and although the American girl was pretty with a cheerleader's smile that revealed (unnaturally) perfect teeth, as Stella moved into her early twenties she was increasingly compared to the Hollywood actress of the day, Elizabeth Taylor. They shared the same delicate but determined chin, almond-shaped eyes, and slim, tapering hands and feet. And while Stella might not have quite possessed Taylor's impressive décolletage, she felt she didn't exactly have to apologise for herself in that department.

In fact, when she had arrived at London Airport's first-class lounge the week before, the freelance press photographers who habitually hung around the concourse hoping to spot someone famous had begun busily taking her picture before they realised their mistake and sheepishly lowered their cameras.

'Sorry, love, we thought you was Liz Taylor for a mo there,' one of them called to her.

'Thanks,' she said wryly, as she went into the lounge. 'She's nearly ten years older than me.'

'Take it as a compliment, darlin'.'

★ ★ ★

40

Sylvia was back with a tube of what looked like green toothpaste.

'It's concealer,' Sylvia explained. 'This'll do the trick.'

'But it's green!' Stella protested. 'I can't put this stuff on. I'll look like — I don't know, the Wicked Witch in *The Wizard of Oz* . . . or a Martian.'

'Trust me,' Sylvia said, confidently dabbing on the cream with her fingertips. 'It'll take the redness down and when you put your make-up on top you'll look fine. Actually, it'll appear as if you have a nice suntan. Our little secret.'

Twenty minutes later, Stella could see Sylvia had been right. All signs of redness had gone, even from her nose, which shortly before had resembled the glowing tail-light on Jeb's Lincoln.

She went to her bedroom door in her dressing gown and poked her head into the hall. 'What are you wearing to the party, Sylvia?' she called.

'Jeans and a jumper and sneakers,' came the muffled reply from the next bedroom. 'Gotta keep it low-key. If Jackie's there, you can bet she'll be in jeans or slacks. You don't want to outshine the First Lady. How about you?'

'I can't decide.' Stella went to her wardrobe and looked unhappily at the clothes she'd brought from England. The summer dresses and skirts and tops she'd worn the year before looked staid and dated to her now. She *had* experimented with some of the new designs that had come out in the spring of '62, but none of them looked right for a beach barbecue. Simple

41

A-line skirts (inspired by Mrs Kennedy's own effortless and much-lauded style) and the chic Harris tweeds with matching satchels that she'd bought from the achingly fashionable Urban Outfitters in London didn't seem remotely synonymous with sea and sand to her.

She went back into the hall. 'Sylvia?'

'What?'

'Help!'

★   ★   ★

And so it was that an hour later, the Rockfairs and their English guest set off for the coast in the Continental. They looked 'pretty damned spiffy', as Jeb put it. Dorothy was in pink slacks and a white fitted cardigan; Jeb wore a sailing cap at a rakish angle above an electric-blue nylon windcheater.

Stella was in pale blue jeans (Sylvia's), a white cotton sweatshirt (Sylvia's) with 'Boston' printed in large black letters across the front and 'Red Sox' emblazoned in crimson on the back, and high-topped sneakers (Sylvia's) on her feet. A Red Sox baseball cap (Sylvia's) with her hair poking out behind in a pony-tail completed her outfit.

Dorothy turned around in the sedan's front seat to admire her.

'Honey,' she said, 'you look more of a Yankee than the rest of us put together. Very glamorous, too. I'll bet Bobby tries to draft you onto his brother's campaign team for the '64 election!'

Stella smiled back at her. 'Who knows, maybe

42

I'll say yes . . . Jeb, how long will it take us to get there?'

'Coupla hours to Woods Hole where we pick up the ferry to Vineyard Haven. Then we'll drive over to Oak Bluffs where the party is.'

'Do the Kennedys use the ferry too?'

The others laughed.

'Sorry, Stella,' Jeb said apologetically. 'No reason why you should know any different . . . see, the Kennedys have their family compound at Hyannis Port on Cape Cod, just across Nantucket Sound from the Vineyard. They have their own, er, water transport. Likely as not they'll sail across to Oak Bluffs in the family yacht, *Victura*. She's quite a sight, that li'l boat, believe me. Nothing but the best for old Joe K's family.'

Stella was thoughtful. 'If JFK *does* come, what do I call him if I end up speaking to him?'

'Mr President,' they chorused.

'But don't worry,' Dorothy added. 'He doesn't stand on ceremony. After a minute or so, you'll forget you're talking to the most powerful man in the world, I promise you.'

'I doubt it,' Stella said. 'But how do you know that? Have *you* met him?'

'Sure, lots of times,' Dorothy replied, surprised. 'Why, hasn't Sylvia told you?'

'I didn't like to brag, Mom,' her daughter said uncomfortably. 'Sorry, Stella — I didn't quite know how to bring it up without sounding swollen-headed. Anyway, there's a sort of convention that you just don't talk about stuff like this. It's really excruciating when you hear

43

people do that, just to show off.'

Stella nodded quickly. 'Oh, I understand,' she said. 'But go on, you might as well tell me now. How *do* you know the Kennedys?'

Jeb slowed down for the toll station and reached for his newly filled ashtray of coins, with a pointed glance at his wife.

'It's no big deal,' he shrugged. 'Bobby asked me if I'd do some historical research for his brother's speeches in the 1960 campaign. I went to Hyannis Port a few times to help out with the early drafts and Jack was usually around. We kinda got along, and when he won the election . . . well, the Kennedys don't forget their friends. Anyway, I'm already signed up for the '64 campaign so we keep in touch.' He handed quarters to the toll attendant and turned around to grin at her.

'Just don't go falling for JFK's deadly charms, Stella. Jackie's the jealous type.'

7

'Holy fuck.'

The picture editor pushed the Polaroid away from him, his face rigid with disgust. He sat in his swivel chair for a few moments, breathing heavily, before lifting the desk phone from its cradle.

'Get me News, please, honey.' He could hear the girl switching jackplugs on the switchboard in front of her and a moment later a man's voice crackled down the line.

'News editor.'

'Henry, it's Glen. You need to get over here. Right now.'

★ ★ ★

Using steel tweezers, the Miami police detective carefully slid the Polaroid into a clear plastic evidence bag. He turned calmly to the two newspapermen with him in the editor's office at the *Courier*. It amused him somehow that both wore a kind of near-identical journalist's uniform — baggy grey suit trousers with braces and turn-ups, white button-down shirts with the sleeves rolled up above the elbows, and cheap ballpoint pens jammed behind their ears. Both men had hair slicked back with oil. They could have been brothers.

'Who's touched this, please?'

45

The picture editor gave a quick nod. 'Only me, before I knew what . . . what it was.' He swallowed. 'Henry here didn't handle it at all — he figured the fingerprint angle from the get-go. But I — '

His colleague interrupted him.

'Now just hold on a second here, officer! That photo was handed in to the *Courier*. Technically, it's this newspaper's property. Obviously I understand you need to take it with you but I have to make copies first. We're splashing this story big-time tomorrow and we'll syndicate it the day after. Hand it back for now, if you please.'

The policeman shook his head. 'No way. Print this? Are you kidding? You'll have half your readers throwing up over their breakfast waffles. Anyway, you splashing this image across fifty states could compromise the investigation.'

'Bullshit! Compromise it in what way, exactly? It's us who decide what our readers can stomach, not the police. And obviously we'd mask the details — put a black block over the knife and her eye at the very least. But that's our business. I want that photo back for copying and I want it now.'

'What about the poor kid's family? Have you thought about the effect seeing this in the morning paper might have on them?'

'Screw the family. This is news.'

'Wow. I'm impressed. You really are a hard-ass, aren't you? Well, you can take it up with my chief. This photo comes back to Miami with me.'

Not in the least perturbed by the stand-off,

46

the detective glanced around the office. Its walls were covered with framed front pages and awards citations. Pride of place above the door was taken by the screaming headline: 'CASTRO FIASCO!' — a reference to America's disastrous rag-tag army invasion of Cuba's Bay of Pigs the year before.

He nodded towards an impressively large but empty desk opposite a picture window which offered sweeping views over Key Largo's Buttonwood Bay and its myriad uninhabited — and uninhabitable — mangrove islands. 'So where's your boss today?'

'The editor's on a fishing trip down in Key West,' Henry replied sourly. 'He's sure as heckfire on his way back now, though. When I tell him about the little stunt you've just pulled he'll probably go straight from the airport to police headquarters. He'll have your badge for this.'

The policeman yawned. 'Well, I've been on the force for twenty years so frankly he'll be welcome to it. Mind if we sit down?'

The news editor glared at him for a few moments longer before reluctantly indicating the small conference table at one end of the editor's office. 'Over there.'

'Thanks.' The detective stretched unselfconsciously. It had been an exhausting few weeks since the first murder and he was damn tired. He felt more like seventy than forty.

'So . . . ' He slid off his suit jacket and hung it on the back of his chair, removing a notebook and pen from his hip pocket before repeating:

47

'*So* . . . like I said, I'm Lieutenant Frank Coulter. And you are? Full names, please.'

'Henry Stewart — I'm news editor here.'

'Glen Morton. Picture editor.'

'Thanks. OK, gentlemen, I'm going to ask you some questions. But anything I say in here is strictly off the record. That understood?'

The news editor frowned. 'No, it isn't. We have some questions for you too — *on* the record.' He pointed to the bagged photo that was protruding from Coulter's jacket pocket.

'Obviously that's Lucy Twain, the Keys victim from a couple of days back. In spite of that God-awful thing sticking out of her head she's pretty recognisable from the family photos we ran yesterday.' Stewart leaned forward. 'But you guys never mentioned *that* little detail. Which leads me to ask — did he do the same thing with the other two? And if so, does he do it before or after he kills them? Why have you been holding out on us?'

Coulter gave the journalist a cold stare before saying quietly: 'Back up, friend. I'll go first with the questions. And I decide how much I tell you about this case. Let's not let the tail go wagging the dog here, OK?'

The news editor's gaze was just as icy. 'Fine. Ask your questions, detective. Then it's my turn.'

Coulter decided to park the point for now.

'Hmm . . . well now, let's see . . . you say the photo was delivered by hand. Was it in an envelope?'

Morton nodded. 'Yup. A regular white one. It had 'For Picture Desk' printed in biro on the front. It's still on my desk across the passage there.'

'Anyone touch it apart from you?'

'The girl on the front desk when it was given to her, I imagine, and the in-house courier who brought it up to me.'

Coulter sat up a little straighter. 'Hold on. You mean it was handed in in person to the front desk? Not dropped into the *Courier*'s mailbox by the lobby entrance?'

'You got it, detective. We have the girl standing by for you to talk to.'

But the girl was of little use. Yes, the envelope had definitely been brought in by a man, she said, but she had barely glanced at him. She'd been on the phone to the circulation department. She'd had the vague impression of jeans and a T-shirt, but she couldn't be sure. No, she hadn't really looked at his face, but he might have been wearing sunglasses and a baseball cap. In fact, thinking about it now, she thought he probably was. No, she hadn't noticed anything about his hands, rings or anything like that. His age? It could have been anywhere between twenty and fifty. No, he didn't speak. He just passed her the envelope and left. She was pretty sure he was white, but then again he could have been Hispanic. She was real sorry not to be more helpful. What was this all about, please?

When she had gone, Coulter asked to be taken to the picture desk. He carefully bagged the envelope that was still lying where Morton had tossed it.

Back in the editor's office he said, 'I'll need

49

the girl's prints and the courier's, as well as yours, Mr Morton. Was the envelope gummed down, by the way?'

Morton shook his head. 'No. The flap was just tucked in.'

'Damn. We might have got some saliva and a blood type from that.'

Coulter sat forward a moment, tapping his teeth with his pen. Then he relaxed. 'All right, Mr Stewart. Ask your questions, but I'm not guaranteeing to answer them.'

The news editor pulled out his own notepad.

'At yesterday's press conference, your spokesman said the police believe the three victims — the last girl, Lucy Twain, and Jennifer Alston and Hester Wainwright — were killed by the same person, due to the specific nature of their injuries. All you've told us about those injuries is that they involve extensive and distinctive knife wounds. Does that include the calling card he left in the Twain girl's eye?'

Coulter smiled and scratched his chin. Then he stood up. 'I can see the way this is going. I'm sorry, Mr Stewart, but questions like that are above my pay grade. You're going to have to put them to my boss. In fact, I suggest your editor does that when he drops by headquarters to collect my badge.' He turned to leave.

'Hey! Now wait just one second! We've been co-operative! At least give me a guarantee we'll be the first to run the picture when you end up having to admit it doesn't compromise the investigation!'

'Again, above my pay grade. There'll be

someone over later to take those prints, by the way.'

'*Jesus!* Answer just *one* thing then, will you? Do you have prints from any of the murder scenes? On that knife left in Lucy Twain's eye, for example?'

Coulter considered the question from the doorway.

'Possibly,' he said at length. Then he was gone.

The news editor turned to his colleague. He was almost purple with rage.

'Can you believe that guy? What a jerk.' He paused for a moment, drumming his fingers angrily on the table. Suddenly he glared at the picture editor. 'And why, by the way, didn't you take a cover shot of the damn Polaroid before Coulter got here? Too busy throwing up? Jesus Christ, Glen!'

Morton sighed as he removed a miniature Leica camera from an inside pocket of his jacket.

'Have a little faith, Henry. Actually, I took three.'

8

'Jack? Can you come in here a minute?'

Bobby Kennedy ducked back out of the glare of the strengthening early autumn Massachusetts sun, running his fingers through his hair as he re-read the docket that had just chattered off the teleprinter in the study.

Jesus. This was a *royal* pain in the ass.

A few moments later, the tall French windows facing onto a wide lawn were pushed open and his older brother came into the room, swinging a white towel. Jack was wearing shorts and a sweatshirt and he was covered in a light sheen of perspiration.

'Your wife and I were about to *completely* take Teddy's team at touch-ball, Bobby! Ethel's furious with you, so this had better be important.'

'C'mon, Jack, TAKE them? With your back? You're coach these days at best. Anyway, it is. Important, I mean.'

'*Family* important, or Attorney General important?'

'The latter. You should read this.' Bobby held out the docket.

Jack slumped on to a cream leather sofa and pushed damp hair back from his eyes with one hand as he reached out with the other. 'Thank you, Mr Attorney General. Where's this from?'

'Florida. The FBI station in Miami. There's a

problem in the Keys. Just read the damn thing, won't you?'

Thirty seconds later Jack Kennedy looked at his brother and gave a low whistle.

'Yeah . . . well . . . what d'you feel we should do about this?'

Bobby flopped down on the sofa beside him.

'There aren't any obvious political complications that I can see — unless this fruitloop is from one of the Cuban exile groups, in which case we may have a problem. It's more a straightforward case of law and order . . . and the effect on tourism. You've seen what the Mayor of Miami has to say about that, in the fourth paragraph there. He thinks that if we don't nail whoever's responsible we'll lose a lot of the snowbirds. People won't want to fly down to the Keys this winter, especially with teenage daughters in tow, with a madman on the loose. Jesus, Jack — three dead in three weeks! At this rate we'll be into double figures by Thanksgiving.'

'Why didn't we, ah, know about this before?'

His brother sighed. 'Probably because the cops down there were trying to keep a lid on it, hoping to catch the guy before things got any more out of hand. But it seems he outsmarted them — sent a photo of his handiwork to the local scandal sheet, killed another one, and then the *Courier* ran the damn thing in this morning's edition. It'll be coast to coast by tomorrow.'

'So . . . who do we call in? Department of Justice?'

'Absolutely, the FBI, yeah. I'll tell Hoover to

53

get someone, someone very good, down to the Keys on the next plane.'

'No, Bobby, you won't *tell* him. I'll *ask* him.'

'Jesus, Jack. Not this again. Who's Chief Executive, you or Hoover? Fine, he's FBI Director but you're the President, for God's sake!'

His brother reached for the telephone on the coffee table in front of him.

'I told you before, Bobby, just like I told the Vice-President. I'd rather have that bastard inside the tent pissing out, than outside it pissing in.' He dialled, and paused a moment.

'I've got this, Bobby.'

'You'd better have.'

9

He hadn't really expected the Courier to run the photo in its original, explicit form but he was pleased at how little they had messed with it. The blade and most of the handle of the knife had been obscured by a black rectangle, and the eye-socket itself was blanked by a larger circle of white, but you definitely got the general idea, especially when you read the caption underneath.

This is the horrific calling-card left by the person responsible for all three of this month's so-called Keys Killings: a knife, believed to be the murder weapon, plunged into the victim's left eye-socket. 'The slayer is clearly a maniac,' Detective Lieutenant Frank Coulter told the *Courier* last night. 'But he's careless, leaving fingerprints and other evidence at the crime scenes. It's only a matter of time before we identify and apprehend him. There is no reason for alarm or panic here in the Florida Keys.'

Full story, pages 3, 4 & 5.

He had to laugh. Hadn't they realised yet why he didn't give a red cent about fingerprints? Or the knives? As for panicking . . . there was plenty of time for that. He'd barely gotten started.

He had no interest in looking at the inside pages. This was his story, not theirs, and anyhow they couldn't even tell it right. 'Keys Killings' — it sucked. What a crappy headline. 'EYE-SOCKET SLAYINGS' — couldn't they SEE it? Maybe he'd write them a letter. But that was the Courier for you. One of the big boys, like the LA Times or New York Times, would be more likely to call it right. He must remember to buy copies from Kmart tomorrow, once the story had been syndicated.

He slid his half-finished breakfast away from him across the diner's Formica table and yawned. It had been a long night and judging by the lack of any significant police activity along the early-morning-sunlit Overseas Highway, which ran right across from the customer parking lot, they hadn't found number four yet.

It couldn't be much longer, though. He peered out of the restaurant window in the direction of the backwater where he'd left her, half a mile south down the highway just before the Islamorada Bridge.

Yup. There they were. At least half-a-dozen buzzards, wheeling in the cloudless sky, right above the exact spot. As he watched, he saw one drop out of formation and swoop low down into the mangroves. Almost immediately, two more followed.

Someone had better find her soon or there wouldn't be a whole lot left to find.

10

The screams were bloodcurdling and came from down by the water. They cut like jagged knives through the laughter and chatter further up the beach, and sunglasses glinted and flashed as people turned their heads towards the sudden disturbance. There were more screams, even louder now, and a long, wailing: 'Noooooooo . . .'

Dorothy turned to Stella, grinning. 'And *that* is why JFK and Jackie won't let Caroline and John-John play with Ethel and Bobby's kids,' she said. 'One, they're hopelessly outnumbered and, two, Jackie says her children would be safer fooling around in the tiger enclosure at Washington Zoo. Look out, here come Kathleen and Joe. They're the eldest and the most dangerous.'

Stella watched as brother and sister whooped past, seawater dripping from their woollen bathing costumes and brandishing enormous water pistols as they ran. 'Ouch! Hey!' she cried, as a jet of water hit her square above one eye. 'I'll get you for that!'

The children chased past her, oblivious, onwards up the shelving sand to the two-storey white-painted wooden beach house that stood behind a raft of picnic tables and several fiercely smoking barbecues.

'The little darlings,' Stella snorted, ruefully wiping her eye with the back of one hand. 'How many of them are there, exactly?'

'Ethel's been pushing one out pretty much every year since 1951,' Dorothy told her. 'I think even she and Bobby are beginning to lose count. God help them if they ever have twins. Let's see . . . Kathleen, Joe, um, Robert . . . her lips silently mouthed the rest of the names, marking them off on one hand and then uncurling the fingers of the other.

'Yeah, I think that's all of them,' she frowned at last. 'Seven, at the last count.'

'*Seven?*' Stella repeated in disbelief. 'But from what I've read, Ethel can only be in her early thirties.'

'Yup, thirty-four last April. Three girls and four boys already. The youngest is Mary — she's two; three in September.' Dorothy shrugged. 'Irish Catholics. It's their thing. Ethel'll be pregnant again by Christmas, I guarantee it.'

Stella turned to take in the scene around her. There were about fifty or sixty people at the barbecue, most standing around on the sand or sauntering down to the ocean, now that Bobby and Ethel's brood had stampeded inside behind their two eldest siblings.

She was sure she recognised some of the men, particularly the older ones. 'Haven't I seen that man's picture in the paper?' she whispered to Dorothy, pointing surreptitiously.

Dorothy shaded her eyes. 'You mean the well-fed middle-aged guy in the Hawaiian shirt?'

'Yes, talking to the tall man in trunks with his back to us.'

'Ha! I can assure you, Stella, when that tall

58

guy turns around you'll recognise *him* all right. That's Ted Kennedy. He's probably the best-looking man here. The pork chop he's talking to is the senator for Massachusetts, Benjamin Smith. Big friend of the family. When Jack won the Presidency two years ago he had to give up his seat in the Senate, of course. Benjamin took his place, but only to keep it warm for Teddy.'

'What do you mean, keep it warm?'

'Teddy was a little too young under the rules to be a senator back then,' Dorothy explained. 'But he turned thirty a couple of months back, so he can take over in the fall.'

'I see . . . and what'll become of Mr Seat-Warmer then?'

'Oh, don't worry about him. The Kennedys don't forget their friends.'

Stella took a thoughtful sip of the peach-coloured cocktail a waiter had handed to her when they arrived.

'They're a bit like a royal family, aren't they?' she said at last.

Dorothy laughed. 'Exactly! Why do you think we call it Camelot?'

Stella was about to ask more when the tall man in trunks turned around and immediately made eye contact with her. He gave a casual wave and raised his glass, bowing theatrically from a trim, muscled waist.

She offered a slightly flustered wave back, turning to Dorothy as she did so. 'Good heavens, you were right, he's gorgeous,' she muttered. 'If he wasn't a politician he could be a film star.'

'He certainly behaves like one, in certain

59

departments,' the older woman said drily. 'Total womaniser. See that girl over there in the green headscarf and matching sunglasses? That's his wife, Virginia. He's steadily driving her to drink, poor kid.'

Stella turned away as casually as she could from Teddy Kennedy's unwavering, knowing gaze. 'So it's true then, what I've heard? About the Kennedy brothers?'

'You mean that they all fool around? Sure. It's just that the papers have made a collective decision not to report it. They love the Camelot image and the happy all-American family thing, beautiful wives and golden children. Why spoil it for everyone? Anyway, Jeb says most editors honestly believe it's better to keep the whole Kennedy cheating story under wraps; they think it'd be unpatriotic to blow the lid on it. Bad for Uncle Sam's image. Besides — they're such impressive, upstanding guys in most other ways. Terrific at running the country, and all that. Taking us into a shining future. Really. Wait 'til you meet Jack and Bobby. Jeb says — '

On cue, Jeb materialised beside them. 'Dottie, Ethel wants to say hi and she and the guys would like to meet our English rose, too. Come on, girls. Where's Sylvia?'

Dorothy nodded towards a riotous group of mostly very young men further down the sands. 'Playing beach baseball with the boys.'

'Oh . . . OK, we'll leave her to it then. C'mon.'

But Stella was rooted to the spot. 'Jeb . . . ' she said hesitantly. 'By *the guys*, you don't mean . . . '

60

He grinned and took her arm. 'I most certainly do. Stella, come and have a drink with the two most powerful men on the planet.'

★ ★ ★

Jeb and Dorothy led her through a light screen of Secret Service men, incongruous on the beach in their dark suits and neckties, forming a loose circle at a respectful distance around the largest of the charcoal grills.

As they got closer, Stella could hear the President and his brother quarrelling over how much longer the T-bones needed on the giant griddle. There were at least twenty enormous steaks smoking and spitting furiously over the coals.

'Take 'em off *now*, Jack — we've turned them twice and they're done already. Jackie, tell him!'

'Don't drag me into this, Bobby,' the First Lady said over her shoulder, breaking off from conversation with her sister-in-law. 'It's not even your barbecue. You two put yourselves on cookhouse fatigue, nobody asked you, so just see it through and stop squabbling like babies.' She turned back to Ethel. 'Sorry, Eth. As I was saying, I felt the only way I could possibly deal with it was to — oh my word, *Dorothy!*'

Dorothy stepped forward across the sand, smiling broadly. 'Hi Jackie — Ethel. We thought now might be a good moment to call time on the grand chefs so we can all actually get something to eat.'

Jeb peered over his wife's shoulder at the

griddle behind the three women. 'Those steaks look done to me, guys. I'm pretty sure the cow's dead.'

Bobby turned round gratefully. 'Now that's exactly what I've been trying to say, Jeb. Hear that, Jack? You've been outvoted and you've chargrill-filibustered yourself into the bargain.' He clapped his hands and called out to the nearest partygoers. 'Chow down, everyone! We're serving up here! Get in line, folks! And Jack, take that ridiculous chef's hat off. It does nothing for you. You look like Macy's Chubby Christmas Cook.'

11

The brothers had been busy for twenty minutes now, serving undeniably blackened T-bone steaks to a line of people clasping paper plates and plastic cutlery. Stella had not been properly introduced to them yet, other than Jeb's 'this is our English rose I was telling you about, guys', which had elicited friendly waves from both men before they were swamped by hungry guests.

She watched them covertly as Jeb stood patiently in the queue for food, clutching plates for himself, Dorothy and Stella.

She tried and failed to picture the British Prime Minister, Harold Macmillan, standing on a beach in bare feet and shorts, laughing and trading friendly insults with a gaggle of barbecue guests as he served them their lunch.

In fact, she couldn't imagine the patrician Macmillan going within a hundred miles of a barbecue. At this very moment, five hours ahead of US Eastern Time, the Prime Minister was probably in his Pall Mall club, or Downing Street, or perhaps his weekend grace-and-favour country home, Chequers. He'd be comfortable in Sunday tweeds, puffing on his briar pipe, and nursing a pre-dinner brandy and soda while perusing *The Sunday Times* over half-moon reading glasses.

Hardly Camelot.

The President was barely twenty years

younger than Macmillan, Stella calculated, yet the American and British leaders belonged to completely different periods. Macmillan still had one foot in a vanished age. JFK stood squarely in the present, and was stepping confidently into the future.

He had, as did his brother, what looked to Stella like an all-over tan, a flat stomach and even now, in his mid-forties, a boyish face. He could be, she thought, a sports hero, even a film star. No wonder women adored him. In fact, if she was honest, she herself could imagine —

A voice jolted her out of the beginnings of a rather pleasant daydream.

'Would you just look at those two! For heaven's sakes, this isn't even their barbecue!'

Stella turned to find a pretty, petite woman in jeans and pale blue sweatshirt standing next to her, extending a slim hand.

'Ethel Kennedy,' she said. 'I'm Bobby's wife. You're Stella, the Rockfairs' English rose, right?'

Stella laughed, offering her own hand. 'Are all English girls described as roses here in America?'

'Hey, don't go complaining about it. We can call you stinkwort if you'd prefer.'

Stella laughed again. 'No, rose is fine with me, Mrs Kennedy.'

'I just told you, it's Ethel. Dorothy said you were the formal type.'

The older woman nodded back towards her husband and brother-in-law, who were now arguing about how many fresh steaks should go on the griddle.

'I swear, plant those boys anywhere and they

just can't help themselves trying to take everything over and run it all. But you'll meet with them later. In the meantime, tell me about yourself. Jeb says you're here to study for your Master's at Smith. What subject?'

Stella described the specialised research she had been conducting into psychopathy.

Ethel was intrigued. 'You mean people like that nutcase in the Alfred Hitchcock movie? What *is* it about you Brits and psychos?'

Stella laughed. 'Actually, some of the most interesting front-line research into psychopathic behaviour is being conducted on your side of the Atlantic, Mrs Kennedy. I was only reading yesterday that at Berkeley — '

'Oh, for Pete's sake! It's *Ethel!* Anyway, go on.'

'Sorry . . . um . . . Ethel . . . ' Stella stammered, 'there are some new ideas floating around now about how to diagnose psychopaths and in particular how to identify them when they're involved in criminal behaviour. Although of course most psychopathic personalities aren't criminal at all.'

But Ethel wasn't interested in the qualification. 'What kind of criminal behaviour?'

'Well,' Stella said carefully, 'at the extreme end of the scale we're talking about repeat killers, like Jack the Ripper, at large in the last century when psychiatry was in its infancy. In fact, it hadn't really been conceived as a science at all, not until Freud and Jung. Even today, people who should know better think it's a lot of mumbo-jumbo.'

'You mean, if folks like you had been around

back then we would have nailed creeps like the Ripper, right?' Ethel smiled to show she wasn't trying to patronise.

But Stella considered the question seriously. 'Well . . . perhaps we would, actually. It's about method. I read a wonderful paragraph on the subject just the other day, written by a German psychiatrist attached to the faculty at Harvard. Let me see . . . ' Stella placed her hands behind her back like a schoolgirl, planted her feet in the sand, closed her eyes, and recited:

'*A young woman's body is found lying on a lonely beach. She has been stabbed to death there. A single set of footprints in the sand leads away from the bloody scene; they are identical to the ones leading to it, which are mingled with those of the victim. Which set of prints is it more important to follow?*'

Stella opened her eyes. 'Well, Ethel. What do you think?'

Ethel's own eyes flashed. She enjoyed a challenge.

'It's obvious,' she said confidently. 'You follow the tracks leading away from the body.'

Stella shook her head. 'No. Not according to this professor you don't. You take the back-bearings. If you follow the signs into the past, you have a chance of understanding who the killer is, where he's been, where he comes from. Then you might be able to predict his next move and frustrate it, even intercept him and catch him.'

Ethel snorted. 'That's ridiculous! You have to chase the killer down!'

66

Stella raised her hands in mock defence. 'Up to a point, of course,' she said, 'but that German professor was really constructing a simple model designed to make us stop and think. If you keep racing blindly towards an unknown, empty horizon, you're never going to give yourself time to assess the larger picture that lies behind, are you? You're always running to catch up.'

A waiter in plastic sandals, Bermuda shorts and a violently pink short-sleeved shirt materialised next to them.

'Drinks, ladies?' He proffered a tray crowded with brimming blue plastic beakers.

'What's in 'em?' Ethel demanded.

'I have no idea, ma'am.'

She pointed to his footprints trailing behind him in the sand.

'Then follow those back to wherever you got them from and find out. OK?'

The waiter nodded uncertainly and retreated.

'See, Stella?' Ethel said. 'I can take new ideas on board as well as anyone.'

Stella clapped her hands delightedly. 'That was a very practical application of a psychiatric theorem, Ethel. I'm most impressed.'

Ethel grinned back at her. 'Yeah, but we didn't get our drinks, did we?'

'No, but we will eventually, *and* we'll find out exactly what they are.'

'If the guy ever comes back.' They both laughed.

After a moment Ethel spoke again, her face now serious. 'So how much do you know about psychopaths, dear? Truly? Are you, for want of a better word, what one might describe as an expert?'

'Yes,' said Stella without hesitation. 'I am. I've been reading all the latest studies and theories for at least the last two years, material from both sides of the Atlantic and the little that's coming out of Australia, too. I've been asked to contribute to several papers myself. I don't think I would have achieved my double-first from Cambridge if it hadn't been for my dissertation on psychopathy. Although to be honest — and I promise I'm not being conceited here — I probably know more about psychopathy than anyone on the examination board that marked my paper.'

Ethel regarded her coolly. 'You're quite the confident one, aren't you?'

'In my chosen field, yes, I am. And there's nothing wrong with that, I don't think. Like your husband and his brother — ' Stella gestured to the pair, still bickering at the griddle — 'it's important to know your value; what you're good at. And anyway . . . ' Stella paused, feeling awkward for the first time since the conversation had begun.

'Go on.' Ethel cocked her head to one side and considered the young woman opposite her. She reminded Stella of an inquisitive bird.

'It's just that . . . well, I don't want to go into detail here, if you don't mind, but I do have personal experience of psychopaths. One, at least.'

A few hours earlier while the Kennedys were sailing across to Martha's Vineyard, a troubled

68

Bobby had confided in his wife, telling her about the crisis down in the Keys.

Now, Ethel came to a decision.

'Wait here, dear.'

She went to fetch her husband.

12

He'd ended up staying put at the diner's window table right through the morning, following waffles and coffee with an early lunch of cracked conch with rice and beans. The waitress had cleared his plates but now he was on his second Bud. This show was just too good to miss.

It had started with a single highway patrol car barrelling down the Overseas Highway from the direction of Tavernier, siren blaring and roof lights flashing. The turn-off to the dirt road that led down to the water was marked by a straggle of Florida pines and, sure enough, he saw the sedan's brake lights glow just before it reached them. A swirl of dust enveloped it as it swung a crazy left off the blacktop.

A minute or two later the buzzards were rising into the air in a cluster of dark specks, but they didn't go far. They settled into a patrol of their own, cruising in slow, lazy circles a few hundred feet above the spot where, he decided, the cops were now busy throwing up.

An hour later Route 1 looked like the Miami-Dade Police section of the Mayor's annual parade — only going a lot faster. Cruisers, black-and-whites, emergency wagons, and three ambulances. Why three? he wondered. There was only one body. Perhaps a bunch of people had found her — a canoeing party, maybe — and they were getting the dizzy-giddies, as his mom would have said.

'What d'you think is going on out there, hon?'

His waitress, with coffee he hadn't ordered. For an insane second he felt like telling the old woman the truth.

'Well, ma'am, I reckon they've found the little girl I cut to death out there last night. She must be a sight for sore eyes after those buzzards got to work on her.'

But instead he pointed to the clock-calendar above the diner's entrance.

'It's the day of rest, ma'am. I do believe those fine officers are out there taking their ease and having themselves a cook-what-you-can-catch Sunday barbecue.'

She looked at him in a puzzled kind of way but her reply, when it came, was drowned out by the thunder of the police helicopter that suddenly clattered overhead.

He nodded to himself in calm self-congratulation.

They were taking him seriously now.

Finally. It was about time.

71

13

'Do you believe in, ah, serendipity, Miss Arnold?'
'You mean happy coincidence, Mr President?'
'Yes indeed.'
'I've never really thought about it, sir.'

Stella heard herself speaking from what seemed like a great distance. She felt as if she was watching a scene in a play or film, except that, absurdly, she was simultaneously appearing in it, too.

A few minutes earlier she had watched, mystified, as Ethel tugged her husband away from the throng surrounding the barbecue and began speaking to him in low, urgent tones. He had glanced across at Stella just once and given her a small, reassuring smile and simultaneous half-wave, before turning back to his wife. When she'd finished telling him whatever on earth she was telling him, he'd nodded and kissed her nose before turning to retrieve his brother who, bored with cookhouse responsibilities, was wandering back down the beach with his wife.

Stella was sitting in the cosy den of their hosts' beach house. Bobby and Jack Kennedy lounged amicably opposite her. No one else was in the room. It struck her as somehow faintly incongruous that all three of them were sitting on enormous beanbags, arranged around a low pine table covered in pieces of twisted sun-bleached driftwood and giant white and pink seashells.

Through the storm-proofed, sound-proofed, double-glazed floor-to-ceiling picture window that looked out over the beach, Stella watched the silent scene of Ethel and Jackie rounding up their children. It must be nearly time for the Kennedys to sail back across Nantucket Sound to Hyannis Port. She could see the prow of their 26-foot yacht nosing around the bluff toward the bay. It wouldn't surprise her in the least if Ethel later took the helm and barked out commands to the crew. She was obviously an extraordinarily —

'Um . . . Miss Arnold?'

Stella jumped. 'Oh . . . I'm so sorry, Mr President; I was drifting a little. You have to understand that this is a very . . . unusual situation for me to find myself in. I've lost my bearings a bit, I'm afraid. A couple of hours ago I thought I might just possibly be shaking hands with you or your brother. Now I'm in this lovely room with you both. It's all rather overwhelming and . . . well, confusing.'

Bobby grinned at her. 'My brother and I call it the five-minute rule. Most, ah, first-timers like you, if I can put it like that, Miss Arnold, feel just fine in the time it takes to smoke a cigarette. I see you've almost finished yours.'

She looked down at her hand in surprise. 'I didn't even realise I'd lit this,' she said, with a short laugh. 'But do you know, I believe you may be right. The ringing in my ears is fading.'

The brothers laughed. 'She's making jokes now, Bobby,' Jack said. 'I think we can, ah, safely start.'

They really *do* speak with a Boston drawl,

73

Stella thought to herself. 'Please call me Stella,' she said. 'And — excuse me — why did you ask about serendipity just now, Mr President?'

'Jack, I'll take point on this.'

Bobby slid down from his beanbag and settled more comfortably on the floor, his tanned feet splayed out on pale floorboards, hands clasped around his knees. He looks about nineteen, Stella thought, especially with his floppy fringe.

'Ethel told us what you are studying, or intending to study, at Smith,' he began. 'It seems you're an expert on psychopaths, Miss Arnold, ah, *Stella* . . . especially dangerous ones.'

She looked at him appreciatively. 'My goodness. You know there's a difference, then? Mention the word psychopath to most people, however educated and intelligent they are, and all they can see is garrottes and flashing knives. But we're beginning to understand that psychopaths come in all shapes and sizes, and many aren't dangerous at all. In fact there's one body of thought that suggests leaders in industry and particularly politics might quite often display psychopathic tendencies. I actually think — '

She clapped a hand over her mouth. 'Forgive me! I didn't mean . . . I wasn't trying to imply . . . '

But the two men opposite her were laughing. 'There you go, Jack!' grinned Bobby, reaching across and punching his brother's thigh. 'I always said you were the psycho of the family. Turns out science agrees with me! Stella, if and when the opportunity arises I'd like to buy you a beer.'

Stella smiled at him ruefully. 'All I was trying to say was — '

'It's OK, it's OK, we get it. Anyway. Let's focus. Dangerous psychopaths. Repeat murderers, for example. Tell us about them.'

She had recovered herself.

'Well, I'm not going to affect some kind of false modesty about this,' she said calmly. 'I'm more or less at the top of my field — my *academic* field, I should say, in terms of the latest thinking on criminal psychopathy. Obviously, not in terms of the psychiatric treatments, and so on — but even there I have a fair amount of theoretical knowledge.'

'That's fine, just fine,' Bobby told her. 'Now, tell Jack and me what you were telling my wife out there on the beach a few minutes ago.'

Stella obediently repeated most of what she'd said to Ethel, adding: 'In fact I was at a conference on the subject a few weeks before I left England and to be honest I came to realise that I knew as much, if not more, than some of the main speakers. I think a lot of European faculties are still a bit snobbish about American academia, to be honest, and they don't read enough of the new research and studies being done over here.'

Bobby nodded, thoughtfully. 'Right. So . . . and this is purely a 'for instance', Stella . . . if someone were to present you with details of a contemporary repeat homicide case — who'd been murdered, how, the way their bodies were left, and so on — you might be able to tell us something about the killer?'

'In theory, yes,' Stella answered carefully. 'But it would totally depend on how much information there was to hand. With a reasonable amount of data, though, I could probably give you a general idea of the kind of person he might be; things such as his likely age, the kind of job he might have, and some reasonably intelligent guesses about his background.' She smiled at them. 'Well, with a bit of luck and a following wind, anyway.'

Jack Kennedy returned her smile, and spoke for the first time in several minutes. 'And you wouldn't object if our people checked you out, Stella? Got in touch with your alma mater in Cambridge, for example? Talked to the people you'll be studying under at Smith?'

Stella's eyes widened slightly. 'Not at all . . . but why would you want to do that, Mr President? You still haven't explained why we're having this conversation.'

Jack Kennedy steepled his fingers and rested his chin on top of them.

'Now *that*, Stella, is where serendipity finally enters the picture.'

14

Todd Johnson wasn't at all sure it had been such a great idea to transfer from Detroit Police to the President's personal Secret Service detail. He'd thought it would be a whole lot more glamorous than this. Todd had envisaged loping alongside the presidential limousine as it drove slowly through vast, cheering crowds, perhaps winning the occasional admiring glance from the First Lady as he pressed a finger against his earpiece and barked crisp, efficient updates into the tiny radio microphone pinned to his suit lapel.

But not this. Not sitting alone in a nondescript mid-range unmarked radio car with busted air-con and nothing to do unless the receiver suddenly crackled to life with a message. Which it hadn't. Not since they'd got here.

All the other guys were down on the beach, eyeing up the women and working on their suntans. When he'd stepped out of the car to get some air and maybe tilt his own face up to the sun for a few minutes, his boss had materialised from the sand-dunes like some kind of frigging magician and yelled at him to 'get back in the goddamn car, Johnson, or get back to Detroit!'

He wondered if he could smoke a cigarette, and then decided against it. Old hard-as-nails would probably pop up from the dunes again like a jack-in-the-box, and he'd be on report. He sighed. Things had better start improving soon or he'd be seriously thinking about going back to work in his brother's car showroom in Dearborn.

'*Jesus Christ!*' He jumped near clear through the car's roof at the sudden hammering on the driver's window. 'What the f — '

It was one of the local Vineyard cops, a three-striper. Todd got a grip and rolled down the window.

'Yeah?'

The sergeant grinned at him. 'Sorry, son. Didn't mean to startle you there.' He held up his ID. 'Trade?'

Todd fished out his Secret Service pass from an inside pocket and flashed it back at the cop. 'What's up, officer?'

The sergeant nodded to the short-wave radio unit bolted to the sedan's dashboard. 'You having trouble with that thing? We been trying to raise you from the station this past twenty minutes. I tried you from the car on the way over here. Nix.'

Todd flicked a few switches, and then thumped the top of the receiver-transponder.

'Stone cold. I was wondering why it had all gone quiet . . . it was fine when we got here,' he added, lamely.

'Yeah, well, praise the Lord for the US Telegram Service, huh?'

Todd looked at him blankly. 'Begging your pardon?'

The sergeant pulled a crumpled telegram envelope from his back pocket. 'Looks like we've not been the only ones trying to reach you, son. This came through a few minutes ago from FBI

78

Miami. Urgent, for the Attorney General. I do believe he's still here.' The sergeant nodded out towards a low headland. 'I noticed the *Victura*'s still at anchor around the point. You take this straight to him, son. It's in plain speech so your boys won't need the codes.'

Todd got out of the car. 'You've read it then.'

'Couldn't avoid doing so, friend. Don't have a single idea what it's about, mind. Maybe it *is* a kinda code after all. All seems to be about the number four.' He nodded. 'I'll be getting back. You get that radio fixed, mind, on the double. Hell, what if the Ruskies are comin'?'

Todd could hear the sergeant laughing as he strolled back to his patrol car.

He looked down at the envelope. This was it. A personal message for the President's brother. And he was the one lucky stiff who got to deliver it.

★ ★ ★

'An FBI *telegram?* What the hell's wrong with the radio, Johnson?'

The most senior of the three Secret Service men guarding the veranda of the beach house glowered at him, chin thrust forward aggressively.

'It's out of service, sir. I only just — '

'Then get straight down on that beach there and tell the old man RIGHT NOW. We need to get the *Victura*'s back-up unit ashore and powered up right away. *Jesus*, Johnson, what if the Ruskies are coming?'

The older man snatched the telegram from Todd's unresisting fingers and turned to go inside the wooden building.

'But sir, *I* was going to — '

The screen door slammed shut and Todd was talking to himself.

'I'd sprint, not walk to the beach, Johnson, if I were you,' one of the remaining guards said dispassionately, eyes hidden behind blank shades. 'Even then I wouldn't bet against this being your last day with the organisation, sport. Enjoy what may be left of it.'

* * *

Before the President could begin, there was a double knock on the den's sliding door.

'*Dammit*. Yes, come in . . . '

The door rolled back and the agent stepped into the room. 'Sorry to interrupt, Mr President, but a telegram's just come through from the FBI in Miami, urgent for the Attorney General here.'

Bobby laughed. 'A *telegram?*' He reached out for it. 'Maybe Hoover's boys will start using the Pony Express again soon.'

The agent looked embarrassed. 'Problem with our radio car, sir. We're on it.'

'Sure.' The Attorney General took the envelope and opened it as the agent slid back out of the room as quickly as was decently possible.

He stared, expressionless, at the sparsely worded paragraph in front of him. After a moment, he closed his eyes and wearily pinched the bridge of his nose between a thumb and forefinger.

'Oh, *shit.*'

'Hey, Bobby ... ' His brother inclined his head towards Stella, still perched on her beanbag.

'What? Oh ... I apologise for my language there, Miss Arnold ... Stella, I mean ... would you, ah, excuse us a moment?'

'Of course,' Stella said, beginning to get up. 'Do you want me to go outside?'

'No, no, you stay comfortable in here. Jack, would you come into the hall, please?'

Stella was left alone in the den. She looked out at America's most powerful at play while their President and his brother whispered outside on the stairs.

She'd always had a vivid imagination, but she couldn't have got close to predicting such a wildly improbable scenario.

Despite everything, she started to laugh.

★   ★   ★

'*Four!* Are they sure?'

'Pretty much. The FBI say everything about the new one found this morning screams the same *modus operandi* as the first three, Jack, even before the post-mortem. We've got a real problem here. And there's something I haven't told you yet.'

The President was sitting on the stairs, his hands cradling his head. Now he raised it to stare at his younger brother. 'Oh man, this thing

81

just gets better and better. What, and *why*, if you please?'

'C. Farris Bryant is flying up to Washington from Miami tomorrow and he wants to see you in the White House first thing Tuesday when we get back. The *why* is that I only took his call as we were leaving Hyannis Port earlier and I didn't see any good reason to burden you with it until the morning.'

The President pushed his hair back with both hands. 'Great. So we have four murdered and mutilated women down there inside precisely three weeks, and the State Governor on the warpath to Washington. Thank the saints Bryant's a Democrat, at least.'

'Small mercies, yeah . . . ' Bobby considered a moment. 'I'll give you the background during the flight down to Washington tomorrow, but the bottom line is that Bryant is attracting serious investment to turn Florida into America's new winter playground. He's building freeways and bridges and green-lighting all kinds of tourist development. There are huge deals on the brink of being signed.

'But the mother of them all — and don't you start in on me, Jack, this was news to me too, I swear — Bryant says he's begun secret talks with Walt Disney to get the new Disney Park located down there and things are at a very delicate stage. Right now, Bryant needs a multiple murderer rampaging round southern Florida like he needs a fucking hole in the head. He wants to know what we're going to do about it.'

'And this conversation with him this morning

was *before* he knew about this fourth one?'

'*Oh* yeah. I'm expecting sweet, loving messages from him waiting for me when we get back to Hyannis Port. I'd probably be hearing them right now if the radio car wasn't out of action.'

The President looked back towards the den where Stella waited patiently for them.

'And Bryant'll be opposite me in the Oval Office Tuesday? Wanting answers?'

'You can bet on it.'

His older brother nodded slowly. 'Right. Then we're going to feed this guy some seriously good news. We'll tell him that we've drafted one of the world's foremost young minds concerning homicidal psychopaths, and she's on the case as a special advisor to the FBI as of yesterday.'

His brother stared at him, and gave a short laugh. 'Isn't that what you might call something of an over-promotion, Jack? Sure, she's as bright as a new penny but Jeez ... she's only twenty-one, twenty-two at most.'

'We know that, Bobby, but Bryant doesn't. We'll sell her to him as a prodigy. Come on, help me fix this. It doesn't have to be for long — maybe a week at most. Meantime you get some kind of endorsement from her senior don at Cambridge, something that looks impressive; something that I can wave in Bryant's face. We just need to keep the guy happy for a few days until the FBI boys get a lead, which they surely will. The Keys aren't the Wild West, for God's sake — we're talking about a handful of small islands here. Anyway, you never know, maybe we'll cut a break. Maybe this girl really *can* help

83

us out. She seems confident enough, that's for sure.'

Jack Kennedy stood up. 'Come on. Let's go pin a deputy's badge on the kid.'

15

Stella heard the den's sliding door opening behind her and she turned from the beach window to see Jack Kennedy entering the room alone.

'Oh . . . where's your brother, Mr President?'

'He's gone to get us some cold beers. I, ah, think you may appreciate a drink when we're done here. We all might.'

He smiled reassuringly at her before beginning to lower himself awkwardly onto one of the beanbags. Suddenly he winced and grunted in pain.

'Um . . . I think I may remain standing, if that's OK with you, Miss Arnold.'

'Of course . . . are you all right?'

'Never better, thank you. I just have a touch of stiffness in my back today, that's all.'

She watched him fishing for something in a jacket pocket before he produced a small brown glass bottle and quickly unscrewed the lid. He glanced at her. 'Aspirin,' he said. 'It takes the edge off. Would you, ah, pass me that water, please?'

There was a pewter tray bearing a blue glass carafe with matching tumblers set on a small table beside the window. Stella poured a glass out and handed it to him. *I'm giving a glass of water to the 35th President of the United States and it doesn't feel peculiar at all*, she thought, as she watched him take a sip from it and throw his head back to swallow the pill. She caught the briefest glimpse of it on his tongue. The tablet was bright red and tiny. It didn't look like any kind of aspirin she'd seen before.

'Thank you,' he said, handing back the glass.

He smiled at her. 'Stella, I have to tell you that I think your presence here today is a remarkable coincidence and, ah, a fateful one at that.'

'In what way?'

'You may be able to help us. Help our country, rather.' He considered her for a moment. 'You've heard of the Florida Keys?'

'Of course. I've seen the Humphrey Bogart film *Key Largo*, just like everyone else. And ever since I watched *White Christmas* and those gorgeous opening scenes set down in the Keys at night, I've wanted to go there.'

The President laughed. 'Another touch of serendipity, then. Because that is *exactly* where Bobby and I want to send you. The Florida Keys. Tomorrow, if possible. Tuesday by the latest.'

Stella felt her jaw falling open and somehow managed to close it again. She swallowed, hard.

'You want me to go to Florida? Why? And why the rush? I'm sorry, Mr President, I just don't understand any of this.'

There was a faint clinking behind her and she turned to see Bobby Kennedy coming back into the den, clutching several opened bottles of iced beer to his chest. He slid the door shut again with one foot.

'Don't worry, Stella, you'll understand well

86

enough when we get round to telling you what's going on down there. *Jesus*, Jack, are you still wandering all over the course here? Haven't you got to the damn point yet?'

He put the bottles down and turned back to Stella.

'OK. Here it is. We've got some crazy fellow running around the Keys, killing young women. Four in the last month — in the last three weeks, to be exact. That's bad enough, of course. But the thing is . . . well, the thing is, he does terrible things to them before they die.'

Stella's air of baffled frustration evaporated.

'I see. What sorts of things? Go into as much detail as you can, please.'

She stared calmly at the younger Kennedy, sat back down on her beanbag and gestured to him to do the same. 'How does he kill them, exactly? No, wait. Whatever he does to them, before and after, it's the same methodology every time, isn't it?'

Bobby Kennedy's eyes widened at the abrupt change in her, and her acuity. He sank back down on the floor opposite her as before, impressed by this sudden cool focus. Maybe his brother's instincts were right. Maybe she *would* make some kind of difference down there.

'Yes,' he nodded, hugging his knees again. 'He abducts them, always in the evening. The local police think he uses something such as chloroform to take them and to keep them quiet. He hides them somewhere for a few hours, and then he moves them down to the water.'

'By which you mean the sea?' Stella interrupted again.

'The ocean of course, yes.'

'Why do they believe he does that?'

'He likes peace and quiet, they think. No one's out there at that time of night. He steals a shallow-draught boat, usually a small skiff, so he can get right out into the mangrove swamps. Once he's there he lets them come round before he . . . ' He regarded Stella cautiously. 'Of course, I don't have the entire picture just yet. All this is still coming in to us here.'

'Please don't pussyfoot around. Just tell me everything you know. Isn't that why you got me in here?'

Jack chuckled softly. 'That's you told off, Bobby.'

Stella wheeled round. 'I *beg* your pardon?'

'Ah, nothing.' The President suddenly became fascinated by the activity on the beach outside.

His brother didn't smile. 'I'll tell you the little I do know, Miss Arnold — but I honestly haven't received anything like a full briefing yet.' He made a vague gesture. 'We've been running to catch up here.'

'Of course . . . look, I'm sorry, I didn't mean to sound rude just now. And I do wish you'd call me Stella.'

'I'll try to remember . . . anyway . . . ' Bobby took a deep breath. 'It's pretty much the death of a thousand cuts, apparently. He keeps them tied up while he takes some sort of knife to them.'

Stella nodded. 'And the wounds are always the

same, aren't they? On all four of his victims, I mean.'

'So I'm told. But you'll see the police photographs, of course, if you agree to go down there for us.'

Stella looked surprised.

'What do you mean, 'if'? Of course I'm going down there. This is absolutely fascinating.'

The brothers exchanged glances.

'You must understand, Stella,' Bobby said after a moment, 'that you wouldn't have any kind of, ah, *official* role in any of this. It would have to be completely informal. You'd be working with but *under* a senior FBI agent. And you wouldn't be placed in the slightest danger. You'd be there as a special advisor, working in the background. I hope that's clear to you.'

Stella brooded for a few moments, hardly listening to him. She absently stroked one bare arm and contemplated the floor. 'You're right,' she said at last, looking up again. 'I suppose I should save my detailed questions for when I get to Florida. But just tell me a couple more things now, if you can. It'll be a big help to me in arranging my thoughts on the way down there. How exactly does he kill them, at the very end?'

Bobby looked sidelong at his brother, who gave an imperceptible shrug.

'Well, OK . . . it's a knife to the heart. But only after he's put them through unmitigated hell.'

'Does he gag them?'

'No.'

'Ah. He likes to listen, then.' Stella chewed her

bottom lip. 'Anything else of significance?'

Bobby Kennedy nodded.

'I was coming to that, Miss Arn — Stella.' He drew a long breath, tilting his head back while he exhaled.

'Yes. He leaves what you might call, ah, a very personal signature.'

16

That night Stella lay up to her chin in soapy water in her bath at the wood-framed house on Bancroft Road. The bathroom door was open so she could talk to Sylvia, who was stretched out on Stella's bed.

She'd have tomorrow to pack. She wouldn't be leaving Massachusetts until Tuesday, it had been decided. After the Secret Service radio car had been fixed, Bobby had spent a good quarter of an hour speaking to various agencies, organising the background checks on her and making arrangements on the assumption she would be duly verified and approved for purpose.

'You realise you were alone with them in that beach house for twenty minutes?' Sylvia was saying. 'Dad says ambassadors, potentates and kings get less than that. *Twenty minutes!* What on earth were you talking about for all that time? Come on, you can tell me now we're safe at home.'

Stella sighed. 'Honestly, I can't, Sylvia, not yet, anyway. I explained on the way back here that they were very clear with me about that.'

'Hmm . . . well, I'll let you off for now. But come on, at least you can tell me who you thought was the more attractive? Bobby's always done it for me. He looks like *such* a beach boy.'

Stella considered the question carefully.

'Yes . . . I know what you mean. Bobby has the youth and all that fizzing energy. He's stunningly good-looking too — it doesn't come across on the TV or on the newsreels where he always looks so thin and serious, and even a bit nervous, but in the flesh . . . yes, he's quite something, I agree.'

'And his big brother?'

'Hmm . . . of the two of them, he's got more . . . I don't know if you use this expression over here, Sylvia, but in England we call it sex appeal.'

'Of course we say that too! But why JFK more than Bobby?'

'Oh, I don't know . . . he's extraordinarily self-possessed and confident and obviously very good-looking, but there's something else there . . . I suppose it's all tied up with power. He exudes it, but not in a horrible, knowing way, like some men do. He almost seems unaware of it. It's very, very male and very, very seductive. Especially when it's just the two of you in the same room.'

'What? I thought you were with both of them the whole time?'

'No, Bobby went outside for five minutes — to get beers for us, would you believe. The United States Attorney General getting the drinks in! So it was me and the President in there for a short while.'

Sylvia seemed to be struggling to speak. Eventually she spluttered: 'Oh my God! With his reputation! What would you have done if he'd made a pass at you, Stella?'

'I dread to think,' she answered calmly. 'But he wasn't like that with me, not at all. I felt completely safe with him, all the time . . . anyway, can we change the subject, please? As long as it's not back to questions about what they wanted to talk to me about.'

Sylvia settled more comfortably on the bed.

'Oh, I know exactly what was going on, really. I've merely been toying with you, my dear.'

'Oh *really?* Enlighten me.'

'It's obvious. You're a British spy, aren't you? You've been unmasked, and now they've . . . what's the expression . . . oh yes . . . they've TURNED you. You're working for us as a double-agent now.'

Stella exploded with laughter. 'I only wish my life were that exciting,' she said. 'But honestly, Sylvia, it's no use. I can't say a solitary word about it, not to you, not to your parents, not to anyone. That's been made crystal clear to me. After the Kennedys left, I had the most horrible conversation with one of those Secret Service men . . . or maybe he was from the FBI, I don't really know, he only showed me his identity card for a split second and then it was back inside his jacket.'

'What was so horrible about him?'

'His crew-cut, to start with. Ridiculous on a man his age. But basically, he threatened me. He said if I breathed a word to a living soul about my conversation with the Kennedys I'd regret it for the rest of my days. I almost felt like retracting my offer to help them.'

Stella heard the creak of the mattress and the

swish of Sylvia's legs against the sheets as the younger girl sat bolt upright on the bed.

'A-ha! Gotcha! Your first slip, Miss Superspy! So, you've offered to help them, have you? Now we're getting somewhere! Help with *what*, exactly?'

A weary groan floated from the bathroom, followed by the sounds of a sharp intake of breath and swirling water and bubbles as Stella submerged herself completely beneath the water.

★ ★ ★

Two mornings later she stood with her hosts on the front porch of the house on Bancroft Road. A shiny black sedan was parked against the kerb, its dark-suited driver behind the wheel. He had already silently and effortlessly carried Stella's bulging suitcase down the front path and deposited it in the trunk.

Sylvia nodded appreciatively at the car. 'The McKewans on Franklin have just got one exactly the same. It's an Oldsmobile Dynamic, right, Dad? Brand new, too. That one there's *got* to be FBI.' She began to hop up and down on one leg.

'I *knew* it,' she continued. 'It's obvious. Stella's going to be an FBI special age — '

'Hush, Sylvia,' her father said, with a crispness that Stella hadn't heard in his voice before. 'You were bad enough during the drive back on Sunday, let alone at supper last night. Enough now. Stella's under a direct presidential order to say nothing. This isn't a joke, or a game.'

Sylvia subsided, muttering under her breath.

Jeb turned to Stella. 'Can you at least tell us when you'll be back?'

She shook her head. 'I honestly haven't a clue. I hope it's before the fall, though. I'd hate to miss my first term at Smith. I haven't even had time to look around the campus, yet. But in any event I'll be well behind in my preparations for next term because of this.'

Dorothy smiled. 'They'll understand. They can make allowances. Anyway, we'll speak to your faculty head for you. Not that there's much we can tell them . . . all this secrecy . . . '

A thought suddenly occurred to her.

'Oh my goodness. I can't believe I didn't think of this before. What about your mother? Can you write to Diana about any of it?'

Stella nodded. 'I think so. A little. I asked old Crew-Cut the same question yesterday and he said provided I don't go into any specific details I can at least tell her I'm going away on official US government business. But I have to hand over any letters I write to his lot to be censored first. I suppose I'll write something to my mother on the plane later on the way down to — '

There was an awkward silence before Stella closed her eyes and shook her head in despair.

'Oh God, I'm hopeless at this, aren't I? I wasn't even supposed to tell you I'm flying anywhere, and now I just have.'

'Don't worry, honey, we didn't hear a thing,' Jeb smiled, nudging her conspiratorially.

The Oldsmobile's horn sounded.

'Well . . . '

The Rockfairs crowded around Stella, taking

95

turns to hug and kiss her.

'We'll see you when we see you, I guess,' Dorothy said, giving her a final squeeze. 'Call or write when you're allowed, even if it's only to let us know you're safe.'

'I will, I promise,' Stella replied, suddenly feeling absurdly emotional. 'You've all been so lovely to me and I've only been here a few days. I've learned so much about life here in America in less than a week.'

'You're not the only one,' Jeb said drily as he took her arm and walked her to the waiting car. 'I've learned *never* to introduce any of my house guests to the Kennedy boys so soon again. Especially if they're as beautiful as you. Clearly, it's just asking for trouble.'

He opened the car's rear door for her and placed both his hands gently on her shoulders.

'Good luck, Stella. We'll be thinking of you every day. Come home safe to us.'

A few moments later, the government car was taking her away from the house on Bancroft and the Rockfairs were dwindling into the distance, still waving to her. Her passenger window seemed to be locked shut so she flapped her hand as best she could behind the car's oddly thick rear window.

The Oldsmobile pulled smoothly round the corner and Stella settled slowly back into her seat.

All at once, she felt utterly alone.

What on earth had she allowed herself to be dragged into?

17

He was puzzled. He had to admit it.

He'd expected the newspapers to reveal the technique he was using to take the girls. The nails, the chloroform.

The cops must have worked it out by now. They would have found the peaches' abandoned cars — he hadn't bothered to hide them, even if there had been the time — and everything would have been obvious. Number two would have strongly suggested how he was taking them; number three would have confirmed it beyond a doubt.

But after the fourth — which one headline had labelled: 'INFAMY IN ISLAMORADA' (he'd liked that; it sounded classy) — there was still no mention of how he was grabbing them; what one puffed-up senior cop had called the 'modus operandi'.

He'd picked up a Keys Courier AND a Miami Herald on the way in to work this morning and sure enough, number four was front-page news in both, but even though he combed through the main articles, and a feature piece inside the Courier headlined 'PSYCHO SICKO' — which was plain dumb, not to mention insulting — there was squat diddly about how he picked the peaches from their trees.

That bothered him.

He signed in at the office, grabbed the keys for

his usual cab from the duty pegboard, and went outside again to the pound.

He wasn't sure where to start his shift today. The supervisor left that kind of stuff up to the boys to decide. He was sorely tempted to drive south to upmarket Cheeca Lodge in Islamorada itself. That way he could swing right by the spot he'd been watching from the diner's window yesterday.

He decided against it. His waitress was giving him some mighty funny looks by the time he left — he'd been at the same table for nearly three hours, watching the increasingly frantic comings and goings outside — and the cops might now have set up a checkpoint where the dirt road peeled off Route 1. Not that that bothered him, at least not now, at this early stage. But it was going to be a long game and he didn't want his face to stick in a watchful cop's mind as the guy who always seemed to be hanging around the scene of the crime. That was how you got yourself caught, if you were stupid.

And so was sticking to the same . . . what was it that jackass had called it? Oh yeah, 'modus operandi'. That was going to have to change sometime soon.

He'd still kill them in exactly the same way, obviously. He'd got that down to a fine art, now, and anyway he enjoyed it way too much to want to change a single damned thing.

But he'd have to start working on a new trick to catch them. The investigation was obviously holding back the nails thing from the papers so they could lay a trap for him. Christ, they must *think he was born yesterday.*

It didn't matter either way. He'd work out a neat little plan B and leave them as flat-footed as before.

He selected Drive on the long lever that poked out of the old dash, and pulled out on to the Overseas Highway, turning north for once. Maybe he'd drive all the way to Key Biscayne, where there was increasingly serious money these days.

And serious money meant perfect peaches.

18

Massachusetts had been oven-hot when Stella flew out of Boston that same afternoon. But the wave of liquid heat that poured into the cabin of her scheduled flight to Miami when its doors opened soon after landing overwhelmed her.

She had never known humidity like it. She was standing a few feet from the nearest exit with stairs that led down to the concrete apron below, and all she wanted to do was retreat into what remained of the air-conditioned atmosphere in the fuselage behind her.

'Good *grief*,' she said faintly to a trim businessman in a light grey tropical-weight suit and jaunty straw pork-pie hat, who was immediately ahead of her in the queue to disembark. 'Is this normal for Miami?'

He turned and gave her a chipper look.

'This time of year? Why sure, honey!' He gripped his black crocodile-skin valise a little tighter as the queue began to shuffle towards the exit. 'Why d'you think they call us the air-con capital of the continent? You'll get used to it.'

She followed him out onto the little metal landing and into the whitest, hottest sunshine she had ever known. She gave a small gasp of shock, and almost at once felt rivulets of perspiration begin to trickle from her hairline and down her forehead, neck and back.

'Oh my goodness! How long does it take to get used to this?'

He shrugged. 'A week or two. But you have to embrace it. Don't complain about it or talk about it. You need to adopt the right psychological attitude.' He squinted at her in the glaring light as they began to descend the stairway. 'Think you can do that?'

Stella didn't reply at once; she was struggling with the unprecedented sensation of inhaling something disturbingly close to liquid air. 'What's that smell?' she managed eventually. 'It's like a bowl of rotting fruit in a steam-laundry.'

He laughed. 'That's the Sunshine State's special scent of summertime, ma'am. But like I told you — you'll get used to it. You might even come to like it.'

He trotted briskly down the stairway ahead of her. She couldn't see even the faintest marks of perspiration on the back of his spotless linen jacket.

Stella looked fuzzily at the airport terminal, sticky beads of sweat now oozing from her eyebrows and dropping down into her eyes, causing them to sting.

This was *awful*.

She remembered the brick of high-denomination dollars they'd given her just before she left Boston.

Maybe she should just buy a ticket home to England and be done with the whole thing.

There was a sudden roar of diesel engine and the airport transfer bus pulled up close to the bottom of the steps. Pork-pie hat turned round and waved at her. 'C'mon in!' he called. 'The air-con's lovely!' He pointed at the vehicle's sealed windows. 'It's gonna be like a Frigidaire in there!' He disappeared inside the bus.

Stella tottered after him. Back in England on hot days you opened windows on a bus; here it seemed that you had to keep them tightly closed.

Maybe, she thought, as she climbed on board into a miraculous coolness, she could contrive to spend most of her time in Florida indoors.

A minute or two later there was a grinding of gears and the vehicle moved slowly across the tarmac to the terminal building.

The journey took less than five minutes but by the time they arrived, the sun had vanished behind the blackest cloud she had ever seen and fat raindrops were beginning to drum loudly on the roof of the bus. Lightning flickered and, as she hurried into the arrivals hall, there was a violent crash of thunder, seemingly directly overhead. It made a cracking, shivering noise, like great tree-trunks being split in two.

Pork-pie grinned at her. 'Another perfect day in Paradise,' he said. 'How long you staying in Florida?'

Stella looked out at the sudden tropical downpour which was now so ferocious that anything further than fifty yards away from the terminal was completely obscured from view.

'I only wish I knew.'

★ ★ ★

The elderly professor replaced the handset in her study and stared blankly at her bookshelves opposite.

'My goodness,' she said at last.

She could honestly say that it had been the most extraordinary phone call she could remember receiving since the war.

It had come from the State Department in Washington, of all places. An extremely polite American had telephoned to ask her — *her* — to provide the White House with her general assessment of a former Girton student, Stella Arnold. Her reliability, honesty, and, specifically and most importantly, her standing in current academia on the subject of psychopathy and criminal psychopaths in particular.

Professor Harriet Donnelly had initially offered a rather frosty response.

'And why should you want to know this, may I ask?'

The pleasant voice, speaking from more than three and a half thousand miles away, had explained that Stella Arnold was being considered for a special internship at the White House, and that this phone call was part of a perfectly normal series of background checks.

'I see,' said Professor Donnelly. 'Well, I don't suppose it can do any harm . . . Miss Arnold is of impeccable character, I can certainly vouch for that. As for her specialist knowledge in the field of criminal psychopathic behaviour, she is, considering her extreme youth, exceptional. At the Paris conference on the subject last summer, she — '

The pleasant voice interrupted her to explain that the decision on the internship had to be finalised within twenty-four hours and therefore something in writing would be required. If Miss Donnelly could possibly put the salient points in telegram form, that would be greatly appreciated. There was no need to worry about the cost; she must feel free to use as many words as necessary, she would be promptly reimbursed.

So now the professor crossed the study to her writing desk and switched on its green-shaded lawyer's light. She opened a large leather-bound notebook and took out a fountain pen and began to compose a restrained eulogy to the most exceptional student of Psychology she had ever had the pleasure — no, the honour — of tutoring.

PART TWO

PART TWO

19

Stella was sixteen when they finally told her everything. About him; about what he really was; what he really had been all along.

She'd suspected much of it for a long time, of course. Most fathers didn't go round kidnapping their own children for ransom.

The biggest shock was to be told that he was dead, and had been for so long. She'd always had a vague idea of him continuing his shadowy, underground existence down on the Côte d'Azur, pursuing a violent criminal lifestyle underwritten by the enormous ransom her grandfather had been forced to pay for her release.

She'd always despised him, and learning that he was long dead changed nothing.

But as her mother sat there before her, steadily turning the secret pages of their shared pasts, her father's death turned out not to be the biggest surprise, after all.

Because there was something else her mother had to tell her.

Or rather, that her grandfather was about to confess.

★ ★ ★

Stella was sitting with her mother in the breakfast room of the Dower House, the country

107

home tucked beneath the Weald of Kent where Diana had grown up before the war; the place where she first encountered James Blackwell, the man who would steal her heart — and, a decade later, for two terrible days, her daughter.

Diana's mother and father had insisted that she and their granddaughter live with them in the Dower House when they returned so unexpectedly and dramatically from the south of France, the very day after Stella's release.

'Just for a while, anyway,' her father Oliver had said. 'Until you both find your feet.'

But the arrangement had become permanent. Stella had been boarding at a girls' public school in neighbouring Sussex for the past six years and Diana had accepted an offer from her old Cambridge college to complete the degree in Politics that the war had interrupted. She'd gone on to take her doctorate at Girton, where she now lectured.

★ ★ ★

Mother and daughter spent their holidays back in Kent with Oliver and wife Gwen and now, on this sunny August morning four months after Stella's sixteenth birthday, Diana was reluctantly embarking on the conversation she had been dreading for so long.

'Do I *have* to tell her?' she'd almost pleaded with her father the night before, with Stella safely upstairs in her bedroom. 'It's not as if she ever asks about it, or him.'

'Which means she probably thinks about it a

good deal,' Oliver had replied evenly. 'One day she'll simply confront you outright, and you'll be caught off-balance. She won't take any flannel, either — you know what she's like. Once she sets her mind to something she's an unstoppable force. You need to seize the initiative, now, my dear. It's best for you and fairest for her.'

'But, Daddy . . . apart from anything else, what on earth do I say about *your* part in it all? Only you and I and Mummy know what you did. Stella will be horrified.'

Her father went across to a silver cigarette box on the card table in the centre of the drawing room and brought it back with him to the sofa they were sharing.

'She'll be shocked, certainly,' he said at last, sitting next to her and stretching his legs out before him, 'but possibly rather thrilled, too. Don't deceive yourself, Diana — Stella holds no sort of candle for her father. She detests him. In any case, she's such an innately rational person that I'm sure she'll see the logic in what I did . . . what I *had* to do, that night.'

He lit a cigarette and waved it expansively in the air. 'Remember how well she handled her kidnapping, Diana. She was only ten but she wasn't the least bit afraid — in fact when I delivered the ransom to that bastard he told me that Stella had been in a constant state of simmering fury throughout. She'd even managed to attack him — remember the scratches and bite marks I saw on his face and wrist?'

Diana smiled despite herself. Her father was so proud of Stella, and of her fighting spirit.

She looked at him sidelong as they both drew on their cigarettes. He hadn't changed much since that last, extraordinary night in Nice. Now in his mid-fifties, Oliver Arnold was one of the leading libel barristers of his day. He was still dressed in the three-piece navy suit he'd worn to court that morning. His cufflinks were unclipped and his tie was loosened, as they always were at this time of the evening. Perhaps his hair was a touch greyer about his temples, and his waist a little thicker, but that was all.

Occasionally, when she was in town and one of her father's more celebrated cases was under way, she would drop in to the public gallery to watch him conducting cross-examination. Sometimes she wondered what a trembling witness might think if they knew that just a few years earlier, the bewigged, gowned and languid figure standing in the well of the court had, without hesitation or a shred of compunction . . .

He broke into her train of thought. 'Diana? Did you hear what I just said?'

'Sorry, no. Just thinking of something. Again, Daddy?'

'I was saying that once you've told Stella everything we know about her father, I'll tell her the final part about me and him. What really happened that night. Unless of course you think it'd be better coming from you.'

She was suffused with relief.

'It was what I was most dreading telling her. And no, I really think it will be better coming from you, Daddy. But aren't you in the least bit, well . . . anxious about telling her everything?

110

What you had to do to protect us both?' He smiled at his daughter.

'Don't worry. Just think of it as a closing speech.'

20

The car had just breasted Cutler Ridge — the only area of raised ground in this part of southern Florida, particularly vulnerable in the hurricane season — and was heading down towards the swamps and marshes that divided the mainland from the first of the Keys, the chain of narrow islands that stretched out like a long string of pearls into the Gulf of Mexico.

Stella leaned forward to speak to the driver. 'How much further?'

He paused in the act of inserting yet another potato chip into his mouth. She had watched in growing amazement as he went through pack after pack of them. This must be his sixth since leaving the airport. It would certainly help to explain the size of his stomach, which was pressing gently against the lower curve of the car's steering wheel. He must be the fattest agent in the entire US Secret Service, she decided.

'To Largo Lodge, ma'am?' he replied, small crumbs of crisp spraying from his lips and landing on the dashboard in front of him. 'Well, let's see now. Key Largo's about thirty miles, the Lodge'll be another five. We'll be there in forty minutes, I reckon, if the swing bridge ain't up to let one of these here luxury launches through the Sound. That always adds another quarter of an hour.'

'Thank you.' Stella sank back into her seat.

The scenery outside was boring; an endless flat expanse of fields sown with regimented fruit trees and bisected by drainage canals. Now and again they passed a scruffy-looking palm at the roadside. She was looking forward to the point where, according to the crumpled map she'd found in the back of the car, the Atlantic began to press up against the highway to the left, and the Gulf of Mexico pushed in from the right. That would be the start of the Florida Keys, and . . .

And what, exactly? She still wasn't sure precisely what it was she was supposed to be doing down here. She fished in her handbag for the handwritten scrap of card they'd given her before she left Boston that morning.

Service car to collect you at Miami Airport. FBI Agent Lee Foster to meet and brief you on arrival at Largo Lodge, KL.

That was it, apart from a scribbled Washington number she was supposed to call in any crisis or emergency.

She wondered what Agent Lee Foster was like. Just as long as he wasn't another Crew-Cut.

21

Stella often wondered what sort of reaction she would have got from the professors on her selection board for Girton if she had answered their very first question with the literal truth.

Why did she want to study Psychology, the youngest woman on the all-female panel had earnestly enquired of her.

'*Because my father was a homicidal psychopath and my grandfather shot him dead. It was an ex-judicial execution. That's rather left me wondering if I've inherited any similar proclivities for ruthlessness from either of them, so I thought I'd thoroughly investigate the question. Good enough reasons for you?*'

She doubted if such directness would lead to the offer of a place at Cambridge so had dissembled accordingly.

But it would have been a completely honest answer. Since the morning Stella had learned that her father was not only a gangster but a merciless killer, and that her grandfather had despatched him with a nerveless touch all his own, she had begun to wonder whether something of either man's ruthless streak infected her, too.

Not that she compared her father with her grandfather; not in moral terms. James Blackwell had been the epitome of selfish wickedness; Oliver Arnold was a good and loving man. She knew that. But somehow it disturbed her that she had found it so easy to accept her grandfather's explanation for shooting her father dead.

22

Key Biscayne hadn't exactly turned out to be the happy hunting ground of his hungry imagination.

But he was stone-cold right about the new money that was pouring in to the island, that was for sure. A lot of modern waterfront developments had sprung up since he was last up here two or three seasons back. Gated communities, mostly, which were no damn use to him. Uniformed guards in spick-and-span air-conditioned cabins behind electric barriers. He quickly registered that cars and delivery trucks wishing to be admitted needed to have special community identity stickers gummed to their windshields, different colours for different condominiums.

As he cruised slowly up and down the newly completed ocean boulevards he noted that the occasional cab was allowed through the gates, but all the drivers seemed to have some sort of specific reservation or booking code which they bawled out to the gatehouse as they pulled up at the checkpoint. Guards inside consulted a clipboard and ticked them off before they raised the barrier.

His own company's booking office back down in Key Largo never received calls from this far north, and the cabs going in and out of these model communities were a lot shinier and smarter than the scruffy sedan he drove. There was no chance of bluffing his way past the gatekeepers, he could see that; he'd stick out a mile.

Anyhow, even if he did talk his way inside, there were far too many residences (pink-and-white-painted two-storey town houses, mostly) with their owners wandering around in a virtual uniform of golf pants and Aertex shirts, to even think about trying anything. Through green-painted mesh fences he could see Hispanic groundskeepers tending perfectly maintained lawns and clusters of sub-tropical plants that lined the pavements. Here and there, classy-looking speedboats were being carefully towed on trailers down to private launch ramps that sloped gently into the lapping waters of the dock.

It was hopeless. He'd wasted the best part of a day driving up here, and then poking around, and he had nothing to show for it — no mark, no plan of action, not even a goddamned legit fare for his trouble. He couldn't understand what he'd been thinking of.

These days, he decided, Key Biscayne had become pretty much a semi-detached suburb of Miami itself. That was mostly thanks to the new Rickenbacker Causeway, which they'd finally gotten around to completing a few years back. Biscayne had lost any remaining atmosphere of the proper Keys — his Keys — which lay sixty miles to the south, where the islands began curving away from the sprawling brackish swamps of the Florida Everglades, down towards Cuba.

117

The real Keys were a sloppy, choppy mix of Caribbean, Cuban, and all-American Joe. Not like this pristine place. Welcome to Perfectsville, USA.

★ ★ ★

Cursing under his breath, he swung the old Buick in a hard, tyre-screeching semi-circle across the street and headed back towards Route 1. He glanced at his watch. It would be dark in a couple of hours. Already, he knew, folks down in Key Largo were beginning to drift towards ocean bars and restaurants on the westward-facing shores. They'd order cocktails, and jostle subtly for the best spots to watch the timeless end-of-day ritual: sunset. They'd raise their glasses as the sun drowned itself in the warm, soupy Gulf of Mexico, only to rise again a few hours later, dripping and renewed, from the cold Atlantic.

Highway traffic was light this evening and if he hit the gas he figured he could be at his favourite Gulfside seafood bar in time to catch the spectacle. The skies were clear, apart from some patches of high, thin cirrus. That promised a fabulous red-and-gold sunset and if the horizon stayed cloud-free and the ocean was calm, there might even be a chance of seeing the mysterious Green Flash — an incredibly rare phenomenon. He'd lived in the Keys for most of his thirty-two years and even he had only witnessed it once: the weird, piercing emerald ray that shot from across the ocean like a searchlight, at exactly the same moment the last fragment of glittering sun winked out below the horizon.

But the bright light that now suddenly flashed in his windshield mirror wasn't green.

It was red.

A moment later, it was underscored by the clipped, on-off whoop and wail of a siren.

★ ★ ★

'State driver ID, licensed cab-driver ID and county certification, please.'

The cop was close to his own age but it was hard to be sure. His uniform cap was pulled down low above the blank lenses of reflective Aviators.

He nodded to the patrolman as he reached up and flipped open his sun-visor, calmly removing documents from the built-in wallet.

'Here you go, officer. I think you'll find everything is in order.'

His personal stuff was in the unlocked glove box to his right.

Including the new knife, the rope, and the half-empty bottle of chloroform.

And his gun.

He told himself to stay cool. This was just a routine check.

'Thank you, sir. Step out of the car, please.'

He loathed being told what to do, but managed to resist the temptation to reach for the gun. He could take this cop here quickly and easily, with his bare hands, if it came to it.

He'd been pulled over at a lonely spot. The

waters of the Atlantic and the Gulf hustled in on both sides of the narrow two-lane highway. There was no dry land for buildings of any kind here in these shallow swamps on the edge of the Everglades, studded with bleached, drowned pines. The dead trees cast thin, gloomy shadows over the two men as the sun settled lower, getting ready for its big finale.

'Move behind the vehicle's trunk and remain there, please. I need to take a look inside.'

'Whatever you say, officer. I hope I wasn't speeding. I wanted to catch the sunset at Sloppy Joe's.'

The cop grunted and bent inside the cab through the driver's door. After a moment he grunted again and opened the rear door, peering around at the footwells and along the empty parcel shelf.

'Open the trunk, please.'

He popped the trunk and the cop made a careful inspection of the spare tyre, the jack and the toolkit. Apart from those, the space was empty.

'OK. Close it, please.'

He obeyed. Instinct told him something else was coming, and it wasn't going to be a ticket.

'You drive for . . . ' the cop looked at the paperwork he held in his hands: 'Pelican Cabs, Key Largo, right?'

'That's correct, officer.'

'So how come you're up here, halfway to the Everglades?'

'I had a one-way fare to Key Biscayne today, officer. Kind of a freelance thing, strictly between us. Off the books. You know how it is.'

The cop grunted once more. Christ, was this guy a terrific conversationalist, or what?

'So you'll have been out of radio contact with your base most of the day.'

Where was this leading? 'Uh . . . yeah, I guess so. The range on these sets ain't so hot once you're off the Upper Keys. Why?'

'Because otherwise you'd know by now we've kinda deputised you taxi drivers, as of this morning.'

'No, I hadn't heard that, officer. What's the deal?'

The cop removed his shades and began cleaning them on the end of his necktie. Without them, he looked older. A network of fine lines spread from the outer corners of his eyes and there were deep vertical creases flowing up towards the forehead above the bridge of his nose, too.

Too much Florida sun over the years.

'The *deal* is this crazy bastard we've been after for weeks now in the Keys. The psycho who's running around down here killing women. There's still a news blackout on how he snares them, but the Sheriff's decided to cut you boys in on that part of the story. He figures maybe you can help us.'

Oh, this was good. This was almost too good. Why did he always want to laugh, at moments like this? It would be the death of him, one day. Somehow, he managed to look concerned.

'A *psycho*, officer? My Lord. How exactly can we help?'

The cop pointed to the cab's dash-mounted two-way radio.

'By using that thing to call in if you see anything suspicious.'

'Hell, we do that anyway, at accident scenes and suchlike, you boys know that . . . but is there anything special we should be looking out for right now?'

'Yeah. Friend Fruitloop wedges three-inch nails under his chosen victims' front tyres, when they're parked up. That means they'll run flat later, around about a mile or two after setting off to wherever they're going, and that's when the son of a bitch takes them. Maybe plays the part of a knight of the road rescuing a damsel in distress. Who knows.'

'Jeez . . . he sure sounds like a calculating bastard, officer.'

'He is. Now, you see any car, any car at all, that looks like it's in trouble at the side of the road, you call right in and you report it. Right then and there, if you please. But you reckon it has a flat, you tell us that faster than you can fucking blink, OK?'

'Sure . . . but excuse me, what if the girl's still inside the vehicle?'

'Sheriff's still working the exact details on that scenario. But we protect our women here in the southland, do we not? So you act like a good citizen. At the very least, you keep an eye on her from a safe distance until we arrive. If it were me, I'd park my sedan right up close next to hers and offer her my gentlemanly assistance.'

122

'And if friend Fruitloop were to put in an appearance?'

The cop smiled faintly as he replaced his sunglasses.

'You done military service?'

'Sure. Korea. Special operations. Two years overseas.'

The cop's smile broadened a little.

'Then I'd say ... feel free to use your initiative, sir.'

23

'Looks like somebody's got themselves a ticket there. Cab driver, too. He oughta know better.'

Stella glanced out of the right-side passenger window in time to see a patrol car, its red roof-light flashing, pulled up close behind a dirty white taxi. The policeman was standing with his back to her but she could see the taxi-driver's face as they flashed past the little tableau. It was only a fleeting glimpse, so brief that the image was almost as frozen as a still photograph, but she had the definite impression that . . .

'I don't think he was getting a speeding ticket,' she said thoughtfully.

'Huh? What? How d'you figure that, ma'am?'

'Well I only got a glimpse, but it looked to me as though the driver was trying not to laugh.'

* * *

Largo Lodge turned out to be agreeable enough. A dozen or so white-painted wooden cabins with little verandas and pretty, bougainvillea-covered porches were dotted around a much larger twin-storeyed main building. This turned out to house en-suite bedrooms upstairs and, on the ground floor, a reception area with a smallish restaurant and bar. There were a few heavy pine tables inside under cover, but most were laid out haphazardly in the open, on the sandy beach that looked out across the Gulf.

Stella's driver, once he'd toted her bag to reception, had driven off without another word.

'*Charming. Probably gone to buy himself more crisps,*' she thought, as she signed the hotel register.

'Would you prefer a cabin, ma'am, or a room right here in the main house?' The desk clerk was a freckled, overweight man in his fifties with a velvet-soft southern drawl and the kindest eyes Stella thought she had ever seen.

'What would you recommend?'

'Oh, the cabins, ma'am. They're three dollars a night extra but they all have unobstructed sunset veranda views. And you're more in your own space in a cabin, I always think. It's the low season right now so I can do you an excellent deal. You can pretty much take your pick. There's only one other that's occupied, if I'm to be honest.'

Stella fumbled in her handbag for the card she'd been given that morning. 'Would that be a . . . let me see . . . a Mr Foster?'

The man looked surprised.

'Why indeed it would, ma'am. But I — ' He suddenly closed his eyes, and his shoulders sagged.

'Oh Lord. Where are my wits when I want 'em? You must be . . . ' He turned the register around so he could read Stella's signature. 'You are Miss Arnold, right?' His kind eyes were now filled with anxiety and self-reproach. 'Mr Foster was *expressly* clear with me that the moment you arrived I was to direct you to him at *once*. He

125

was most insistent. I do believe he may be here in some official capacity. Oh dear, oh dear . . . '

Stella tried to reassure him.

'Look, it's quite all right, I've only this minute checked in, haven't I? You've done nothing at all wrong. Where might I find Mr Foster, please?'

But the clerk remained flustered. He gestured nervously towards the beach restaurant, visible through sliding glass doors that were firmly shut to allow the air-conditioning to keep the building cool.

'He's out there right this minute, at the beach restaurant. Young guy sittin' on his own wearing Bermudas. Changed out of his coat and tie as soon as he checked in. He's government issue or I'm a Frenchman. I hope we're not in any kind of trouble here. This is a respectable hotel. I'll have your bag taken straight to your cabin. You're in Conch — last one before the ocean. Oh dear oh dear.'

Nervous, disconnected sentences stuttered out like tickertape.

Agent Foster, Stella thought, as she was shown to her cabin, must have quite a forceful personality.

★ ★ ★

Despite the clerk's agitation she decided to unpack first and freshen up. She was still wearing the navy skirt and cream blouse she'd put on in Boston that morning, and they were both creased and grubby from the flight. Also, she noticed with some embarrassment, there were

126

dark perspiration stains under both arms of her blouse and even down the back.

She dropped the clothes, including her underwear, into the laundry basket in the bathroom and decided to take a quick shower.

She was towelling herself dry a few minutes later when the phone on her bedside table rang. She hurried over to pick it up.

'Stella Arnold.'

'Agent Foster. What the *fuck* do you think you're doing?'

'I . . . I *beg* your pardon? I was — '

'You were what? Taking a siesta after your arduous three-hour flight down here in first class? You were specifically told to check in with me the moment you arrived.'

Stella snatched the phone away from her ear and glared furiously at the receiver. She was tempted to slam it back down on its cradle but somehow managed to resist the impulse. Instead, she counted to ten before returning it to her ear. By now Foster's voice had gone up a semi-tone and he sounded angrier than ever.

' . . . Hello? HELLO! Are you still there? Jesus Christ . . . *hello*?'

Stella took a deep breath. 'Yes, I'm still here. Be quiet.'

'*What?* Now see here, you have to — '

'No, YOU have to. Be quiet, that is. To start with, I did NOT fly here first class and neither am I having a nap, although if I chose to, I certainly would. All right? As for seeking you out the moment I got here, if it was that urgent and important, why weren't you waiting for me in reception? Instead of sunning yourself in your Bermuda shorts out there on the beach, hmm? *Agent* Foster?'

The line popped and crackled with static before he answered, in a slightly more measured tone.

'OK, OK . . . I can see we've got off on the wrong foot here. I — '

Stella decided to match his more conciliatory tone, but without giving an inch. 'No, Agent Foster, *you* got off on the wrong foot.' She paused for emphasis, before adding curtly: 'I'll be with you in five minutes. Will you ask for some menus, please? I'm absolutely starving.'

★ ★ ★

Stella took her own time and it was closer to twenty minutes before she chose to walk outside to the hotel's beach restaurant. Her hair was still damp from the shower and she had only bothered to put on a little mascara and a swipe of lip-gloss. Her sunburn of a few days earlier had evolved into a healthy-looking tan.

The sun was now extremely low on the horizon, although it still radiated a surprisingly fierce heat in a way it never would this late on an English evening. But there was no sign of the reds and pinks and yellows in the western sky that Stella had heard accompanied so many Florida sunsets. Maybe all that was a bit of an exaggeration, a self-serving myth to draw in the tourists. Currently, the heavens were a uniform azure blue.

She could see at least a dozen tables set out on the soft, white sand. Most were empty, although one or two had seated couples, sipping beers and cocktails and waiting patiently for the free lightshow to begin. But all the tables had glowing hurricane-lanterns above them, their aluminium casings painted in jolly greens and reds and attached to hooks screwed into the tops of tall, thick bamboo poles that had been driven deep into the sand. The flickering lanterns were beginning to sway in the strengthening evening breeze.

The hotel had its own inlet and dock cut into the southern half of the beach, and as she watched, a speedboat nosed its way carefully into the little harbour, its outboard burbling quietly on low revs. She saw a slim, tanned woman in a yellow bikini emerge on deck from the cabin and throw a mooring rope ashore in one practised movement. A waiting attendant deftly caught it and quickly tied it off onto a metal cleat.

There were a few other motor boats rocking gently at their moorings; maybe they were for hire. Stella made a mental note to find out: if she got a chance it would be fun to go out on a fishing trip, and certainly a lot cooler than staying ashore. It was still oppressively humid, although down here by the water the breeze felt a little fresher.

Agent Foster was sitting at the table nearest to the ocean. It had to be him, she decided; he was the only solitary diner there and she could see two absurdly large menus in the shape of lobsters had been placed on both sides of the table. But he wasn't wearing Bermuda shorts; he was in khaki chinos and a white cotton shirt. He must have gone in to change after she'd mocked him earlier.

She was in white too; she'd put on the simple lace dress that Sylvia had given her the morning she left Bancroft Road.

'Unless they're sending you to Alaska you'll need something smart and summery,' the younger woman had told her. 'This is a bit on the short side but you've got terrific legs, so you can carry it off.'

Stella was finding it difficult to walk on the soft, shifting sand so she slipped off her sandals and carried them in one hand as she made her way across to the table.

She couldn't see Foster's face because he was reading a paperback, holding it high to catch the last of the sun's rays behind him. The book completely obscured his features. The novel, she noticed as she drew closer, was *A Tale of Two Cities*. For some reason it surprised her that an FBI man should be reading Dickens.

'It was the best of times, it was the worst of times,' she called when she was a few feet away from him.

He lowered the book.

'It was the age of wisdom, it was the age of foolishness,' he replied.

No crew-cut. A short-back-and-sides, rather, and although his brown hair had been combed back from his forehead it was sneakily trying to tumble back down into a fringe above his right eye. He looked, she thought, more English public schoolboy than American agent and he couldn't be all that much older than her. Thirty, at most.

'I always forget the next part,' she confessed, holding out her hand. 'Something about it being the spring of hope and the winter of despair. I'm Stella Arnold. How d'you do?'

'Lee Foster.' He stood up, took her hand in his own and gave it a quick shake. 'Yes, that bit comes after the stuff about the season of light and darkness, blah-blah. But to be honest I reckon Dickens was squeezing the lemon pretty dry in that opening, anyway. He'd done the job with his best of times, worst of times line. He should've left it there.'

He hesitated. 'Look, Miss Arnold ... I'm sorry I was so, well, terse on the house phone just now. I had a long flight from LA and a truly annoying message from C. Farris Bryant waiting for me when I landed in Miami.'

Stella sat down opposite him, unwilling to let it go just yet.

'You weren't terse, you were extremely rude,' she said flatly. 'I'm supposed to be here to help, not to be insulted ... Bryant's the state governor, isn't he?'

He nodded. 'Yup. And he's in a real fix, thanks to these killings.'

He put both hands into his trouser pockets and leaned back in his chair, staring at her. She realised that he was sizing her up, and she folded her own hands in her lap and waited.

'Now look here, Miss Arnold.'

'It's Stella.'

131

He hesitated, and then said, with quiet emphasis: 'I'll stick to Miss Arnold, if that's all right with you. I don't believe we're going to know each other long enough to get on first-name terms. Anyway . . . ' He removed his hands from his pockets and folded his arms on the table in front of him. His body language could not have been clearer: he was shutting her out.

'Anyway . . . here's the thing. I have no real idea why Washington sent you down here but to speak plainly, you're in my way, Miss Arnold. Hoover's drafted me in to oversee this investigation because I have a track record on this kind of stuff. I catch repeat killers. I'm good at it. I've been in California wrapping up my third multiple murder case and J. Edgar hauled my sorry ass across the continent to handle this one.'

He tried and failed to attract the attention of a distant waiter before continuing.

'So, I get here to find a goddamned *writ* from the state governor telling me I have to work with a kid who's not even out of college. An English kid, too. I'm sorry, but it's all way out of the ballpark, Miss Arnold, and it's not going to happen, OK? Anyway, I answer to J. Edgar, not C. Farris or any other fucking politician. Excuse my French.'

He sat back, waiting for her reaction.

Stella looked at him calmly.

'I completely understand your feelings, Mr Foster. Now, have you decided what you'd like to eat? I want to order. I told you, I'm starving.'

132

He hadn't expected her to fold quite so easily and he looked surprised, and relieved.

'Um . . . well . . . me too, I guess. I'll have the little-neck clams with linguine. You?'

'The same. I'll order for us both while you make your phone call.'

He stared at her. 'What phone call?'

She fished into her handbag and brought out the scrap of paper she'd been given that morning.

'To this number. I was told to ring it if there was any kind of serious problem, but I rather feel you're the one with the problem, Mr Foster, not me. So you'd better be the one to call.'

He took the note and peered suspiciously at the digits scrawled across it. 'I don't recognise this, other than the Washington code. Whose number is it?'

Stella waved to a nearby waiter. 'We're ready to order now, thank you,' she called. The man nodded and hurried over.

She placed their order, then smiled at the mystified agent opposite her.

'You mentioned his name just then. I think you need to have a little chat with your boss. Have you actually spoken with him personally before? I'd have a care, if I were you. The Attorney General told me Mr Hoover can be awfully grumpy when people call his home at dinnertime.'

★ ★ ★

He was back five minutes later, flushed and angry.

'Great. Thanks for the ambush.'

She raised her eyebrows. 'How so? I told you who you were calling. Anyway, why would I want to ambush you? As I said, I'm here to help you. Although I certainly didn't ask to come down here. I was politely, if extremely firmly, *sent*.'

'Sure, Hoover made it clear to me you're here on the highest authority but he didn't deign to give me the details. What the hell is going on? You made some crack about the Attorney General just now. Are you serious? You know Bobby Kennedy? Is he behind this? I don't believe it.' Foster was seething with a combination of curiosity and anger.

Stella closed her eyes and slowly pushed both hands through her hair. She'd come to America to study for her PhD. Right now she should be amongst her new friends in Massachusetts, preparing for her studies. Not wrangling with a resentful detective down here in the near-tropical late summer swelter of the Florida Keys. Maybe she should have transferred directly to the international departures lounge at Miami Airport after all, and bought a ticket for the next plane home. None of this was her problem.

Before she could answer, the waiter was back with their bowls of steaming clams and pasta. Stella felt slightly restored by the sight of food.

'We'd like some wine too, please,' she said. 'Mr Foster . . . what would you recommend?'

'What? Oh . . . well, a Californian Chardonnay usually hits the spot. Two glasses, please.'

'Sure,' the waiter answered. 'By the way, I'd leave those clams to cool for a few minutes. The

134

sauce is just a shade below boiling.'

When they were alone again, Stella leaned across the table towards him.

'I'd be happy to explain all this to you, Mr Foster, but I'd appreciate it if you took that ridiculous frown off your face first. You've been glowering at me since I sat down.'

For the first time he looked slightly off-balance. 'I wasn't aware that I was frowning,' he said stiffly.

'Well you are. Ah . . . that's a little better. Now, please listen to me. None of this is complicated. I'm here because I happened to bump into Ethel Kennedy last Sunday at a beach barbecue in Martha's Vineyard. Her husband was there too. And JFK and Jackie, if you want to know.

'Ethel asked me why I was in the States. I explained I'm here to take a PhD in Psychopathy at Smith. I know a *lot* about psychopaths, Mr Foster, especially the dangerous ones. When you've calmed down, I expect you and I will have some interesting exchanges about them. Anyway, Mrs Kennedy got very excited and went to find her husband.

'The next thing I knew I was in a room alone with the Attorney General and the President, and after a conversation I won't burden you with, followed by a rather unpleasant grilling from the Secret Service, I found myself on a plane to Florida.'

She leaned back and reached inside her bag for cigarettes and lighter. 'Which is why you and I are sitting here having dinner together. I told you, it's not complicated. You're frowning again, by the way.'

He glared at her. 'Oh boy, this is just *great*. You walk into this, this, this high-society *soirée* in the Vineyard and — '

'It wasn't a *soirée*,' she calmly interrupted him. 'It was lunchtime.'

'Who the hell cares. You walk in looking like a million dollars, no doubt, with your cute English accent and batting your eyelashes every which-way, you do a great snow job on the President and his brother, and *I'm* the sucker who ends up landed with you the first day I get down here. I'm an FBI agent, Miss Arnold, of many years' standing, not a babysitter. I've got a killer to catch, and an extremely active one too. We could wake up tomorrow morning and discover he's murdered his fifth. Frankly, at the rate he's going, we probably will.'

He pulled a breadstick from the packet between them and broke it in half, staring moodily out at the setting sun.

'Sure,' he continued a moment later, turning to her again. 'You've read all about psychopaths in your textbooks and research papers and discussed them at conferences and you've written your double-A-star essays, and you think that makes you the jumping-jive expert, right? But have you ever tracked a psychopathic killer, Miss Arnold? Arrested one? Pulled a gun on him a split second before he pulled his on you? Jesus wept. I can't believe this.'

The waiter arrived with their drinks, apologising profusely for forgetting them. Stella leaned

136

down and quietly stubbed out her cigarette in the sand. 'Now we can eat.'

They ate in silence for a couple of minutes before she spoke again.

'You asked me three questions, and the answer to all of them is no, obviously. I'm not a policeman. I don't arrest people, still less point guns at them. But I know how these men *think*, Agent Foster. I know how they *feel*. From the little I've been told about your killer down here, I've already managed to build up a rough profile of sorts.'

He forked a clam into his mouth and washed it down with a gulp of Chardonnay.

'Oh you have, have you? Then please enlighten me, limey. Who exactly should I be looking for, in your elevated, academic opinion?'

She stared at him. 'Please don't call me limey. It's just silly. Would you describe Charles Dickens as a limey? Or Cary Grant? Or Charlie Chaplin?'

He sighed and rubbed his eyes with the heels of his hands. 'No, of course not. I'm sorry. Like I said, it's been a helluva day and I'm just letting off some steam here. Look . . . why don't we pick this up in the morning? It's obvious we're gonna have to work together, J. Edgar couldn't have made that plainer to me just now. You can make your pitch to me over breakfast.'

Stella stood up and tossed her napkin on the table.

'I have no intention of making any kind of *pitch* to you or anyone else for that matter,' she said coldly. 'But I *will* tell you what I know about repeat killers and how they behave, and how I believe one can seek them out. I was given some very basic case notes on this one to read on the flight down, and as I say, I've had one or two general ideas already. But if that's not good enough for you, Agent Foster, then I'll fly back to Boston. Frankly, I'd be glad to. It's your choice. In fact, it's your problem. It certainly isn't mine.'

He looked at her in surprise.

'Look, hold on. Where are you going? I just said I'd work with you, didn't I? Anyway, don't you think you should finish your meal and your wine, and watch the sunset? Look at that sky now. It's all coming together. Jeez, it's so *fast* down here.'

She glanced out at the skyline. The fading blue had been replaced with daffodil-yellow streaked with red. It had happened almost as quickly as a theatre lighting change.

'I have my own veranda for watching the sunset, thank you. As, presumably, do you.'

She slipped her sandals back on and put her bag over her shoulder before picking up her barely touched glass of wine in one hand and her dinner in the other, and began to head back carefully across the beach towards her cabin, but after a few steps she halted and looked back at him.

'I really would like to help, you know. Oh, I don't mean help *you*, personally,' she added quickly. 'I mean *them* — those poor girls out there. We have a very intelligent, very dangerous creature to catch. He's your enemy. Not me.'

138

She hesitated. 'And I agree with you. He may very well take another one tonight. Whoever he is, he makes Jack the Ripper look like a slouch. But I presume you've already spotted his Achilles heel?'

Fortunately for Agent Lee Foster, Stella had turned away again before he could think of a suitable reply.

24

There was no fifth killing that night. The *Courier* had splashed with the fourth murder two days earlier and this morning the paper had to be content with a lesser story about how the girls were being snared.

KEYS KILLER: PUNCTURES VICTIMS' TIRES FIRST

It wasn't a bad lead, Henry Stewart thought, as he left that morning's news conference and returned to his own office. And it was a bona fide scoop, thanks to a taxi driver who'd been on the paper's payroll for years.

Circulation had gone through the roof since the first killing just over three weeks ago, spiking on the mornings following the discovery of a new victim. Today's sales figures would be good; people were avid for details of the case.

But nothing sold like fresh blood.

A handwritten note from his secretary was waiting for him on his desk. One of the Governor's press aides, a former *Courier* reporter, in fact, had telephoned during morning conference and would appreciate a call back. *Says he might have something interesting for you*, the note finished.

The news editor poured himself a black coffee from the pot that was kept permanently filled on his window ledge, before returning to his desk and dialling the number. The man at the other end picked up on the second ring.

'Greg! It's me, Henry. How are ya? You called.'

A few seconds later Henry Stewart stiffened, and screwed the receiver tighter into his ear. 'Yes, I'm getting this, Greg. Go on.'

When the journalist spoke again, it was a one-word question. 'Source?'

After a moment he chuckled. 'Nah, neither would I. But you can't blame a guy for trying. I'm happy to take your word on it, though, Greg. Just one more question — why are you being so good to me?'

Now he burst out laughing. 'Always negotiate your price before you drop your tip, my friend. The old man won't come through with that much gold but I'll see what I can do. He's in a pretty good mood at the moment, what with the upped circulation and syndication fees from that photo. I'll get back to you. And Greg? Thanks.'

He disconnected the call before dialling a single digit. His secretary picked up in her office next door.

'Sheila? Tell the old man I'm coming through with news; news to warm the cockles of his chilled and pickled heart.'

★　★　★

'So how much does this guy want? What's his source?'

Stewart grinned at the *Courier*'s editor-proprietor, who was sitting behind his vast teak desk like a wrinkled old terrapin. William Brinks's appearance hadn't altered a scrap in the ten years the news editor had worked for him.

'As if he'd tell me, Bill. Or you, come to that. But from the way he was talking, I'd say it's got to be someone in the White House. As for how much he asked for, if I told you, it'd probably put you in hospital with your third coronary. But I reckon he'll be happy with a couple of hundred bucks and tickets to the top table at this year's Miami Press Ball for him and his wife.'

'He's goddamn lucky I didn't sue him for crooking his expenses when he was still with us,' the old man replied. 'But I suppose that's OK. I've paid more for less.' The editor pushed gold-rimmed glasses to the top of his bald, deeply tanned head. He always reminded Stewart of an elderly bank teller when he did that. An elderly bank teller with a loaded shotgun resting on his knees under the counter.

'How you gonna run it, Henry?'

'Front lead; big picture.'

'Of the girl?'

The news editor nodded. 'Of course. We'll get one later today. Greg says she's a real English rose, by all accounts. I have her name and where she's staying. I doubt we'll get a quote from her but I've already got a guy on the way over and whatever's there to be got, he'll get.'

'Syndication rights? The UK papers will want it, too, remember.'

'Jeez, Bill, I haven't even written the damn story yet.'

142

'And yet still the schmuck sits here in my office.'

Laughing, the news editor went back to his own desk and sat down in front of an old battered Corona, his companion ever since he graduated from journalism school twenty-five years earlier.

He took a sheet of blue carbon paper and sandwiched it between two blank pages of cheap letter paper, rolling them around the typewriter's drum and snapping the spring-loaded restraining bar over the top two inches of paper.

Normally he let the chief sub-editor compose the headlines, but not this one. It had come to him even before he'd put the phone down on his contact not ten minutes earlier. He flexed his fingers the way he always did before writing a story. Then, with the crude typing style of journalists the world over, he began stabbing the keys with both forefingers.

A moment later, he was looking appreciatively at tomorrow morning's headline.

'AN ENGLISH ROSE FOR A KEYS KILLER.'

25

Stella didn't know it, but Henry Stewart was putting the finishing touches to his story about her as she finished her breakfast of sliced melon, pineapple and French toast in the lodge's air-conditioned dining room. She pushed her plate away and picked up Lee Foster's note to read it again. He must have slid it under her door while she slept.

Dear Stella (if I may belatedly now call you that),

I owe you an apology, and a much better one than my half-assed attempt yesterday evening.

In mitigation for my rudeness, let me explain that I have just worked twenty-three days straight in LA on my last case and I got no sleep at all the night before I flew down here (it's a long story but it was the only way to close the case).

So I was pretty frazzled when I got to the Keys, but I had no business at all taking it out on you.

This morning, after my first good night's sleep in a month I woke up to a wire from the FBI in Washington. You weren't kidding when you told me you knew a few things about psychopaths. Your former university tutor has vouched for you, and how. I was wrong to doubt your qualifications, in fact I can see now they could come in very useful. So, once again, I apologise.

I've gone to the local police headquarters for a full update on this Keys case, but I should be back mid-morning when I can fill you in too, and then we can get started. I'm sure we'll work very well together.

   Until later,

   Lee

PS Grab yourself a copy of this morning's Courier (they have them in reception) — there's a not half-bad account of how he catches them before killing them, and profiles of all the victims so far. Still four — we were wrong about waking up to another. Maybe he struck out for once. He's certainly had more luck so far than any killer has a right to.

Stella folded the note back into its envelope and put it in her bag. It was, she decided as she reached across the table for the *Courier* a waiter had brought her, a gracious apology as far as these things went and of course she would accept it. Anyway, it would be nice to be on better terms with the young FBI agent. He was obviously intelligent and, now her anger with him had subsided, she had to admit to herself that he was . . . well, rather attractive. But as she shook her paper open, she firmly doused the faint excitement that she could feel stirring inside her. For all she knew, Agent Foster could be married.

But she didn't think so.

A few minutes later Stella put her newspaper down and stared with unseeing eyes through the restaurant's plate-glass windows towards the beach that lay beyond, all thoughts of Lee Foster gone.

The man she had come all this way to help track down was certainly methodical. The article she had just read reported that the nails he used to puncture his victims' car tyres were of a uniformly heavy gauge and exactly three and a half inches long. He placed four of them, in pairs, leaning backwards into the treads of the tyre on the front passenger side of his chosen vehicle. As soon as it moved off, the tyre was pierced, running flat within a mile or two. Police speculated that the killer chose to sabotage a front tyre because the driver would 'feel' the puncture through the steering column as their car veered increasingly to one side, and be more likely to promptly pull over. It was possible to drive on a rear flat for some distance before realising there was a problem.

There was no sign of a struggle at any of the abandoned cars. The doors had usually been carefully locked, and the girls' handbags and personal valuables had, in every case, been removed. It was impossible to say for certain, but it seemed the victims may have gone willingly with their killer.

Stella picked up the newspaper again and turned to the profiles of the dead women. They had been allocated a quarter of a page apiece, each mini-biography accompanied by a black-and-white high school photograph of the victim. Slightly eerily, all the girls were portrayed wearing the mortar board and gown of their graduation day and all but one clutched a furled diploma in its shiny embossed cardboard tube. The photos were relatively recent. The oldest victim, Stella noted, was twenty-four, the youngest nineteen.

She began to read:

VICTIM ONE — HESTER WAINWRIGHT, b. 06/13/1942

Hester Wainwright was last seen alive by her parents three weeks ago as she left the family home on Sawgrass Blvd for night college at Homestead. She never arrived. Her car, a white Chevy Convertible, was later found with a shredded tire neatly parked on the central grass verge of Overseas Highway, less than two miles from the Wainwright residence.

Of Miss Wainwright there was no sign, until the following morning when her body was discovered by a fishing party in mangrove swamps south of the soon-to-open John Pen-nekamp State Underwater Park in upper Key Largo. As with all the Killer's subsequent victims, she had bled to death from multiple stab wounds and cuts to all parts of her body.

Miss Wainwright was a trainee hotel manager and mid-way through a business studies course at night school. She was intending to marry next summer and her distraught fiancé, who was arrested and questioned by police hours after the body was discovered, has been cleared of any knowledge of or involvement in the slaying.

VICTIM TWO — JENNIFER ALSTON, b. 04/23/1940

Kmart checkout attendant Jennifer Alston was born Jennifer Davies in Southampton, England, but was almost immediately evacuated to the

147

United States at the start of WW2. Her parents were killed during a German air raid in 1941 and Miss Alston was adopted shortly afterwards by Harold and Becky Alston, her US sponsors here in Key Largo.

She became a naturalised US citizen while still at high school and was saving much of her Kmart salary to finance a one-year full-time course in make-up and beauty treatments, after which her adoptive parents say she had hoped to open her own salon.

Miss Alston disappeared on her drive home from work and her car was later found abandoned, one front tire heavily punctured. Like all the Killer's victims thus far, Miss Alston's body was discovered floating in mangroves well out of sight or sound of any dwellings or business premises. Initial examinations indicate that she died of blood loss, shock, or a combination of the two.

VICTIM THREE — LUCY TWAIN, b. 03/03/1938

Lucy Twain was an experienced scuba diver and part of the advance team preparing the world's first underwater national park, John Pennekamp, for its grand opening on Key Largo next year.

Born and brought up in the Keys, Miss Twain, in an interview with this newspaper last year, declared that Pennekamp would attract visitors from all over the United States and beyond.

Miss Twain was driving to her home from a planning meeting at Pennekamp when she was abducted. But as she lived alone in a one-bedroomed apartment in Homestead, no one reported her missing.

Police eventually found her abandoned red Ford pickup two miles north of Pennekamp on a deserted gas station forecourt. But this was after a coastguard vessel on routine patrol checking for boat-wash erosion to mangrove channels near Buttonwood Sound had discovered Miss Twain's body there. At twenty-four, she is the oldest woman to die at the Killer's hands.

VICTIM FOUR — BECKY HOOPER, b. 06/30/1943

It was with the discovery of the Killer's youngest victim earlier this week that signs of a bizarre sub-pattern may have begun to emerge.

Becky Hooper was the 19-year-old only child of married Key Largo general practitioners Stephen and Samantha Hooper, who have been practicing in the Upper Keys since they arrived here from New York in 1955.

Like Wainwright, Alston and Twain, Miss Hooper was young, slim and considered to be pretty. But was her hair color of significance too? The first victim was dark-haired; the second fair; the third a brunette, and Miss Hooper a strawberry blonde. Dark, fair, dark, fair. Will the Killer's next target prove to be dark-haired?

Stella snorted. Silly, speculative nonsense. It was far too soon to read any significance into the question of hair colour. Irritated, she bent over the paper to read the final paragraph.

Miss Hooper's mutilated body was discovered by a canoeing party close to the Islamorada Bridge, the furthest south of any such gruesome discoveries to date. As with all the Killer's victims, she had suffered multiple stab wounds, severe blood loss, and the knife used to inflict the fatal injuries was left deeply embedded in the left eye-socket.

'It's his signature,' a source close to the investigation told the *Courier* last night. 'He's telling us: 'Make no mistake, it's me again. I'm back.' He's proud of his work. This here's one very, very sick guy.'

Stella left the newspaper on the table behind her and slid back the restaurant's plate-glass exit to the beach, pushed open the sprung screen door that fitted snugly behind it, and stepped outside. It was barely nine-thirty but the sun was already high, though not yet burning with the intensity it had on her arrival in Miami the afternoon before.

As she walked across the sand back to her cabin, a young man in a crumpled linen suit materialised beside her.

'Stella Arnold?'

She stopped and turned towards him. 'Yes, I am she. Who are — '

He smiled engagingly at her. 'I'm to give you this.' He handed her a long-stemmed red rose.

150

Stella looked down at it with a puzzled smile.

'But who is it from?' She raised her head again. She was staring into the blank lens of a camera.

'Compliments of the *Courier*, Miss Arnold,' the young man said, snapping off three or four quick frames. 'Welcome to the Florida Keys.' He turned on his heel and walked swiftly away.

26

'*Shit.* Sorry, Stella. But this could be a damn nuisance.'

Lee Foster and Stella were sitting on high stools at the hotel's beach bar. She hadn't noticed this place the evening before; it was tucked behind the little dock where she'd observed the motor boat tying up.

He had called her in her room when he returned from the police briefing; they'd arranged to meet here and she had told him straight away about her encounter with the *Courier*.

'Why would they want to take my picture? And how did they know my name, and that I'm staying here? I'm baffled.'

'I wish I was,' he said, taking a swig straight from the neck of his bottle of Coca-Cola. 'There must have been a leak, I'm afraid. Someone in the administration — or in Bryant's office — has been talking to the *Courier* about you.'

'Why would they do that?'

He shrugged. 'You're currency. All stories are currency. I can just see tomorrow's headline — 'JFK Drafts Beautiful English Killer-Catcher To Help Nail Keys Slayer'.'

'But I've never caught a murderer in my life,' Stella protested.

'No matter, Stella, that's how they'll run it. It's a good story. It reflects well on Washington and

Bryant — makes them look focused on cracking the case. They want folks down here to think they're on the ball.'

She toyed with her orange juice and shook her head in genuine bemusement. 'It never even crossed my mind that this would happen. Isn't there anything we can do to stop them?'

He finished his Coke. 'Nope. Not a damn thing. We have a free press in this country, Stella, and in their book you *are* a killer-catcher. You're an expert on psychopaths, aren't you?' He scratched his chin reflectively. 'Hell, apart from some temporary embarrassment to the Bureau — Hoover will *not* have wanted this story to break — I can't see there being much harm done, now I really think about it. A few stupid headlines won't make any difference to the investigation, or your contribution to it.'

He stood up. 'C'mon. Let's forget about it. I've requisitioned the hotel's one and only suite as our office while we're down here. They should've finished installing the extra phone lines and teleprinter by now. Let's go get settled in and I can tell you everything I know about this case. You can start by reading the files.' He tapped a thick manila envelope under his arm and grinned at her. 'And then you can tell me who our man is; I'll arrest him; and you and me can go fishing for a day or so before they wise up and send us both home.'

He signed the bar bill and handed her his ballpoint. 'Better keep this pen handy. When the *Courier* comes out tomorrow with your picture all over page one you might find yourself having to sign autographs.'

★ ★ ★

When the two of them reached their converted suite, Foster explained to Stella how things were going to work.

'The State Police are doing their thing; the local FBI are doing theirs, and I'm meant to be Mr Go-Between, co-ordinating everything. But I can't take you with me when I go to combined headquarters — that'd go down like a bag of cold sick, trust me. They're funny about women down here. No one on the force will admit it, but they operate an informal 'keep women out' policy, a bit like the colour bar in some of the states down here.'

'You're joking.'

'Nope. I know, I know, this is 1962 but you're in the southland here, Stella. The sight of you walking in by my side would be marginally less welcome than Castro coming ashore on Miami Beach waving the red flag. It's just how it is. And as for your being English as well as a woman . . . ' He shrugged expressively.

'Do your colleagues even know I'm here?'

He shook his head.

'So what happens when I'm all over tomorrow's *Courier*?'

'I'll handle it. I'm senior case officer. They'll think what I tell them to think. Let's just not rub their noses in it.'

He handed her the manila envelope. 'C'mon,

154

we need to get going. You should start with these.'

Stella shook out four separate files, each with one of the dead girl's names printed on the front cover. She carried them across to an office bureau by the window and sat down in a creaking chair mounted on castors. She flipped open the first file.

As the minutes passed, it became clear to her that in every case the killer's *modus operandi* was the same — or very nearly. The victims' hands and feet were bound with the kind of medium-gauge hemp rope sold in any hardware store. There was no trace of any gag or other attempt to silence them, but skin tests around the mouths and noses of the victims all revealed identical chemical traces. Two of the girls — the ones whose bodies had been discovered soonest after they were killed — gave off a faint but distinctive odour of solvent or cleaning fluid.

Tests showed this to be chloroform, just as Bobby Kennedy had indicated to her. Stella knew it to be a heavy, volatile liquid once widely used as an inhalation anaesthetic, particularly in dentistry. Detectives believed it had been used specifically to incapacitate the victims for capture and transport, and that they were allowed to regain consciousness once they had been securely bound and transferred to the location chosen for slaughter.

In each case, the left eye-socket had been punctured by a blade at least five inches long, which had been buried in the skull. The knives were high-quality brands and of the same design

— narrow-bladed stilettoes. Quantities of eye-fluid had spread out across the victims' faces, but the absence of any significant blood flow from the socket suggested that the trademark wounds were inflicted postmortem.

The main theatre of death was, it was abundantly clear, performed on the girls' torsos, legs and arms, and genitalia. Once again, the wounds were strikingly similar in every case. There were at least fifty to sixty puncture marks, none of them deep enough to be fatal on their own. Many cuts were more like elongated runnels, stretching in neat parallel lines down all four limbs. There was clear sexual mutilation, with both breasts deeply and repeatedly punctured, and beneath them the abdomen and vulva were cross-hatched with a dozen or more curving, scimitar-shaped slashes. The *coup de grâce* was always a stab to the heart.

There was only one exception to the uniformity of the mutilation, and Stella immediately grasped its significance.

The first victim's wounds were noticeably deeper than the following three: it was plain she must have bled to death quite quickly, probably within ten minutes.

But the cuts and puncture wounds on the other girls were shallower. This, the report suggested, would have resulted in a more lingering death, possibly lasting up to half an hour.

'He's a fast learner,' Stella said aloud.

Foster looked up from his own desk opposite. 'How's that, Stella?'

156

She gestured to the files. 'He's deliberately refining his technique so he takes as long as possible to kill the girls. You don't just have to look at the depth of the knife wounds — the first victim; what was her name?' Stella flipped back through the original file — 'Yes, Hester Wainwright, poor girl. The ropes binding her wrists and ankles left some pretty bad burn marks where she strained and twisted against them while he went to work.'

She pushed the file away and picked up the next in the sequence.

'But see what happens when he gets his hands on Jennifer Alston? These aren't just friction burns, Lee. One of her wrist bones is exposed and her right Achilles tendon is almost severed. It's even worse with the next two.'

Foster shot her a narrow look. He had been browsing through a stack of scene-of-crime photographs, but now he tossed them back onto the table and leaned back in his chair, clasping his hands behind his head. 'You OK, Stella? These here pictures are bad enough but I always think the cold-blooded descriptions are worse. You look a bit pale to me.'

She shook her head impatiently. 'Nonsense. I'm fine. But this case is, well, it's *exceptional*, isn't it?'

He nodded, and walked over to a coffee percolator he'd had installed for them. '*Oh* yeah. This guy makes the Marquis de Sade look like jolly old Saint Nick.' He poured out two mugs. 'Cream? Sugar?'

'Both, please.' Stella pushed the files a little

further away. 'I've studied a lot of historical psychopathic killer cases,' she said slowly. 'Most have had elements of sadism, often sexual sadism, but *this* . . . be honest, Lee, have *you* come across one as bad as this before?'

He shook his head. 'If I'm honest, no. Most of the crazies I've chased down, or read about, are more jazzed up about the actual killing part, you know? But like you say, our man here seemingly puts it off for as long as he can manage. For him, it's all about the pain, and inflicting it for as long as possible. I think their deaths are almost an annoying inconvenience to him. Obviously the dagger to the eye isn't meant to kill; they're already dead. It's his flourish. Have you got to the part about the fingerprints yet?'

'No, but I already know he doesn't use gloves or make any attempt to wipe his prints from the scene.' Stella reached for the file again.

'Don't bother; I'll spare you the trouble. His dabs are all over the knives — well, their handles, anyway; they're automatically wiped off the blades when he stabs the girls. He just doesn't care.'

'Isn't that a bit odd?'

'Yup. Even with crimes of passion you usually find some attempt to wipe prints afterwards. But these aren't crimes of passion, are they? They're more like surgical procedures, meticulously planned from start to finish. Yet this fingerprint business is unbelievably sloppy and careless. I can't begin to work out what the guy's playing at.'

Stella looked thoughtful. She absent-mindedly tapped out a cigarette from the pack on the table beside her and lit it. 'Oh, I'm so sorry, Lee,' she said suddenly, 'I didn't offer you one.'

He waved the pack away. 'Not right now, thanks. But I'm glad you've started calling me Lee.'

'What? Oh . . . yes, of course . . . now, these prints. Presumably no one's found a match for them yet.'

'Not in police records down here in the Keys, Miami, or Southern Florida, no. Obviously we're spreading the search.'

'Hmm.' Stella blew out smoke, shaking her head as she did so. 'I'll bet you won't find anything, however much further afield you look.'

Foster raised an eyebrow. 'You sound very sure.'

'I'm sorry, but I think it's rather obvious. Leaving prints like this is so completely out of kilter with all the rest of it, isn't it? I propose that we assume our killer has never been in any kind of trouble with the law, and therefore he's confident his fingerprints aren't held on records anywhere. He knows he can't be tracked down that way.'

'Sure! But when we catch him through other means we'll get a match in about ten seconds and straight to Old Sparky he goes.'

'*If* you catch him, you mean. *He* doesn't believe you will. That's the explanation for this, Lee. Like a lot of psychopaths, he'll be a complete, raging narcissist. He's getting a huge kick out of taunting you by deliberately leaving

159

his fingerprints behind. It's classic catch-me-if-you-can behaviour.'

Foster looked distinctly put out. 'Well, that's no good to me, is it? If you're right, these prints won't be the slightest use in catching him until we've . . . well, caught him, if you get me.'

She shook her head. '*Nil desperandum*, and all that. The fact that he's arrogant and over-confident enough to play such a reckless game means, in itself, that he's vulnerable. That's what I was referring to last night when I mentioned his Achilles heel. I need to do some thinking on this but we may have identified his chief weak point: hubris. We should be able to play on it. Give me time.'

The FBI man stared at her.

'You certainly think differently, I'll give you that,' he said at last. 'But when we *do* get the cuffs on him, surely he'll be sorry about the prints then?'

For the first time in the conversation, Stella laughed. 'Good God no!' she replied. 'Once he's got over the shock of being arrested, he'll want full credit for what he's done. I guarantee you he'll plead guilty. He's so proud of himself; of his ingenuity, his cunning.'

The FBI detective scratched his chin.

'OK. So what does that make him? Crazy-clever, or crazy-stupid?'

Stella didn't hesitate. 'Oh, despite flawed behaviour and thinking resulting from excessive self-adoration I think he's a very, very bright individual. I know you use the terms blue-collar and white-collar worker over here.'

'Go on.'

'Well, I think he's more likely to be blue-collar, but that doesn't mean he's not extremely clever. He's a practical man, but instinctive and persuasive. He's probably quite charming, too. Charm is a common feature of the most dangerous psychopaths — I'm sorry, I'm sure you knew that already, Lee, I don't mean to patronise — and that's how he's managing to get these poor women to go off with him without a fuss. He'll have some convincing cover story or other; I'll bet he even manages to makes them laugh, too. They'll feel perfectly safe with him.'

He looked at her uncertainly. 'You *know* all this, Stella?'

She shook her head. 'Not exactly . . . but I do seem to have innate understanding about such things. Did that telegram from England mention the Edinburgh conference I attended in May?'

He shook his head.

'It was a three-day affair for psychiatrists and psychologists . . . I presented a paper on predictive behaviour. Anyway, on the last day they gave us an exercise in something quite new, something called profiling. We were given details of six separate repeat-killer cases from Europe and America, with certain key information altered or withheld so we couldn't identify them. All the cases had been solved. We had to predict what the personality types of the murderers turned out to be.'

'And?'

Stella looked slightly embarrassed. 'Well,' she said, hesitating, 'the fact is that in each case I got

161

the killer more or less bang to rights. Social background, approximate age and IQ . . . there was one strangler who killed five women in Brussels before he was caught and I said he was probably a bus conductor and he *was*, Lee . . . and there was a poisoner in Italy, I forget where exactly, who I *knew* would turn out to be a schoolmaster, and he was — a deputy head, actually.'

The detective whistled. 'So I'm impressed. What do you think our man here in the Keys does for a living?'

She wrinkled her nose, surprised at the question. 'Really? It's obvious, surely . . . I mean, in a general sort of way, if you think about how he snares them and presumably bears them off before he overpowers them.'

'So enlighten me.'

She neatly stacked the files and slid them back into their envelope before replying.

'Whatever it is, it's definitely got something to do with cars.'

'I'm listening.'

'Well, in every case, the victims' cars have been locked, the keys are gone, and the girls have taken their things with them — handbags and so on. No signs of any kind of a struggle. I think that gives us the basis for the reasonable belief they went willingly, even calmly. They remembered their things and they remembered to lock up.'

He nodded, disappointed. 'I think all that's already accepted, Stella. I don't see what that's got to do with — '

She gestured to him to be quiet. 'I haven't finished, Lee. We have to ask ourselves *why* four bright young girls would go off with a stranger like that, assuming he *was* a stranger. In most cases it would have been getting dark, too, which you'd think might add to their feelings of insecurity.'

She put her elbows on the table and steepled her fingers under her chin. 'I've been trying to put together what would be necessary for each one of them to drop their guard so completely.'

Stella began counting off on the fingers of her right hand.

'One. He would have been very persuasive and reassuring. In other words, a charmer. That's a classic psychopathic trait, as we said. But if he was doing the knight in shining armour bit, why didn't he offer to jack up the car and put on the spare? We can only theorise, of course, but he must have come up with a believable reason not to do that. Maybe he lied and told them the spare was flat, or it was too dangerous to change the wheel in the dark, or the toolkit was missing. The point is, he must have demonstrated a lot of *authority*. They accepted whatever he came up with at face value.'

'Very good, Stella. But I still don't see the car connection.'

'I'm coming to that.' Stella paused, frowning. 'OK. *Two.* I think he didn't just sound convincing; he *looked* convincing, too. I realise this is extended conjecture, Lee, but my instincts are telling me I'm on the right track, they really are. I believe this man carried extra authority, especially on the subject of cars, because he has something to do with them. Professionally, I mean.'

The FBI man stared at her intently. 'Are you trying to say you think this guy could be cop? A patrol car officer?'

'It's possible. You should certainly examine the local police car patrol records for the four nights we're talking about, see if there's any kind of suspicious pattern. But aren't there two officers to each car?'

He nodded. 'Usually, though not always. All the same, I'll get it checked out. Go on.'

'*Three.* I believe the clinching factor in the girls going off with him was something to do with the actual car he was in. It represented an added element of reassurance. Presumably he offered to give them a lift home in it and clearly they were happy to climb in.'

She paused for a moment, thinking hard. Eventually she continued: 'I said earlier that we've been assuming this man was a stranger, largely because there's no known connection between any of the victims. But what if they all *did* know him, even if only by sight? Or at the very least, were familiar with the car he was driving? Familiar enough with him or his vehicle, or both, for all four girls to feel perfectly safe going off with him.

'Which brings us to *four.*'

Stella took a deep breath.

'I think he's probably a local taxi driver.'

27

He awoke restless and distracted. Pages of Milton's masterpiece lay scattered on the floor by his bed; the poem had done nothing to calm or comfort him the night before.

The 7 a.m. thump of the rolled-up Courier thrown by the paperboy against his cottage's screen door got him out of bed, but he was lethargic as he went to collect it. He wouldn't make page one today. He'd done nothing to earn it.

Five minutes later, he was pacing between his tiny studio kitchen and the TV lounge and back again in a tight figure of eight, the twin chicanes curving sharply at the Baby Belling stove at one end of his compact home and the portable TV at the other.

He couldn't recall being this excited. Not since the day he'd finally decided to act out the fantasies that had remorselessly consumed him for almost as long as he could remember.

The Courier's headline alone had almost arrested his heart and breathing. His hands had begun to tremble so badly that he'd had to lay the newspaper flat on the tiny kitchen table so he could read the paragraphs beneath that glorious, glorious banner and accompanying photo.

An English rose, indeed.

For him.

Just for him!

And by order of the fucking President of the United States of America. This wasn't a dream come true because he'd never had the audacity to imagine even for one second that such a glittering reward would be his. And after less than a month's work!

He forced himself to calm down and switched on the coffee percolator in the kitchenette. Only when he had a steaming mug of Colombia's finest cupped between both hands did he return to the Courier. Now, he read its astounding front-page story with meticulous attention.

AN ENGLISH ROSE FOR
A KEYS KILLER
By Henry Stewart

JFK has personally intervened in the ongoing Keys Killer case. The President this week requested a British expert on repeat slayers join police and FBI investigators as special advisor.

The *Courier* can reveal this specialist to be stunning English psychology graduate Stella Arnold (pictured). Miss Arnold, believed to be still only in her early twenties, has rapidly acquired a formidable reputation in Europe as a prodigy: a youthful yet leading authority on homicidal psychopaths.

Sources close to Fla. Governor C. Farris Bryant last night confirmed that Miss Arnold flew to Miami as early as Tuesday this week and has already held an initial meeting with the senior FBI officer in overall charge of the investigation.

The *Courier* knows the location at which Miss Arnold has been placed during her attachment but is withholding this information for the security of the investigation.

He burst out laughing. What a joke. He studied the photo again. He'd recognised the picket fence and palm trees in the back of shot the moment he picked the paper off the porch. The clincher was the fragment of clapboard building with wooden steps down to the beach that was visible on the extreme right of the picture. That was the hotel dining room. He'd delivered and collected around a dozen or so fares there this year alone.

She was staying at Largo Lodge. He turned back to the closing paragraphs of the story.

It is understood that Miss Arnold's specialist knowledge includes the relatively new science of 'profiling' — predicting the personality type, social class and sometimes even the profession of a wanted killer, a factor which can significantly reduce the scale of the task facing investigators.

'Profiling is a very promising field of study,' Miami University criminologist Professor Ernest Raymond told the *Courier* last night. 'The hunt for the killer becomes more centred. It's like using a sniper's rifle as opposed to a dragnet. If this English expert is everything the White House clearly believes her to be, the days of the Keys Killer remaining at large may well be numbered.'

Another burst of laughter forced the gulp of coffee he'd just swallowed back up from his throat and out of his mouth and nose, spraying across the lower half of the newspaper in front of him. He managed to sweep it to one side just in time to preserve the sanctity of her photograph. HER, hunt HIM? Didn't they understand anything? After all that he had achieved? All that he had proved? He studied the photograph again.

She was remarkably beautiful. And she was his. She belonged to him. His gift. The paper said so, didn't it?

Very well. He would claim her.

28

'How long you known 'bout this bitch for, Foster?'

The pudgy Miami detective threw the newspaper to the floor and glared at the FBI man opposite. There were scattered mutterings from other officers standing around the room.

Lee had arrived at Key Largo's police headquarters to discover a mutiny of sorts had already begun. He realised immediately he must neutralise it before the investigation was derailed by injured professional pride and wounded southern male vanity.

He'd walked into the temporary operations room to find a gaggle of detectives crowded round that morning's *Courier*, Stella's startled face staring out at them from the front page. One of the men was poking at her image with a stubby forefinger, saying: 'I ain't taking no advice or orders from some goddamn stuck-up English-her-ladyship, I'm tellin' you guys that for free.'

Now they were glaring at Lee, waiting for his reply. He made direct eye-to-eye contact with the man who'd challenged him.

'How long? For a whole lot longer than it'll take me to bust you clean off this investigation, lieutenant. I can have you directing traffic by noon, trust me. Christ, in my time I've canned guys I'd call friends. You, I don't even like.'

The man opposite blinked and licked his lips, glancing at his fellows. 'Sounds to me like you been pussy-whipped good and proper already, Agent Foster.'

Lee crossed the space between them in three strides and pushed the lieutenant hard against the wall. As the man bounced off it he twisted him through 180 degrees, shoving his face into the whitewashed brickwork and sliding his right arm under the astonished detective's jaw, putting him in a fierce choke-hold. The man spluttered ineffectually.

'Hey!' one of the others shouted. 'You assaulting a fellow officer there!'

Without looking round, Lee snarled: 'Not for the first time, pal, and if you don't shut your yap I guarantee you it won't be the last.' The man fell silent.

'Right.' Lee tightened his grip on the lieutenant's throat and the man's chokings were cut off. He raised his voice. 'Listen up, every one of you. Stella Arnold knows more about the kind of man we're after than you guys put together. She knows more than I do, come to that. She's not here to give anyone orders: she's here to give us the kind of advice we need to nail this bastard before he tortures another kid to death. Meanwhile, the only orders around here come from *me*. You got that, everyone? *You* got that, lieutenant?'

He suddenly released his grip and the man slid down the wall, coughing and retching.

Lee ignored him and turned to face the others. 'Show of hands. Anyone who wants off this case

170

raise your arm NOW. I don't want pussies on my investigation who feel threatened by a twenty-two-year-old girl. Go on — raise your chickenshit hands. Then you can clear your desks and go home. I'll decide what to do with you later.'

No one moved a muscle.

Lee let the moment hang a little longer before nodding briefly. 'OK. So let's get back to work. Someone bring the lieutenant here a glass of water.'

He walked across to the blackboard in the corner of the room and wiped it clean with the sponge hanging from a cord at the side. Then he chalked a single word in capitals and tapped it with a fingernail.

'Cars.'

The squad looked at each other, mystified.

'He's something to do with cars,' Lee explained. 'Mechanic, maybe. Car rental.

'But most likely he's a cab driver. We'll start with the latter. I want every taxi outfit here on Key Largo visited in person. Then if necessary we move on to garages, then the rental companies. We're looking for a youngish guy, probably under forty, probably good-looking, probably smooth-talking, probably been on the job a while. We need them to account for their movements on the four nights in question. Anyone who can't do that, or you have even the slightest bad feeling about — bring them in. Cuff them if you have to. We'll fingerprint every damn one of them until we find our man.'

The half-throttled lieutenant spoke in a rasping croak. 'That's a lot of guys. It'll take us

171

days. And we're short here. Coulter — he's been running the case until now — called in sick yesterday. Suspected appendicitis. He'll be out for — '

Lee turned to him. 'Breathe easy, pork chop. I spoke to Coulter by phone from the coast before I flew down here. We'll manage. Right now I want you to go down to the control room and bring up the patrol car records for all four nights. Look for anything unusual or suspicious.'

'What? You think he's a *cop?* Seriously?' someone asked after a shocked pause.

Lee shrugged. 'He could be. Now, let's get on it, gentlemen.'

★   ★   ★

Lee Foster had been born in the middle of the Great Depression twenty-nine years earlier. His father Laurence was then a Phoenix-based architect with no commissions to build anything any more, and his mother Frances was a hairdresser with her own salon and no customers. By the time Lee was six months old, the mortgage company had foreclosed on the loan his parents had taken out to buy the salon two years earlier, and Laurence had sold his Ford for 200 dollars, their furniture for not much more, and bought one-way train tickets to Los Angeles.

'Everyone says it's not as bad in LA,' he told his wife. 'We'll rent somewhere and start over. We'll be fine.'

And by Lee's third birthday, they were.

172

Laurence had landed a job at City Hall thanks to FDR's huge public investment programme and Frances was waiting for their son to start school so she could enrol at law college. By the time Lee was in high school, his mother had graduated and was practising in the rich field of accident and injury litigation. In 1941 she won a major case for the Teamsters union — Frances masterminded their strategy in a class action revolving around truckers' safety on long-haul trips — and the Fosters bought a three-storey house on the outskirts of Beverly Hills.

By the mid 1950s Lee had graduated with honours from UCLA and was wondering exactly what to do with his crisply furled diploma in English Literature. He toyed with the idea of teaching but the idea didn't really appeal to him.

★　★　★

Then one evening, alone in the house while his parents attended a charity ball downtown, he idly switched on the family's TV set. The titles of a brand-new weekly cop drama were playing.

By the time the credits rolled thirty minutes later, Lee's world had somersaulted.

City Detective told the story of a tough-but-bright New York police lieutenant, played by an actor called Rod Cameron.

Lee was captivated before the first commercial break. He realised it was a stupid popcorn cop drama — he'd worked out who the killer was inside ten minutes — but it lit a fuse deep within. Crudely but effectively, the programme

173

had revealed his destiny to him.

He was going to catch killers. He was going to save people.

He was going to be a police detective.

★ ★ ★

Officer Foster spent less than three years on the LA force before he was talent-spotted by the FBI and quietly suborned into its ranks. His skill was to be able to look at a case, any case, in three dimensions. He could see into and around and behind whatever facts were assembled before him, however sparse.

'You have perspective, Mr Foster,' his FBI recruiting officer had told him. 'You see round corners. Most of us see stuff flat, like in a regular movie.' He mimed putting spectacles on. 'But you have those 3D glasses, don't you? You have depth of field. In this business, that's a rare and precious gift, son.'

★ ★ ★

Now, pairing off his officers to begin the trawl around Key Largo's cab firms, Lee privately wondered where that 3D vision had gone. He couldn't believe he hadn't grasped the potential car link before Stella had. She was right; it was obvious. In fact, he hadn't had a really useful insight into this case since arriving in the Keys. Mind you, that was less than twenty-four hours ago and he was unbelievably tired. It had been an exhausting summer on the west coast and he was still coping with the three-hour time difference between here and California. He should stop beating himself up.

He yawned. Something was tickling the back of his brain; a dawning realisation he couldn't quite grab a hold of. Absent-mindedly, he bent down to pick up the *Courier* from where it was still lying, crumpled and scrunched up from where the stupid, rebellious lieutenant had thrown it twenty minutes earlier. He shook it open and looked at Stella's innocent, lovely face staring out at his.

And the shadowy, hazy thought quietly moved into focus.

Of course. If she was right about his being a cab driver — and every instinct told him she was — the maniac they were after would very shortly be checking out of the whole damn scenario. The moment he realised that men in his line of work were being trawled by the police, *en masse*, he would be out of Key Largo and off into the blue yonder.

'We've been too clever for our own damn good,' he muttered to himself.

There was the sound of a heavy tread on the stairs leading up to the office and the fat lieutenant he'd half-strangled earlier reappeared. The man was clutching a month's worth of patrol car schedules and he dropped them onto his desk with an exaggerated sigh.

'Leave those for now,' Lee told him shortly. 'I've got something more important I want you and me to do together, as fast as we can.'

'So what might that be . . . *sir*?'

175

Lee ignored the man's barely concealed insolence.

'Grab us both a Yellow Pages. We're gonna call every cab company on the Key. If a single one of their drivers doesn't show up for work over the next couple of days, or calls in sick, their office is to phone us immediately. I mean, right then and there. This is red flag stuff — be sure to make that clear.'

His interest clearly piqued, the man lumbered off to get the directories.

When he returned, Lee flipped both copies open at the section listing taxi firms. 'You work backwards from the Zs, I'll take it from the As,' he ordered. 'Ask for the boss and tell him he's not to discuss this call with anyone.'

'Gotcha. Do we tell 'em to expect a visit from one of our boys over the next day or so as well?'

Lee considered that a moment, then shook his head. 'No need.'

They might not be able to stop their bird flying the coop, Lee thought as he began dialling the first number, but they'd be on his tail so damned fast he'd go down harder than a bird bounced by a diving falcon.

The bastard wouldn't know what hit him.

29

It was a young uniformed sergeant by the name of Hicks who was one of the first to grasp the nature and scale of the problem facing them, after they'd visited just two taxi call-rooms. Unlike the cautious older officer he'd been partnered with, Hicks was untroubled by being the bearer of bad news to a senior so it was he who volunteered to radio in and speak direct to Foster.

'It's like this, sir,' he said, leaning on the roof of the squad car in the sunshine and idly flicking the spiralled cord that connected the oval microphone to the transmitter fitted under the dash. 'These local firms don't keep records worth diddly. Just a note of who was on duty on what shift, the mileage done, and how much was on the meter when they clocked on and off. There *is* a log of pre-booked pick-ups and regular jobs, but not of cold calls, or casual pick-ups at hotels and bars.'

Lee scowled as he listened. 'So what you're saying to me is, the records don't really tell us anything.'

'Other than which drivers were operational on the nights we're interested in, no, not really. I've radioed some of the other guys and they're saying the same thing, sir.'

Lee drummed his fingers on the desk, concentrating.

'OK,' he said at last. 'I think I know what we're gonna have to do — but I need to make my dispositions first. And I have to place a call.'

*   *   *

Back at Largo Lodge, Stella was getting bored. There was nothing much more she could glean from the files, and she was beginning to wonder if there was actually any further value in her staying down here in the Keys. Unless she was wrong about the whole car connection, of course. That would involve some serious re-thinking.

If anyone gave a damn any more what she thought.

She was about to go for a walk along the beach before it got too hot, when the phone in her room rang.

Lee.

'I need you to make your very best call on something. Right now,' he said as soon as she'd picked up.

'I'll try.'

'OK. Things are moving fast here. I'm going to have to bring in a lot of taxi drivers for questioning and fingerprinting at once, now, today. Logistically it'll be a nightmare so I need to keep the numbers down as far as possible and not waste time with guys you think are outside our frame. What I'm asking you for, Stella, is a definite age cut-off. You told me you thought our man was probably under forty. Why? The psycho I just nailed back in California was nearly sixty.

178

He killed five women. What makes this one here so much younger?'

Stella tried to marshal her thoughts.

'Look, Lee . . . this isn't an exact science, you know. Profiling is more or less in its infancy. I won't lie to you, there's a lot of stabbing about in the dark and — ' Her hand flew to her mouth. 'I didn't mean that the way it sounded.'

He gave a graveyard chuckle. 'It's OK, Stella. That was pretty apt, as it happens. But go right on, please. I don't have a whole lot of time this end.'

'All right . . . well . . . the reason I think this killer may be — and I emphasise, *may be* — under, say, forty, or even thirty, is because there's something . . . you'll think this is so strange . . . well, there's something almost *puppyish* about the way he goes about it all. I've been looking at the post-mortem photographs again, and you can almost sense his sheer enthusiasm when he marks them. The wounds are so prolific and extensive; he just can't hold back.

'And then there's that first girl, and the relative speed at which he killed her compared to the others. I know it sounds bizarre but it speaks to me of an almost youthful impatience and exuberance. I'm going to blush now but it reminds me of the way a young man is said to be when he takes a woman to bed for the first time. Very often it's all over before it's begun, isn't it? But they learn and go slower the next time . . . just like our man here.

'Two more things. There's the rate at which

he's killing them. He's in such a *rush*, Lee. Excitement again, like a kid in a sweetie shop. And lastly, this fingerprint business. It's *so* over-confident and arrogant. I just can't see an older man being quite so reckless.' She paused for breath. 'Does any of that help at all?'

Despite the brutal subject matter, he found himself smiling into the receiver.

'More than you can imagine. Right . . . I've got some buttons to push here now, but I'll see you later. I have a portable shortwave radio so there's no reason I can't have dinner with you at Largo Lodge — it's only a mile or so from headquarters and I can be back inside five minutes if I get the call. Anyway, I might have more stuff to run past you by then. I hope I do. Because so far, I have to say you've been a bloody goldmine, Stella.'

30

There was something going on. He knew it. It was goddamn obvious.

He'd come on shift at ten this morning and not only did there seem to be a lot more black-and-whites on Overseas Highway today but most of them were pulling over outside the offices of rival taxi firms. That wasn't right. That wasn't right at all. In fact, on the way down to Cheeca Lodge to pick up a regular fare — the lodge's owner's mother who had her hair permed every month — he'd heard his own radio controller put out a jokey call to all the boys.

'Hey guys, we got the Highway Patrol here asking questions. So, who's been a bad boy, huh? Who's been — HEY! What the heck, officer, I'm just — '

Transmission had ended abruptly with a squawk and it didn't take a whole lot of imagination to work out why.

He chewed his lip as he drove sedately on south to Islamorada, the deep blue of the Atlantic to his left and the aquamarine of the Gulf to his right as he breasted another summit of one of the spanking new concrete pontoon bridges. The old wooden ones had been pulverised so often by hurricanes that Florida and Washington had bowed to the inevitable and invested bucket-loads of tax dollars on these indestructible replacements.

The dependability of the new upgraded road link that connected Key Largo the whole ninety miles down to the last island on the chain, Key West, was already taken for granted. Next stop, Cuba? People speculated that if Castro took a hike, maybe someday there'd be a soaring, arching highway all the way from Key West across the shallow, narrow straits to Havana. That'd be some bridge to drive over for sure.

But he wasn't thinking about that this morning. He was wondering how the hell the cops had worked it out — or at least this much of it. The taxi connection.

He'd been so damned careful.

He was always scrupulous about pulling up on the blind side of the girls' cars so drivers approaching from either direction would find it difficult to see the mostly obscured cab. He switched his lights off, too, and it was usually getting dark. He was positive he hadn't been spotted. If so, surely the Courier would have carried something. The police would have an obligation to warn young women not to accept unsolicited help from a taxi driver, if they'd broken down or gotten a puncture.

It had to be this fucking English girl. HAD to be. His rose, indeed. The bitch had a sharp thorn on her. The White House guy was right when he told the Courier she was good. She was damned good. He couldn't for the life of him think how she'd put it together so fast — she'd only been down here in the Keys, for what, two, three days? But he could worry about that later.

And work out how to make her pay.

182

For now, he had a small and fast-closing window of time to decide what to do. Not long — but enough.

He forced himself to think calmly. The only way they could pin the killings on him was by taking his fingerprints, and there were scores of other cab drivers working Key Largo who'd have to be eliminated first. It would take hours, if not days, to round everyone up.

And he'd be long gone before they got to him.

He knew that vanishing overnight would put him top of the list as prime suspect for sure, but that didn't matter. He was going to disappear in a way that would make Houdini look like an amateur.

Suddenly he pounded the taxi's steering wheel in frustration. He'd counted on a much longer run than this; in fact he'd figured he might be able to go on indefinitely, even if that meant eventually quitting the Keys. Look at that London guy — Jack the Ripper — never been caught and no one knew who he was to this day.

He slowed to a crawl and when the highway was clear, made a careful U-turn, heading back north.

That old lady wouldn't be getting her hair done today.

But he would.

31

Lee put the phone down and kicked back his chair on its castors, stretching his long legs out in front of him as it rolled smoothly away from his desk on the wooden floor. He rubbed his face with both hands and managed to resist the temptation to pour himself another coffee. He was wired on caffeine already after at least six cups of the stuff over the last few hours.

Mentally, he replayed his checklist. Was there anything he'd neglected to do? He didn't think so.

Downstairs in what the uniformed guys called the 'front office', dozens of youngish cab drivers had already been efficiently processed, their fingerprints taken and compared to the killer's. So far there had been no match, but there were at least twenty more men to bring in. He reckoned they'd be pretty much through by this time tomorrow.

Realistically, though, he didn't think their man would show. Lee increasingly regarded the whole mass fingerprinting operation as an exercise in flushing out his quarry. Once the killer realised what was going on, he'd shimmy right out of the picture.

Every taxi firm had been phoned back and it had been emphasised that they must call the police the moment they suspected any of their drivers had dropped off the radar.

The call Lee had just completed was the last in a rapid series to organise the effective sealing off of Key Largo. He'd put police roadblocks at bottlenecks at the top and bottom of the island — one to the east, at Little Blackwater Sound, where Route 1 veered sharply north over the shallows towards Homestead and Miami, and the other at the south-western end, straddling the approach to the swing bridge at Tavernier. All vehicles were being stopped and their driver's identity checked. Officers had been fully briefed on the profile of the wanted man and mobile fingerprint units rushed down from Miami had been hurriedly set up alongside the roadblocks. Any man even vaguely fitting the profile was having his dabs taken. Lee thanked God they weren't in the holiday season yet — the queues would have been enormous if the snowbirds were down here in force. But Thanksgiving was still weeks away and his men were dealing with limited numbers of mostly local, if infuriated, drivers.

He looked at his watch. Close to suppertime. Almost all the cab drivers on dayshift had been fingerprinted and eliminated; it was going to get interesting in a couple of hours when the nightshift guys checked in for work.

Especially if — or more likely, *when* — one of them didn't.

Lee grabbed his jacket and swept up the pack of cigarettes and his lighter from the desk in front of him. He turned to the overweight lieutenant who was methodically, if resentfully, working through the patrol car records.

'Anything, lieutenant?'

The man shook his head. 'Nah. But we're just covering our bases here; we don't really think we're looking for a cop, do we.' It was a statement, not a question.

Lee felt a twinge of guilt about his earlier physical aggression.

'Yeah . . . it's got to be done, though . . . Look, lieutenant . . . about this morning . . . '

The other man regarded him coolly. 'If you're gonna apologise, Agent Foster, save your breath. For the record, I'd say you overreacted, big-time, but I can live with it. Where'd ya learn that choke-hold, anyway? Korea?'

Lee shook his head. 'I was never drafted.'

The other man grunted. 'FBI boot camp then, I guess. Shame they didn't train you how to put a choke-hold on that temper of your'n at the same time.'

'Well, anyway, I'm sorry.'

'Well, anyway, fuck you.'

★ ★ ★

The sunset was, if anything, more spectacular than the evening before. Stella and Lee were sitting at the same table on the little beach but tonight the atmosphere between them was frost-free.

Lee's black FBI two-way radio was parked in the sand next to them, squawking and crackling every so often.

'Good God,' Stella had said when she saw him lugging it across the beach towards her. 'I

186

thought you said it was portable. That thing's the size of a pirate's treasure-chest.'

'I'll have you know this is state-of-the-art communication technology,' he said grimly, dropping it with relief next to the table. 'Have you ordered?'

'Yes — same as last night. And I got us these Key Lime Cocktails, too. Will that do?'

'Perfect.'

He spent the next few minutes bringing her up to date on the day's developments, omitting the part about the tinpot rebellion he'd nipped in the bud that morning. Stella smiled at him when he'd finished.

'You haven't told me what your team made of the *Courier* story.'

He was blasé. 'Oh, one or two grumbles, sure. No big deal. They needed a little straightening out, but everything's fine now.'

She shook her head at him. 'Come on, Lee. They were absolutely furious, weren't they?'

He hesitated. 'OK, yeah, they were. I told them not to be such jerks or they'd be off the investigation. Seriously, Stella, it's OK. It's all moved on. Like I told you, now we're just waiting for the killer to break cover. Which he will — in the next few hours or so. Someone's not gonna check in for work. And a dime to a dollar says that'll be our man.'

The waiter arrived with their steaming little-neck clams, and the usual solicitation to avoid scalding themselves.

Stella sipped her wine, deep in thought. She'd kicked off her sandals and was curling her toes into the soft sand, still warm from the late evening sunshine. She looked out across the sea at the improbably red, yellow, and azure sky, backlit with golden shafts from beneath a huge, shimmering pink cloud that floated just above the horizon. But the beauty of the sub-tropical sunset was lost on her.

'What if I'm wrong, Lee?' she said suddenly. 'What if all my grand theorising about cars and callow, murderous youth is bunkum? What if this revolting man is . . . oh, I don't know . . . a sixty-something school janitor? Or a hotel-owner? Or a fisherman? In fact, what if he's — '

'Hush. Stop it. Listen to me, Stella.'

He moved his hand down to take one of hers, and folded it firmly in his grip. Her eyes had widened at the gesture but she didn't withdraw from him.

'You've never done anything *like* this before,' he told her quietly. 'Oh, sure, you've studied case files and gone to university conferences and written papers and given talks, but you've never actually gone on the trail of a repeat killer, Stella. This is where theory and reality connect; where intelligence and information and instinct fuse. And it's about real people in the here and now, and that makes it frightening because if you make the wrong call, there are consequences. Of course you have self-doubt. I certainly do, on every single case I'm assigned to. But you have to trust what you know, what you've learned. Because that's what so-called intuition or instinct is actually founded on — our accumulated knowledge and experience.'

He smiled at her. 'Let me tell you, Stella, I've never heard such a penetrating evaluation of such limited facts in a breaking case as I did from you today. You're remarkable — truly, you are. I have a whole operational strategy unfolding out there, based almost entirely on your analysis. And I wouldn't have authorised it if I didn't feel, deep in my gut, that you were right. That means we're in this together — so give yourself a break.'

He released her hand and waved vaguely at their plates. 'Now let's eat. I don't know about you, but I'm starving.'

But before a distinctly flushed Stella could reply, or either of them had even lifted their forks from the table, the radio under the table crackled fully into life and curtailed their meal with unconditional finality.

32

He backed his cab into a space behind the hotel's green-painted emergency generator that stood at the rear of the guests' car park, ready for use if a hurricane or tropical storm brought down overhead power lines.

He parked on the far side of the big machine, so that nobody in the lodge or eating at the tables outside on the beach could see the car. Not that it really mattered; no one would be looking specifically for him yet, but it seemed the wise thing to do.

There was no guarantee he would see her and he had no intention of risking going into reception to ask for her by name. But it had occurred to him, as he was driving back home to collect his things, that he would pass Largo Lodge on the way. It was the dining hour and she might well be having her supper while watching the sunset.

It couldn't hurt to take a look.

He took off his coat and tie and shoes and socks, and placed them in a neat pile on the back seat. Then he rolled his jeans up a couple of turns, and unbuttoned his shirt all the way down. Now he looked like any other vacationer wanting to get some sand between his toes and catch one of Florida's legendary sunsets.

The parking lot's black tarmac was still hot from the afternoon sun and burned the soles of his feet. It was a relief to reach the relatively cooler sand of the beach, where he immediately scanned the tables. About half were occupied, mostly by couples, but over to one side he could see a woman sitting on her own, her back to him. She was studying the menu.

He walked casually across to the nearest empty table to hers and sat down. After a moment or two he glanced over at the woman, who was now in profile.

It was her.

She was even more beautiful than in her picture, he thought. Stunning, in fact. She turned towards him as she cast around for a waiter. Extraordinary, almond-shaped eyes that glowed like soft lamps in her lightly tanned face, framed by dark hair that tumbled down to her shoulders. A stunning figure beneath a close-fitting cream silk blouse — not quite what you'd call voluptuous, but head-turning, for sure. She was in white cotton short-shorts and her long bare legs stretched out onto the beach, the toes of her slim feet wriggling slowly in the sand.

The thought of exactly what he was going to do with her, when the time came, made him slightly dizzy and his breath caught in his throat. He found himself wondering if her screams would sound different because she was English. As if to whet his appetite, he realised he was about to hear her voice as a waiter hurried to her table.

'Good evening, ma'am, welcome back. Are you ready to order?'

191

'Yes, hello again . . . I'd like to order for my friend as well, please. I'm expecting him in a few minutes. We'll both have what we had last night — the steamed little-neck clams. And two glasses of Chardonnay as well, please.'

What an accent! She sounded like the Queen of England. He'd never heard such fucking cut-glass tones in his life, except in the movies. Did all English girls sound like that? He loved it.

The waiter was asking her if they'd like to try the house sundowners.

'I'm awfully sorry . . . what's a sundowner?'

The waiter laughed. 'I think you'd call it a cocktail, ma'am.'

She laughed with him, showing perfect white teeth and the pinkest of tongues.

'In that case, yes — you can bring two of those straight away. Lots of ice, please.'

He could sit here listening to her and watching her all evening but his instinct for self-preservation was nagging at him: it really was time to move.

Never mind. The next time he saw her, which would be as soon as the heat was off and things had calmed down, it would be just the two of them. Alone.

They'd have all the time in the world, then. He'd be very sure to arrange that.

He stood up and began walking back to his taxi. When he turned round at the edge of the beach for one last look at her, she had risen to her feet too and was walking away from him down to the ocean's edge. The rays of the setting sun bounced and reflected off the rippling water and back-lit her breeze-blown hair with a shimmering halo.

Christ, she looks like an angel, he thought.

Which gave him a sudden idea of what to do with her when their time came.

It was something really cool.

And especially, exclusively, for her.

33

Lee grabbed the radio's microphone.

'Yes, sergeant, this is Agent Foster. Go ahead please.'

Lee looked across the table at Stella. 'I think this could be it.'

The speaker hissed static for a few seconds before crackling to life again.

'Pelican Cabs have just been on the phone, sir. They say one of their drivers has gone off the job and they can't raise him on the radio. He was meant to pick up a woman at Cheeca Lodge, coupla hours back, and take her for her regular monthly appointment at her hairdresser's down in Marathon Key but it was a no-show. Over.'

Lee pressed the mic's transmit button. 'Two *hours?*' he barked. 'Why have they taken this long to tell us? Over.'

'Seems the fare was an old lady and when the cab didn't show she figured it was her mistake and she'd gotten muddled; had the wrong day. It wasn't until she got around to calling the cab company half an hour ago to check it out that they realised something was out of joint. Like I say, they've tried calling him up but no dice. They say he's never done anything like this before, by the way. Usually as reliable as they come. Over.'

'Does he fit profile? Over.'

The other man chuckled.

194

'Like a glove, sir. He's thirty-two, been a driver with them for nearly four years, so a lot of people on the island will have got to know him by sight, just like you said.

'His name is John Henry Woods. Lives right here in the Key. We've got men going to his home address now and we've put out an all-car alert with the registration of the cab he was in, and his own private car, too, a Dodge Dart. Over.'

'Have the guys on the roadblocks been informed? Over.'

'Like I said, sir, it's an all-car alert. We've got men at the cab company getting photo ID of the guy from their records. We'll photocopy it here and get copies out as soon as we can. Over.'

'That's terrific work, sergeant — great going. Right, I'm coming straight in to co-ordinate everything from here on in. Meantime, call the TV stations in Miami and give them everything we've got. You can name a John Henry Woods of Key Largo as our prime suspect. Say we'll get photos of him to them inside a coupla hours. And organise a press conference at headquarters for' — he checked his watch — 'an hour from now. Seven-thirty. I'll be with you in ten minutes, max. Over and out.'

He stood up and grinned at Stella — whose face was suffused with relief — with a mixture of triumph and admiration.

'What was that you were saying to me just now about thinking maybe you got this all wrong? Jesus Christ, Stella, you're a goddamned *witch*.'

195

He leaned forward impulsively and kissed her full on the lips.

Startled, she momentarily tried to pull back, but almost at once she instead found herself beginning to respond. The kiss gradually lost its urgency and became a gentler, more tender exchange. Eventually, they slowly drew apart and stared at each other.

'Tell me I don't have to apologise for doing that,' he said at last, putting the back of one hand up to her cheek and stroking it.

She smiled at him. 'Hmm . . . I'm not sure . . . do you always kiss members of your team when they've done something to win your approval?'

He laughed. 'There's a first time for everything and believe me, that was a first.' He hesitated. 'Listen, Stella . . . I wish I didn't have to — '

She took his hand from her face and brushed his fingers with her lips.

'I know. You've got to go. Call me when you can.'

'I will.'

He hefted the radio up from the sand and turned to leave.

'With any luck, it'll be to tell you we've got our hands on the son of a bitch. He can't have got far.'

'Let's hope so. Remember, Lee, he's clever as a fox and slippery as an eel.'

'Yeah, well, so am I, Stella. We'll get him.'

34

The owner and crew of the breaker's yard had gone home for their supper more than an hour ago and the place was deserted. The chain-link gates were ajar — who was going to steal cars headed for the crusher? — and he punched them open simply by driving at them. A few scratches and dents to his beloved Dart hardly mattered now. He promised himself one day he'd get another.

He drove slowly along the lines of deceased sedans, pickups and the occasional rusted shell of a van until he found a gap big enough to accommodate the Dart, driving it in as far as he could go, its front fender wedged hard up against the wreck in the next line in front of him.

He took a screwdriver from the glove box and managed to squeeze his body out into the narrow gap between his car and a totalled Chevrolet, working his way to the rear of the Dart and getting to work on the licence plate. In a couple of minutes he had it off and shoved it under the crumpled, rotting Chevy.

Next, he popped the trunk and took out the bag he'd rapidly packed back at his house — the house he'd probably never see again.

He checked the hold-all, not that he could go back now for anything he'd forgotten. The cops would be there anytime soon, once they realised he'd done a duck-dive. He'd left the company's cab parked openly on the street; there was no point in hiding it. Anyway, he wanted them to focus on looking for the Dart.

Everything he reckoned he'd need seemed to be safely in the black canvas bag. His stash of money — a couple of grand, maybe a little more; it'd last him a few months if he was careful — plus all the usual stuff a guy needed for a spur-of-the-moment vacation. He rummaged for the most important item of all, his heart beginning to thump a little faster as, at first, his groping fingers failed to find it.

Then they touched the plastic bottle and he sighed with relief as he tugged it out. Of course it was there; he'd packed it not fifteen minutes before. He told himself to stop being a jerk.

He shoved the bottle back and zipped the hold-all shut again, slammed the trunk lid down and stepped out onto the cindered track he'd just driven down.

This was good. The Dart was at least four feet deeper into the line of wrecks than the ruined cars on either side of it. Unless you inspected this spot closely — and why would anyone do that? — his car was for all practical purposes invisible. Unless he caught a very unlucky break it would be many days before anyone paid the slightest attention to it. All the same, he picked up some handfuls of dirt and dust and smeared them across the lid of the trunk. Then he stomped down as hard as he could on the rear fender until it was sagging at a drunken angle toward the ground. As an afterthought, he picked up a chunk of shapeless metal lying

198

nearby and smashed it repeatedly through the rear window. Now his car appeared as ruined and forlorn as its neighbours.

He walked back towards the yard's entrance. Next stop, a dark little bar he knew of three or four minutes' walk away. It would take him five minutes to do what he needed to there, and then he'd be on his way.

He knew exactly what he was going to steal to replace his beloved Dart. He'd swung by the spot on his way to the breaker's yard and of course, it was there as usual, waiting patiently for its owner — a snowbird and his family who wouldn't fly down south from their home in Richmond, Virginia until the week after Thanksgiving, still almost two months away. The guy hadn't been behind the wheel of the thing since Easter.

But he had.

And he had the ignition keys right here, snug in the back pocket of his jeans.

35

'He's gone to ground.'

Lee's voice, down the phone to Stella, was calm and unflurried, she thought. The voice of experience.

His roadblocks at both ends of Key Largo were still firmly in place, and would be so for the foreseeable. But they had yet to pull over the Dodge Dart they were looking for (although several young male drivers of the same model had enjoyed some close personal attention in recent hours).

It was past eleven now, and all the local late-night news shows had led with the story. On the networks it was high on the running order too, mostly going out as the second or third item.

Stella, lying on her bed with the television on, interrupted him.

'Hang on, Lee — WBFS are about to run it again. I missed it earlier — let me watch this.'

'OK, Stella, I'll watch it too. Call you back.'

She reached for the remote control box on her bed. It had taken her a while to work out what the thing actually was, and she had been astonished to discover that she could change channels, or adjust the sound, or brightness, without going near the television itself.

Now she pressed the volume button, and the newscaster's voice boomed out of the set.

'A suspect *in the Keys killings has been named at last. State police and the Federal Bureau of Investigation late tonight jointly named 32-year-old local cab driver, John Henry Woods, as prime suspect in the brutal slayings of four young women in recent weeks. All of them lived, and died, in Key Largo.*'

A black-and-white full-face photo, probably lifted from Woods's driving licence, was flashed onto the screen. Stella sat a little straighter against her pillows, full of curiosity. This was the man she had apparently successfully profiled, on such slender evidence.

She knew from her academic work that these monsters rarely, if ever, looked the part, and at first sight the face that stared out at her from the television seemed no exception to the rule.

The newscaster was saying that Woods had brown hair, but it looked pretty mousy to her, even in monochrome. Similarly the eyes, also described as brown, appeared as if they might be a watered-down shade of the colour.

No one ever looked remotely like their normal self in formal, official photographs like this; Stella knew that. Indeed, her own passport photo was, to her eyes, the quintessential portrait of a near-imbecile.

But all the same . . . there was an ephemeral quality here, flickering just beneath the surface. It reminded her of something, something elusive she couldn't quite grasp. The newscaster's stentorian words seemed to fade away as she stared at John Henry Woods's neutral features and blank, expressionless eyes. He seemed

. . . she strained to hear what the instinctive part of her mind was trying to whisper to her . . . he seemed to be . . .

The phone rang again and she snatched up the receiver. 'Lee? Hang on, just let me turn the volume down on the television . . . OK, go ahead.'

'Great coverage, huh? This really oughta help some. A few more of these teleshots, plus tomorrow morning's papers, and believe me, we'll — '

Something in her mind softly clicked into focus.

'He's mocking us, Lee.'

'What? What's that, Stella?'

'He's *mocking* us. He's mocking the whole world. Oh my God, the *ego* of the man! Couldn't you see it in his face just now?'

There was a distinct pause at the other end.

'Stella, have you been at the mini-bar?'

She laughed, despite herself.

'No, of course not . . . look, Lee, I realise I must sound like some kind of ghastly fake stage medium, but I mean it. I know it's totally unscientific, but . . . remember what you were saying on the beach earlier about trusting one's instincts? How they're really based on experience? Mine are trying to speak to me now. Oh, I wish I could explain this properly . . . ' Suddenly she snapped her fingers.

'Of course. Those pictures of the Nazis. Their official party photos, I mean. You can practically see the malevolence in the faces of some of the leading Party members — Himmler, Heydrich,

Hess — their photos *reek* of arrogance and conceit. I felt exactly the same about our man just then. He'd composed his features for an official photograph, but just like those gangsters in uniform, he couldn't hide his inherent arrogance.'

Now it was Lee who laughed. 'Well, forgive me, Stella, but we kinda deduced that about the guy already, now, didn't we?'

She nodded to herself, plunged back deep in thought. 'Yes, of course, but that's only part of what I'm trying to say. There's something else.'

After a long silence he spoke. 'Stella? You're not saying anything. You still there?'

'Just a minute, Lee. There's *something else*! Dammit, what the hell is it? Something else about that face . . . '

'Take your time, Stella. I've learned to trust your instincts.'

Next moment sudden realisation flooded through her like white light and she gasped in shock.

'*I've seen him! I'VE SEEN HIM!*'

'What? Where? When? How can you be certain it was — '

'I've seen him twice, Lee! The first time on the day I was driven down from Miami. We passed a taxi that'd been pulled over by a police car with its roof-lights flashing and everything. The officer was talking to the driver and he was facing me — the cab driver, I mean. It was *him*, Lee! I'm certain of it. I remember saying to my driver that I got the impression the man was trying not to laugh, which I thought was really odd under the circumstances. *Exactly* the expression he's wearing in that photo.'

Lee whistled. 'Jesus, Stella, that's some coincidence, if you're right.'

'Of course I'm right!'

'OK, OK . . . so when was the second time you saw him?'

'Tonight! On the beach here at the hotel.'

'*What!?*'

'No doubt about it. There was a man sitting by himself at a table near mine. This was about ten minutes before you arrived, Lee. He was staring at me. I felt distinctly uncomfortable so I went down to the water. When I came back, he'd gone. But I'd swear on the Bible he was the person whose picture I've just seen on the television, and the man who was standing by the side of the road three days ago. What on earth can it mean?'

His mind raced.

'Well, the first sighting must have been, like I said, a coincidence,' he decided at last. 'A weird one, but still a coincidence.'

His tone flattened. 'Tonight is different. I reckon he recognised the background to that *Courier* photo of you this morning. He's probably picked up and dropped off dozens of fares at Largo Lodge over the years. I guess he was curious to see you before he got out of town and took a chance you'd be having your evening meal out on the beach. Jesus, it's creepy as all hell though.'

'Do you think I'm in danger?'

He considered the question carefully.

'Don't take this as a yes, Stella, because I don't seriously think you are, but from this moment on you're going to have round-the-clock protection, starting with me. I'm coming straight back there now. In the meantime, lock the door and don't leave your room.'

She took a deep breath. 'Thank you. Good God, Lee, this man is even more extraordinarily self-confident than I thought. He has *such* an innate sense of his own superiority to everyone else. What a risk for him to take tonight! What if you'd already identified him, seen his picture, and you'd been here when he turned up? But all the same . . . '

She fell silent.

'All the same, what?' he prompted.

'Well . . . character is fate, isn't it? Overweening self-belief and arrogance may be disagreeable characteristics but they can carry a person a long way, especially if they have the kind of luck this man seems to enjoy.'

'What do you mean?'

'I suppose what I'm trying to say is that I don't think you're going to catch Woods in one of your roadblocks, Lee. In fact, you may not catch him at all.'

'Well, thanks for the vote of confidence.'

'Don't take it personally. I just mean . . . oh, I don't know what I mean. I'll explain it better when you get back here. I'm all hot and bothered. I'm still feeling a bit funny after that kiss on the beach, to be honest.'

'Me too. Would you mind if I kissed you again?'

After a distinct pause, she heard herself saying: 'Actually, I think I'd be rather disappointed if you didn't . . . did you say you were coming back here now?'

The sound of the phone being quietly replaced at the other end was all the answer she needed.

36

He went straight into the men's room when he got to the bar. The middle-aged bartender was flirting heavily with two thirty-something women, the only other customers in the place. They didn't even see him come in.

It was a small set-up and there was only one WC and washbasin in the men's room, so it was OK for him to lock its door. Secured against surprise, he fished out the plastic bottle and a small comb from his bag and moved to the cracked mirror over the basin.

It didn't take long to work the peroxide-based lotion into his hair and then his eyebrows. The instructions on the bottle said the stuff should be washed out between thirty and forty-five minutes after application, and he reckoned he'd just about meet the deadline. He'd have to — much longer and his hair would end up bright yellow.

He dumped the empty dye bottle in the trash and rinsed the comb and his hands. When he slipped out of the room the barman was still fully occupied with the women. He left entirely unnoticed.

His ride was a good twenty minutes' walk away but it was almost dark now — dusk was brief here in the sub-tropics, where the sun dropped almost vertically below the horizon. He just had to stay off the main Overseas Highway and out of any patrol car's way, and that was easy; there were plenty of quiet residential back roads he could use to get to where he was headed.

He must have been walking faster than he realised because just over a quarter of an hour later he was practically there. He cut across a small patch of waste ground and onto on a palm-lined residential street. It was a dead-end: the bougainvillea-covered cottages and conch houses finished abruptly a few yards from where the Gulf washed quietly onto a beach of white sand.

He took a left at the waterline and picked up the sun-bleached boardwalk that led to a small marina at the southern end of the beach. The dock only had one modest slipway, but a good metalled road connected it to the Overseas Highway so folks could get their trailers right down to the water.

There were only six or seven vessels in the marina's thirty mooring bays, and there didn't seem to be a soul around. It was still off-season, after all.

The biggest boat there was a 40-footer with twin outboards, a good-sized cabin with a kitchenette and shower room, and two small but comfortable bedrooms. It was bobbing gently in the furthest bay.

He walked straight to it, taking the cabin keys from his jeans pocket as he stepped on board.

For the last two years he'd had an arrangement with the snowbird who owned the boat. For twenty dollars a month he kept an eye on it, making sure the batteries stayed charged, the hull and deck were hosed clean of pelican shit, and the engines had their legs stretched every now and then. He took it out for a few hours on his days off, sometimes combining his legitimate responsibilities with an unofficial fishing charter for local guys, at ten bucks a head. What the owner didn't know wouldn't trouble him.

And what the owner certainly didn't know tonight was that he would never, ever see his beautiful boat again.

He headed straight for the tiny shiny cubicle aft.

He had to rinse this crap out of his hair right now.

37

Stella's reference to an inexperienced young man's perfunctory performance with a woman was not entirely theoretical.

During her three years at Cambridge she had been the focus of unceasing attention from male students (and occasionally, members of the faculty) and by the time she graduated Stella was, in the words of a friend, 'not without some experience'.

Most of it had been with boys of her own age, although on one occasion she had surrendered to a married Philosophy don's impressively determined campaign, only to be disappointed when he was so overwhelmed by the reality of conquest that he was unable to perform. His repeated protestations of: 'Honestly, this has never happened to me before,' eventually became even more tiresome than what had given rise to them. Or rather, she'd thought wryly as she got dressed again, had not given rise to them.

Lee Foster was knocking on her cabin door and calling softly to her barely ten minutes after she had, to all intents and purposes, invited him to kiss her again. But she wasn't sorry, she thought, as she went to let him in. After their ill-tempered and prickly introduction they had quickly found each other's measure and were increasingly at ease together. She liked the fact that he hadn't been fazed by her uncompromising way of standing up for herself. So many men, in her experience, felt threatened by her intelligence and forthrightness: here was someone who actually seemed to welcome and encourage it.

Anyway, she thought as she looked at him standing in the doorway, grinning at her and holding a bottle of what might be champagne — he was undeniably attractive. Not just because of his looks. He had an unquestionable air of competence and authority. She had no doubt that he had faced some sort of insurrection that morning because of her, but the voice of the officer on the radio earlier had been respectful and deferential. And she appreciated the way Lee had praised the man, too; clearly he was a good team leader.

And now here he was, waving the bottle at her and saying: 'I'm sorry, Stella, the liquor store didn't have any champagne so I had to get this — it's some sort of Californian fizzy blush and I'm sure it's revolting, but needs must.'

'What needs would those be, Lee?'

He laughed.

'My need to kiss you again, for a start.'

Without another word he took two steps into her room, wrapped one arm round her waist and pulled her to him for a far more comprehensive exchange than they had enjoyed on the beach earlier.

They were interrupted by a squawk and electronic burst of tone from the corridor outside.

He looked slightly abashed.

'I'm sorry, Stella . . . I had to bring it with me. The moment we get the bastard, I need to be told. You understand . . . '

She kissed his forehead. 'Of course I do. Just tell me they can't hear *us*.'

'What if they can?' he asked innocently as he went back out to collect the short-wave radio. 'We're only drinking a glass or two of Pommery together and discussing the case while I act as your overnight bodyguard, aren't we?'

'If that's all you're planning to do, Agent Foster,' Stella said drily as she ushered him back inside, 'you can leave the bottle with me and go sleep in your own room. I'll take my chances.'

★ ★ ★

They had left one lamp still burning and afterwards by its glow she looked at the sleeping FBI man's face. His fringe had fallen all the way forward now, covering his right eye. Stella thought he looked all of fifteen years old.

She gradually slid her arm out from underneath his body, trying not to wake him. Eventually she was free and able to massage her wrist and fingers, which had gone to sleep.

Circulation restored, she reached for the bottle they'd left on her bedside table and poured what was left into the tooth mug they'd had to share when he realised he'd forgotten to bring any glasses.

His prediction had been right: the wine was awful — sweet and sticky. But it was better than

212

nothing, Stella thought, as she sipped the last few mouthfuls. Anyway, she felt like holding a private celebration, however silent and solitary.

Their lovemaking had been *wonderful*. His body was lean and firm and brown and she'd teased him about his tan. 'I thought you told me you were *working* in California,' she said when she'd eased his shirt from his shoulders.

'You can go through case notes by the pool just as well as in the office,' he grumbled as he unbuttoned her blouse. 'Anyway, look at you — you're one to talk. You're not exactly Miss Milkskin yourself, are you? I assume you got that colour hobnobbing with the Kennedys on the beaches of Martha's Vineyard.'

After that they hadn't done a lot more talking.

She looked at her watch. It was almost two in the morning. On the dressing table on the other side of the room, she could see yesterday's *Courier* with her photograph staring out from page one.

She chewed her bottom lip for a few moments before reaching a decision.

'Lee. *Lee* . . . ' She stroked his shoulder. 'Lee, wake up. You have to go back to your room.'

'Huh? What? Stella?' He gulped and surfaced, noisily. 'What's up?'

'You — or you should be.'

'Why?'

She slipped out of bed and went over to the dressing table where she picked up the newspaper and held it up to him.

'This. Now you've named a suspect the story will go up to another level. They'd *love* to report

213

that the President's protégée and the FBI's finest are . . . well . . . how would they put it?'

'Screwing?'

Her hand flew to her mouth. 'Oh God, surely not! They wouldn't be so crude as to — '

He gave a sleepy laugh.

'No, of course not. I'm teasing you, honey. But you're right. It *would* make a good story, even if they just ran it as innuendo. I'll get my things — but I'm not going anywhere before we have a cop car parked outside this cabin, OK?'

He dressed while Stella, unselfconsciously naked and cross-legged on the bed, watched him.

'That was incredible,' she told him. 'Just now, I mean.'

He smiled at her and crossed the room, sitting beside her on the bed and taking her face gently in both hands.

'It was for me too, Stella. And I'm only leaving now because . . . well, because . . . ' He gestured towards the crumpled newspaper.

'I know. Anyway, it was my suggestion you should leave.'

'Sure.' He kissed her forehead, and moved his hands down to take both of hers in his.

'Look, Stella. I realise we've barely got to know each other, despite, well, just now . . . and that you're going to have to go back to Massachusetts before long and I'll be sent *God* knows where next, but . . . I really, really like you. And I'd really, really like to go on seeing you. Even if that means getting on a plane and crossing three time zones to do it. Do you feel the same?'

She nodded. 'I do. I think you're lovely, Lee, and admirable, and I — '

She was cut off by the portable radio.

'Headquarters to Agent Foster.'

He looked at her triumphantly. 'This could be it.'

He grabbed the radio's microphone and squeezed the transmitter.

'Foster here. Who's that? Over.'

'Sergeant Thompson, sir. Sorry to wake you. There's no sign of Woods. He's done a complete vanishing act. As you know, he got to his house before we did, but I took it on myself to order a second search of the property and we just found a wall safe hidden behind a locker in the den. The safe's open and empty, so we can reasonably assume he took some cash and maybe other valuables before he cleared out.

'Also, sir, there's no sign of his Dart anywhere on the Key. He's not approached either roadblock and as per your instructions, we've trawled every street on the island. Nix. Maybe he's pushed it off a jetty into one of the deeper docks, or even the ocean, but if he has, how's he planning to get off the island? Over.'

Lee rubbed his stubbly chin. 'You've got men covering public transport? Over.'

'Of course.' The sergeant sounded aggrieved. 'We've got this place sealed off tighter'n a duck's ass, sir. Over.'

'And you're liaising with the Coastguard, as per my orders, in case he tried to leave by boat?'

'That's a bit trickier, sir, at such short notice. They've sent a coupla cutters down from Miami

215

but with so many private boats coming in and out of all the marinas and harbours down here, they need some kinda steer on what to look out for. I've said that if we get a report of a stolen vessel, we'll pass it on to them.'

'Hmm . . . OK, sergeant, I'm coming in. We need to figure this out. Meantime I'd be obliged if you send a patrolman over to Largo Lodge to park his sedan outside Miss Arnold's cabin. I'll explain when I get there. Over and out.'

He dropped the mic, and saw that Stella was wearing a strangely abstracted look.

'What? What is it, Stella?'

Stella climbed slowly off the bed, and reached for the bathrobe that was hanging on the back of the bathroom door.

'Well,' she said, turning to him as she tied off the robe's belt and pushed her hair back from her forehead with both hands, 'I'm grateful for the police protection, really I am, but listening to that little exchange I honestly don't think a patrolman is going to be necessary here. I'm awfully sorry, Lee, but I think our Mr Woods is long gone from this island. He probably got away sometime soon after sunset.'

He shook his head obstinately. 'Not possible. He *must* be here still, lying low. Otherwise we would have picked him up, either in one of the patrol sweeps or at a roadblock.'

She sighed. 'Oh Lee . . . I told you that he's as slippery as an eel. It's obvious. He's wriggled into the water, hasn't he? He's already left by sea.'

216

PART THREE

PART THREE

38

Fall had definitely come to Massachusetts. Although the days remained gloriously sunny and defiantly clutched the tattered skirts of summer about them, nights were chilly now and their darkness lasted longer than the diminishing daylight hours. From Stella's bedroom window in the house on Bancroft Road, she could see that the leaves on the American elms planted down both sides of the street were already turning from green to gold.

'You've come home at my favourite time of the year,' Dorothy told her as she hugged Stella at Logan Airport. She'd had to collect Stella by herself; Jeb was giving his first lecture of the new term and Sylvia was back in class. 'October's a wonderful month here. Oh, it's *so* good to see you again, darling Stella! And look at you! All brown and glowing and sparkly-eyed! My *goodness*,' she said suddenly, 'you haven't gone and fallen in love with someone, have you?'

Stella had blushed and stammered and ended up in a coughing fit. Dorothy laughed: 'Well, well! You must tell me all about him during the drive home. And then I want to know everything else that's been going on. Oh, Stella, you can't imagine our astonishment when we saw you in the papers and realised where you were and what you were up to! And then just a day or so later the police named their prime suspect! That was of course *your* doing, wasn't it?'

Stella nodded. 'Well yes, some of it. Much good it's done them, though. They can't find him. Frankly, I'm not sure they ever will.'

John Henry Woods had indeed vanished into thin air. But in the hours and days after his disappearance a steady stream of details about his background had emerged thanks to a squad of investigative reporters, America's finest, and were published in the fullest detail by newspapers across America.

Agent Foster and his colleagues had found themselves temporarily eclipsed by the press.

'I got bawled out by Hoover himself today,' Lee told Stella gloomily over dinner at their hotel three nights after Woods's disappearance. 'He phoned me direct from Washington first thing this morning and told me he was considering giving my job to the chief reporter of the *New York Times*. Christ.'

It was quickly established that Woods's father walked out on his wife when she was pregnant with their only child. As his son would do thirty years later, Woods *père* had dropped comprehensively off the radar. When last heard of, he was working in a packing factory in the Mexican border town of Tijuana. That was fifteen years earlier and there were rumours he was now somewhere in Venezuela. Some said it was Bolivia.

Woods's mother had died of stomach cancer when her son was twenty. She had worked as a hotel cleaner all her life and to everyone's surprise, it turned out she had managed to

220

squirrel away a considerable sum in her savings account. She left it all to her son and as soon as he could he moved out of their rented apartment and put down a deposit on the cottage he'd lived in since then.

Military records showed that around the time his mother died, Woods had been overseas with the US Army in Korea.

This was where the story took its first sinister turn.

Reporters tracked down some of Woods's former army buddies, and while these veterans took great care not to incriminate themselves, a few of them spoke guardedly about persistent rumours of an atrocity involving civilians in the spring of 1951, when Woods was a 21-year-old G.I. attached to special forces on the Asian peninsula.

For years there had been word-of-mouth reports of civilian massacres in Korea, barbarities committed by both sides, but no one was admitting to anything. However, under pressure from hard-nosed reporters — and with envelopes stuffed with twenty-dollar bills quietly changing hands — some of the men in Woods's outfit began to open up a little.

'I ain't saying I know this for sure,' one former member of his platoon told an *NBC News Tonight* film crew, 'cos I was on furlough down in Seoul at the time, and I weren't up there on the line. But I heard some of our planes shot up some refugees in a village called No Gun Ri — by mistake, of course, lousy intelligence, the usual screw-up — and Woods was part of a

221

detachment of specials sent in on the ground afterwards to see how bad it was. What I heard was that some of those Ko-reans were still alive, but in a pretty bad way. Dyin', I means. The detachment didn't have chopper back-up or medical supplies worth a good goddamn so they did the kindest thing and put those poor heathen souls out of their misery. Shot 'em in the backa the head.'

The off-camera reporter's voice cut in. 'And John Woods was part of this alleged incident?'

The man hesitated. 'I ain't sayin' he was and I aint sayin' he wasn't. But that's what I heard, anyways. Someone tol' me he was the guy that suggested the whole mercy-killin' thing, to be honest, almost as soon as they reached the village.' He looked down at his hands, and added, so quietly that the sound man was forced to quickly push up the recording level: 'I heard he enjoyed it. Enjoyed it a *lot*. And that some of those people he shot probably woulda made it, you know?'

Woods had taken a sniper's bullet to the shoulder later that same year and been shipped home to the States with a Purple Heart and a pension. Back in Key Largo, he'd worked as a car mechanic for six or seven years before joining Pelican Cabs in 1958. He'd been with them ever since. They described him as a model employee with a blameless record. He'd never been in any kind of trouble with the police, either, not even a speeding ticket.

A search of his cottage revealed remarkably little apart from a Polaroid camera, 900 series, which police believed Woods had used to take the photograph he had delivered to the *Courier* offices. But no other photos were found, and no knives. It was thought that these and other compelling evidence, such as the chloroform he used on his victims and the rope he bound them with, had either been disposed of or were in the trunk of his Dodge, which was still missing.

To no one's surprise, the fingerprints taken at the house matched those on the knives used to kill the girls. Woods moved up from prime suspect to Most Wanted.

Stella felt increasingly surplus to requirements as the days dragged on. There was nothing more she could usefully offer the inquiry and Lee was away at headquarters for much of the time, coordinating the hunt for Woods. When he did manage to rejoin her at Largo Lodge, it was invariably late in the evening and he was exhausted and preoccupied. They had slept together once more but it had lacked the spark and romance of the first occasion. He had apologised to her afterwards.

'I'm sorry, I wasn't much good there . . . I'm just so damned tired, honey. And I can't stop thinking about the case. Where the fuck *is* the bastard?'

She understood, but a week after Woods vanished, and after a solitary lunch on the beach — solitary apart from the uniformed cop that was never loitering far from her side during the day — Stella made up her mind.

Lee phoned her that afternoon from head-quarters. 'We've cut our first real break,' he told her jubilantly. 'The Coastguard have found an abandoned motor yacht adrift about twenty miles south of Key West, over toward the Dry Tortugas. The rudder was locked off and the boat had run out of fuel. They've traced the owner. He's a snowbird and — '

'Sorry, Lee,' Stella interrupted. 'What's a snowbird?'

'Oh, it's what the locals call visitors from the north who winter here in the Keys . . . anyway, the last this guy knew, his vessel was safely moored right here in Key Largo. But here's the solid gold part, Stella — the guy says Woods had the contract to keep an eye on it while he was up north. So *that's* how the son of a bitch got away.'

'This is tremendous news, Lee,' she told him. 'But why didn't the owner call the police when the TV and newspapers carried Woods's photo and all the rest of it?'

'Been in Europe on a business trip. Woods's luck strikes again, huh? We tracked the guy down to West Berlin this morning. I spoke to him at his hotel there.'

'I see . . . so, what, then — you think Woods is in Key West?'

'Probably, or hiding out thereabouts. The boat's little inflatable's missing so he must have set the launch's controls to automatic, then abandoned ship and rowed ashore in the dinghy. The bastard tried to open the main seacocks so the launch would eventually sink but he made a half-assed job of it and they got jammed with seagrass and all the junk that comes up with the Gulf Stream. Even so, it was settling in the water

224

when the Coastguard boys showed up. Much longer and it would have gone down without a trace. We're dusting it for fingerprints right now but that's a formality.'

He sighed.

'As usual, Stella, you were one hundred per cent right. The bastard got out by sea.'

She smiled into the receiver. 'Well, you sound happier than you have for days, Lee. I'm pleased for you. But look . . . I've got something to tell you too.'

There was a pause at the other end. 'You're going back to Massachusetts, aren't you?' he said quietly.

'Yes, I am. Tomorrow. My course starts in a few days and I can't see that there's any more I can do to help down here. I need to pick up the threads, Lee.'

'Of course you do,' he answered. 'Don't worry, I completely get it. But listen — the moment we get our hands on Woods and he's looking out at the world from behind bars, I'll be on the first plane to Boston to see you. I'm gonna miss you.'

'I'll miss you too, Lee. Really. I'm only going back because . . . '

'Stella, I *get* it, really, it's OK.' He paused again. 'But look . . . I've got something else to tell you. Well, ask you, actually. It'll keep until supper, though. I'll see you then.'

★ ★ ★

Now, sitting next to Dorothy in the front passenger seat of the Lincoln, the arc of Stella's

225

story had reached the events of the previous night on the beach at Largo Lodge.

She explained that they had just been served their sundowners when he'd leaned forward and reached for her hand.

'Listen, Stella, I said there was something I wanted to say to you . . . well I'm just going to get right to it.'

He'd used his free hand to push his fringe out of his eyes. Stella realised that for the first time since she'd known him, he was nervous.

'It's like this . . . I think I love you. Hell, that's just stupid: I *know* I do. I'm definitely *in* love with you, for sure . . . but I truly don't think this is some kind of silly . . . *infatuation*. I'm nearly thirty and believe me I've had a few of *those* before . . . but Stella, this is totally different. You are the most incredible person I've ever met in my life, and you have to be the most beautiful woman I've ever laid eyes on. I'm dreading having to say goodbye to you tomorrow. I know you have a huge career ahead of you and that means spending at least four years up at Smith, and God knows where you'll go after that, but so long as I'm a part of your life I don't care.'

Stella smiled at him. 'Um . . . don't you think this is a little soon for a proposal?' she teased.

He laughed, embarrassed. 'Of course it is. Don't worry, I'm not going to go down on one knee and produce a ring. But I guess this *is* a proposal, of sorts, Stella. I'm asking you if we can . . . this is going to sound ridiculous from someone my age but I can't think of any other way to put it . . . go steady. You know, not see

226

other people. Give this thing a go. What do you say?'

She leaned forward and kissed him gently on the lips.

'I say I think you're a lovely man and no one's ever asked me to *go steady*, as you put it. And I can't think of anything nicer. The answer is yes.'

★ ★ ★

But Stella couldn't resist pulling Dorothy's leg a little now.

'I suppose I'd have to say he proposed to me, really.'

'What? You're *kidding*. You've only known each other for a couple of weeks! What did you say?'

Stella leaned back on to the soft, smooth leather bench seat, stretched her long legs all the way into the Lincoln's capacious footwell, and began to sing, waving both forefingers to and fro in time with the words.

'Here comes the bride, here comes the bride . . . '

Dorothy gaped. 'I don't believe it! You can't marry someone you've barely — '

Stella burst out laughing. 'I'm sorry, Dorothy, I'm *joking*. But he *did* make a proposal of sorts. He asked me if we could — oh, it was so sweet — 'go steady', and I said yes. He's lovely, Dorothy, and considering the rocky start we had . . . well, we're becoming very close.'

Dorothy was fanning herself with one hand in relief. 'Well, for goodness' sakes don't go rushing into anything, dear . . . are you in love with him, would you say?'

Stella smiled happily. 'If you'd asked me that yesterday morning, I'm not sure what my reply would have been. But when I woke up today I realised I *am* in love. He told me last night that he loves me too and that sort of unlocked something in my head, I think. And I know this is a horrible cliché, Dorothy . . . but I'm missing him already.'

39

'That's odd.'

Stella walked back into the living room where the Rockfairs were settling down to watch the early evening television news.

Sylvia glanced up at her. 'What is?'

Sylvia had run all the way home from class that afternoon, bursting through the front door and leaping on Stella — who'd just come downstairs after unpacking in her old room — with screams of delight. 'You caught him, Stella! You caught that monster, that horrible, horrible man! I'm so proud of you! We're all so proud of you!'

Stella staggered back under the onslaught and almost fell. 'Hey, steady on, Sylvia!' she laughed. 'You'll have me over.' She managed to recover her balance and put her arms around the younger girl, hugging her tight. 'Anyway, I haven't caught anyone, I just helped identify him, and God knows where he is now. But never mind all that, it's wonderful to be back. I wanted to call you all every day but it was made pretty clear to me that I couldn't. I haven't even spoken to my mother since I went down to Florida.'

Stella could have sworn that Sylvia and Dorothy exchanged some sort of coded glance but the next second Jeb, who'd cancelled his last class of the day, was striding through the front door and sweeping her off her feet and whirling her around and around, and the moment was swept away by another joyful reunion.

Now, several hours later, she sank down on the sofa next to Sylvia, shaking her head.

'It's just that I've tried to call my mother at least four times now, but she isn't answering. I even rang her college and they said they think she's gone away on holiday, which is very strange — her lectures will be starting in a week or two and she should be preparing for them now. She always does that in her study at home, where our phone is. I so want to tell her the news about Lee and me. I can't understand where she's gone.'

Jeb was fussing with his pipe.

'Well, I'm sure you'll talk to her soon,' he said from behind a cloud of smoke. 'You must try again later. It's lunchtime in England right now — she's most likely out with a friend. And, by the way, please stop offering to pay for the call, Stella. Transatlantic telephone connections aren't nearly as expensive as they used to be. In fact, I read the other day that British and American television stations will soon be able to talk to each other live, in sound and pictures. Imagine that! In fact, I — '

He was interrupted by a knock on the front door. Jeb jumped up and went to one of the windows that looked out over the street.

'Well now, there appears to be an airport taxi outside our house,' he said, turning to the others with an exaggerated expression of surprise. 'I wonder who this could be. Dorothy? Sylvia? Are you expecting someone this evening; a weary traveller from afar?'

Stella looked suspiciously at the three of them. They all seemed to be struggling not to laugh.

'What's going on here, you lot?' she demanded. 'You're up to something . . . and why isn't anyone going to open the door?'

Dorothy managed to bring herself more or less under control. 'Well,' she answered, a touch unsteadily, 'that's because we figured it might be better if *you* did, dear. Go on. Go see who's out there on the porch.'

Stella rose from the couch, half-smiling now. 'I have *no* idea what this is all about but fine, I'll go.'

She strode across the Turkish rug and onto the polished wooden floor beyond it that led into the hall. A moment later she was pulling the front door open.

A woman on the step was paying off the cab driver, so she had her back to Stella. Then she turned around to face her and cocked her head to one side, frowning in mock reproach.

Stella gaped.

The woman spoke. 'Come on, Stella. Don't you have a hug and a kiss for your mother? After all, I've come all this way to see you.'

'*MUMMY!*'

Behind her, Stella heard the Rockfairs' triumphant shouts and slaps of palms. Beginning to cry with laughter, she fell into Diana's open arms. 'I'm so glad to see you. I've missed you *dreadfully*. I have so much to tell you and I'm SO happy you're here!'

Diana clasped her daughter to her. 'Well, dearest, I believe I know the headlines already,' she said, repeatedly kissing Stella's cheeks and nose and forehead. 'Jeb and Dorothy have been reading me the American newspapers over the phone every day, although you've been in ours too of course. I'm very, very proud of you, my darling.'

After a moment or two, Stella pulled away, wiping her nose with the back of her hand.

'Ah, but there's one headline you can't possibly know,' she said, hiccupping and laughing at the same time, 'because it's about something that only happened yesterday evening.'

Diana's eyes widened. 'My goodness! Have the police got their man already?'

Stella shook her head. 'No. But I think *I* might have.'

40

He'd never lived like this before. Under a new identity. In disguise.

He found it oddly liberating.

Going blond would probably have been enough in itself, he reckoned. No one looked past first impressions. But he was taking no chances. As soon as he'd slashed the rubber dinghy and rammed its ribboned remains into the nearest dumpster, he headed straight for Duval Street, Key West's throbbing main artery.

It was past nine in the evening but most of the crummy, tacky shops on Duval were still open. He went into the men's fashion store opposite the Hog's Breath bar — 'HOG'S BREATH IS BETTER THAN NO BREATH AT ALL!' the crudely painted sign hanging over the bar's western-style saloon swing-doors proclaimed — and picked out the clothes he calculated would best complete the transformation.

Skin-tight white jeans. Pointy-toed Chelsea boots. A short corduroy jacket in beige with matching cord trousers (if anything, tighter than the jeans). Some high-collared cotton shirts with purposeless buttons running along both sleeves from flounced cuffs to elbows. A large, light blue canvas shoulder-bag swinging from a long cream-colored strap.

Three doors down he found a cheap jewellery store and bought some brightly coloured bangles and plastic rings, and a pair of steel-wire sunglasses with narrow rectangular frames and pale yellow lenses.

As an afterthought he went back to the fashion store and bought a jaunty cap in white denim with a peak made from faux mother-of-pearl.

He crossed the street and went inside the Hog's Breath, heading straight for the restroom. Inside a locked cubicle he stripped out of the clothes he'd been wearing since that morning and put on the white jeans, boots, and a purple shirt. Outside in the restroom he balled his old things into the trash and transferred the rest of his new purchases and contents of the old hold-all into a new blue shoulder-bag. He crammed the battered grip and empty fashion store bags on top of the rest of the stuff in the bin.

He put the yellow sunglasses on and slid every single bangle, bracelet and ring on his wrists and fingers.

Then he inspected himself in the cracked and dirty restroom mirror.

His own mother wouldn't know him.

He grinned at his reflection.

He was ready.

41

'I honestly don't know when you'll be able to meet him.' Stella pushed the marmalade jar across to her mother and used the butter knife to spread the dollop she'd just scooped onto her own slice of toast. 'Lee's not even in Key Largo any more — he went straight down to Key West with most of his team almost as soon as that boat turned up.'

Stella took a large bite out of the toast and reached for her tumbler of orange juice. 'The thing is,' she went on indistinctly, 'he can't just take a couple of days off and fly up here to see me — and meet you, of course — much as I know he wants to. He phoned before breakfast. Reckons he's getting close to finding his man. But he can't afford to let up for a second. Woods is trickier to pin down than smoke.'

Diana nodded. 'I understand, darling, of course I do. It's just that I fly home in a week and it would have been lovely to meet Lee. From everything you told me about him last night, I like the sound of him.'

'I like the *look* of him,' Sylvia chimed in from her end of the table. 'Has Stella shown you his photo yet?'

Diana shook her head while her daughter smacked her own forehead with the palm of her hand.

'How idiotic of me to forget! Lee gave me a

photograph of himself before I flew back yesterday morning. I'll run and get it.'

A few moments after she'd left the room, Jeb walked in carrying the morning mail.

'Greetings all,' he called. 'Morning, Dottie; morning, Dee-dee. How ripping you both look this lovely October morning. It will break my heart to have to leave for work. Now, let's see . . . letter for you, Dottie . . . one, no, wait, *two* for me . . . nothing for the darling daughter, but that's hardly surprising, is it? For Sylvia's generation the sixty-minute unbroken telephone conversation long ago replaced the art of writing a letter.'

Sylvia stuck her tongue out at her father.

'But perhaps I'm wrong — there is one more here,' Jeb went on, turning over a thick white envelope so he could see who it was addressed to.

He raised his eyebrows.

'Well, well! My oh my! Who'd a' thunk it? Our Stella continues to move in exalted circles.'

Stella came running back in, oblivious. 'Here you are, Mummy. This is Lee. Isn't he a bit of terrific?'

Diana took the photo from her daughter's outstretched hand and almost immediately raised her eyebrows.

'He certainly is. My word, you weren't exaggerating last night, Stella — he's . . . what do they say over here? 'Straight out of central casting.' What a dazzling couple you must make!'

Stella laughed, embarrassed. 'Well, I don't know about that . . . but I knew you'd like the

236

look of him. Just wait 'til you actually meet him, though, Mummy. He's so incredibly — '

'Ahem,' Jeb interrupted her. He waved the white envelope above his head. 'Your attention, please, everyone. I believe I hold in my hand something almost as glamorous as that photograph. Stella, see what the mailman's brought you. A letter from Washington.'

She frowned at him. 'But I don't know anyone in Washington.'

'You most certainly do,' he said. 'A person who lives at 1600 Pennsylvania Avenue, to be precise.'

Stella was mystified. 'I've never heard of that address in my life,' she told him.

Sylvia and Dorothy were now both sitting bolt upright.

Thoroughly enjoying himself, Jeb shook his head in mock regret. 'Tsk, tsk,' he clicked, 'such ignorance even in one so young, and despite the so-called special relationship, too. Still, I suppose I — '

'Jeb! Stop teasing the child,' Dorothy chided him. She turned to Stella.

'1600 Pennsylvania Avenue is the address of the White House, dear,' she informed her. 'If my ridiculous husband's histrionics mean what I think they do, you've got a letter from the President.'

Stella gasped and Jeb laughed.

'Sorry, Stella,' he said. 'I'm annoyingly playful at this time of day; I have no idea why. I know it's intensely irritating. Yes, this is from the White House all right. Look.' He held the front of the envelope towards her; the Presidential crest and stamped lettering: 'From the Office of the President of the United States of America' were prominent.

She gulped. 'Would you open it for me, Jeb, please?' she asked him. 'I'm a bit overwhelmed here.'

'Sure, honey.' He picked up a knife from the table and slit the envelope open. 'I'm probably committing a federal offence by interfering with a Presidential missive to a third party, but what the hell . . . ' He extracted the single folded sheet of paper inside. 'OK. Here we go . . . '

After a moment, Jeb gave a low whistle.

'I don't even have to turn it over to see the signature — I'd recognise this handwriting on anything.' He glanced up at Stella. 'JFK's written this himself, Stella. I'm seriously impressed. I had a coupla letters from him during the last election campaign but they were mostly typed, dictated, with just a few scribbled notes from him in the margins.' He looked appreciatively at the piece of paper he was holding. 'You're gonna want to have this framed. This'll be in pride of place on your study wall when you're an old lady.'

Sylvia smacked the table with the flat of her hand. Everyone jumped.

'Stop waffling, Dad, and let her read the damn thing! We're all dying to know what it says and all you can do is talk!'

Jeb looked abashed, as he always did when Sylvia told him off.

'Sorry, Sylvie, you're quite right . . . Stella?'

He handed the note out to her.

She shook her head. 'No, you read it out loud, Jeb. I'm not the only one here dying to know what it says.'

'You can say that again,' Diana sighed. 'For heaven's sake, get on with it, Jeb.'

Jeb needed no further encouragement. 'Well, if you're sure . . . ' He cleared his throat. 'OK . . . there's a kinda formal stamp here at the top that says: 'From the desk of the President' — I guess that means he actually wrote this in the Oval Office itself — and then his handwriting begins underneath that. He uses a fountain pen, by the way. Well, here we go, folks . . . '

Dear Miss Arnold,

Firstly, I should say that my brother Robert and I had high hopes of you when we asked you to travel to Florida last month to help with investigations into the recent terrible events in that state.

I have to tell you that you have exceeded our expectations beyond measure.

I have before me on my desk a summary of your contribution to the case, prepared at my personal request by the senior FBI case officer, and fully endorsed by the agency's Director. It makes for remarkable reading and I have personally marked both these documents for immediate release to you and/or your family the moment national security considerations allow. This may be some time hence but a Presidential order is binding and will be executed in

239

the fullness of time, I assure you.

At the time of writing, the suspect in this case designated by the FBI as Most Wanted is still at large but the fact that he was so presciently identified by you — or at least, that his profile, age, job description, and likely escape route were all accurately forecast by you based on the slenderest of facts — is extraordinary. I offer you my warmest congratulations and deepest thanks on behalf of the people of the United States of America.

I now wish to make two proposals.

Firstly, that alongside your forthcoming studies at Smith, you make yourself available, entirely at your convenience, as an unofficial (but appropriately remunerated) consultant to the FBI in any future cases where your considerable gifts may be of assistance.

Secondly, that you and any members of your close family who may presently be visiting with you in the United States join myself and Mrs Kennedy, and the Attorney General and his wife, here at the White House for dinner later this month. I hope the evening of October 14 is convenient.

My office will be in touch in due course to confirm your acceptance.

With my warmest personal wishes, and thanks,

John Fitzgerald Kennedy

42

Lee Foster was far from the confident FBI agent who'd just told his girlfriend he was close to cracking the case.

The truth of the matter was he was baffled, frustrated, and increasingly at a loss over what to do next.

Logic dictated that John Woods *had* to be somewhere here in Key West.

The island was dominated by the huge Naval Air Station on neighbouring Boca Cheeca Key, four miles east of downtown Key West. Warplanes busily took off and landed every few minutes, like suspicious wasps patrolling their nest. The town that lay just to the west was relatively small by comparison — a colourful, motley, cosy grid of a few streets of mostly wood-framed buildings that straggled down to Southernmost Point — not only the most southerly place in Florida, but in the entire United States. Next stop Cuba, which squatted just below the horizon on the other side of the Tropic of Cancer. Any of the fighter jets that continually roared into the air from Key West's military runway could, if their pilots chose, be streaking over Fidel Castro's communist strong-hold in minutes. The wooden sign marking Southernmost Point informed tourists that Cuba was exactly ninety miles away.

Lee stared gloomily out of the window of the

boarding house he'd commandeered for himself and his men. He was looking down along Duval Street and its motley collection of bars, restaurants and shops. It was quiet at this time of the morning but by lunchtime the place would be thronged with tourists, hustlers, prostitutes and drifters. As he watched, a squad of leather-clad bikers cruised slowly down the sun-drenched avenue, heads wrapped in red and blue bandanas, the backs of their jackets studded with the insignia *Hell's Angels — Tallahassee Chapter*. Duval had a seedy charm all its own, any time of day or night, an atmosphere now enhanced by the wanted posters Lee's team had nailed to every telephone pole, tree and any available flat surface from here at the northern end of Duval, all the way down to Southernmost Point.

The face of John Henry Woods stared blankly out at passers-by, beneath two words, printed in red letters: *MOST WANTED*.

Under the photo was the terse caption: *HAVE YOU SEEN THIS MAN? JOHN HENRY WOODS, BELIEVED TO BE IN KEY WEST. $10,000 REWARD FOR INFORMATION LEADING TO ARREST.*

Apart from a couple of chancers and attention-seekers, there had been no response. Extra officers had been drafted in from the upper Keys and as far as southern Florida. They had knocked on just about every door in Key West, trawled every bar, visited every hotel and bed-and-breakfast, and examined every boat docked in the harbour.

Lee had personally taken part in the shake-down and his hopes had been briefly raised when the owner of one of the larger conch houses being run as a small hotel had said a youngish man had checked in several evenings earlier and had yet to leave his room, asking for all his meals to be left on a tray outside his bedroom door. The owner had just taken the man his lunch and called through the door to tell him it was there. He had heard a muffled response so the guy was definitely inside. He hadn't really looked at him that closely the evening he arrived, but he was certainly about the same age as Woods, early thirties.

Lee had instantly summoned back-up and a few minutes later had men stationed on all sides of the wooden veranda that, in typical conch house style, ran around the entire building. Others stood guard outside the white-painted picket fence that surrounded the property which, with all its pink louvred shutters demi-closed against the fierce afternoon sun, appeared to be taking a siesta.

'Jeez,' one of the cops had muttered to the man nearest to him. 'Looks like we're gonna bust the Gingerbread Man's house.'

Minutes later Lee was crashing into the mysterious guest's room, gun drawn and three burly armed officers at his back.

It turned out the recluse was a thriller writer, behind deadline with his next novel and determined to finish it free from any distractions or interruptions from the young family he had temporarily deserted back in Tampa. Once he recovered from the shock of having his sanctuary stormed by gun-toting state and federal law-enforcers, he'd been almost grateful for the incursion, telling them enthusiastically he could 'really use this' in a subsequent chapter.

★   ★   ★

The plain fact was that Woods was nowhere to be found and not a soul had seen him anywhere in Key West. The previous evening, Lee and his men had mingled with the crowds that by tradition gathered every day to watch the sunset from Mallory Pier. All the officers carried Woods's photograph, but the picture merely provoked shrugs and shakes of the head.

Lee's conviction that Woods was somewhere close had been bolstered by the discovery of the tattered remnants of the stolen yacht's missing dinghy. A sharp-eyed refuse truck driver had spotted it poking out of the dumpster where Woods had jettisoned it two days earlier. The man had read in the *Lower Keys Shopper* that morning that the 'Keys Killer' had probably rowed ashore in a now-missing inflatable. He made a shrewd guess at what the rubber ribbons dangling from the dumpster were, and called the police.

'He *has* to be here,' Lee muttered aloud to himself for the second time that morning.

But for the life of him he couldn't think of a new way to flush out his quarry. Also, he had no way of knowing if Woods was in deep cover or hiding in plain sight, camouflaged in some ingenious way against Key West's multi-coloured, kaleidoscopic backdrop.

Whichever it was, he decided, at some point his man would have to break cover; that was inevitable.

The sixty-four-thousand-dollar question was — when?

43

Down here they'd been calling Key West 'the Gulf of Illinois' since 1961, when the midwest state became the first in America to repeal incredibly repressive laws outlawing homosexuality.

In fact, the bar he'd been working in since the evening after he rowed ashore had recently and proudly renamed itself 'The Springfield Tavern' in honour of the Illinois state capital.

Local police tolerated what they called 'twinkie bars' well enough. For some reason Key West had become a refuge for men who preferred each other's company, along with parts of New York and San Francisco.

What was more, down here the so-called pink dollar talked. The authorities increasingly turned a blind eye to the types of bars and their attendant micro-communities that in other parts of the Deep South would have sparked vicious mob attacks, violent arrests and aggressive prosecutions.

He'd known all that, of course. It was why he'd chosen this identity, and it had served him well thus far. Very well indeed.

The barman in the Hog's Breath had grinned at him when he'd emerged from the restroom, propped himself elegantly on a high stool the other side of the counter and asked for a glass of Chardonnay.

'Sure, man, comin' right up. I'm thinking you're new in town.'

'Yes, I am, as it happens . . . how can you tell?'

The other man laughed as he scrutinised the blond customer's ultra-fashionable, flamboyant clothes and yellow-tinted spectacles. He gave a friendly nod as he pushed the drink across the polished bar top.

'Cos you're in here dressed like that, is why. Plus what you're drinking there. There's a coupla bars a little further down the street, towards Mallory, that I reckon you'd probably prefer. More your style, if you follow me.'

He had affected haughtiness.

'I don't know what you mean. More my style? What are you sayin', that I'm a friggin' — '

The barman had laughed, not unkindly.

'Hey, it's cool, man. You're in Key West, remember? All I'm sayin' is you might feel a little more comfortable somewhere like the Springfield Tavern, more at home, and all. I'm just tryin' to be helpful, OK?'

'Well, if it's like that . . . OK. Sure. Thank you. Anyway, what do I owe you?'

'Zip. First drink before nine is on the house. Welcome to Paradise, my friend.'

⋆   ⋆   ⋆

The Springfield Tavern had turned out to be pretty well damned perfect for what he needed. To begin with, they were looking for an extra bartender as the coming season approached and he'd fluked straight into the job. It helped that in between coming back from Korea and starting work as a mechanic he'd taken a part-timer at the Blue Flamingo in Key Largo for a few weeks. He at least knew how to mix a drink.

What's more, the job came with a small but decent room upstairs.

It was an ideal set-up.

The bar's owner, Tom, was from Arkansas. He'd come down here in the late '50s when his necessarily secret boyfriend — Little Rock had zero tolerance of men like them — had told him that he'd heard they could live and breathe a lot easier on the last fragment of the United States before you got to the tropics.

So they'd sold their respective apartments and bought this place together — it was whimsically and incongruously called The Coral Heifer back then — before said boyfriend had fallen head over heels in love with a visiting lawyer who was passing through the Keys on his 60-foot yacht, and had sailed off to live with him back home in the Bahamas.

Tom had taken this abandonment with good grace and bought out his partner's share in the business. He now ran one of the best and most profitable taverns in the Key.

Woods had worked out his cover story while he chugged down to Key West in the stolen boat. He told his new boss he was on the run from the authorities in Texas. He said he had been caught in a classic police sting operation — an undercover cop had come on to him in a Dallas hotel bar and when he'd responded to the man's clumsy and, with hindsight, pretty obviously fake advances he'd found himself under arrest and down at city police headquarters being charged, outrageously, with soliciting. It was a brazen set-up.

Luckily he'd made bail and immediately skipped town. He'd heard how things were down in Key West and had driven directly here from Dallas, completing the journey in two straight days' driving, sleeping in his car overnight.

Tom had offered him a parking space out back but, thinking on his feet, Woods told him he had no further use for the car and had sold it for cash at a car lot up where Route 1 connected with the Key. He added that for the time being he was going under a false name, Dennis Clancey, and he'd appreciate it if his new boss didn't mention he'd just arrived to any police who might come snooping around, not that he thought they would, but you never knew.

Tom, appalled at the persecution and perfidy from which this pleasant young man had been forced to flee, promised complete discretion.

'I'll have a quiet word with the other guys, too, er . . . Dennis. Trust me, no one here's gonna give you away to those bastards.'

He had smiled gratefully and gone upstairs to his room to unpack.

He hid the gun and what was left of the chloroform under the spare blanket on top of the wardrobe.

He wouldn't be needing them again for a while.

So he thought.

44

Jeb's Lincoln Continental had gone through the little-known security checkpoint at the back of the White House and was now following two dark-suited Secret Service men who jogged easily in front of the car at a steady 5 mph.

'Bet those guys wish we weren't having this Indian Summer,' he said to no one in particular. 'They'll be sweating through their coats by the time we pull up at the side-door.'

Jeb had visited the White House several times before and he knew the routine. On the drive down from Northampton he'd regaled Dorothy, Stella and Diana with stories about the celebrations there in the heady days after Kennedy had won the presidency two years earlier.

'It was all still pretty rumbustious by the time Jack and Bobby asked me down to raise a glass,' he told them, 'and that was three days after Jack and Jackie and the kids moved in. But apparently their first day was wild. Bobby said he slid all the way down the bannisters in the main part of the house and Ethel said she'd have done the same if she'd been wearing pants.

'The kids — mostly Bobby and Ethel's, obviously — ran riot through the rooms and everyone went for a swim in the pool in the basement. Then they had a bowling competition in the President's private alley.'

'Who won?' Stella had asked him.

'Are you *kidding?*' he'd laughed. 'Ethel's team. Ethel Kennedy is the most competitive female in America. I swear if she'd been born fifty years later she'd be the first woman president of the United States. You've met her, Stella. Every one of that Ethel's switches and buttons is permanently set to ON.'

'Will she be there at dinner tonight?' Diana asked. 'I'd love to meet her. I know everyone's obsessed with Jackie but it's Ethel I'm fascinated by.'

'Sure she will. It'll be the four of us, plus the President, Jackie, Bobby and Ethel.' Jeb had turned around to grin at mother and daughter and the car swayed alarmingly on the turnpike.

'Jeb!' shrieked Dorothy. 'Keep your eyes on the road!'

'Sorry, honey.' He steered the Lincoln back on to the line. 'All I was about to say was . . . well, Stella, the Kennedy boys are genuinely grateful to you. One, you got C. Farris Bryant off their backs — I hear the talks with Disney are on again — and two, everyone agrees it's only a matter of time before golden boy down in Key West gets the cuffs on whatshisname . . . Woodward . . . no, Woods, right? Anyway, that won't really matter either way to the snowbirds. All they care about is that the bastard's on the run and the Keys are safe again for their wives and daughters. Crisis over. Mostly down to you, my dear. Light me a cigarette, would you, Dottie?'

A few moments later Jeb returned to his theme.

'And Jack's serious about making you a hired gun for the Feds. He'd never have suggested it without running it past old J. Edgar himself. Hoover may be a son of a bitch but he's a son of a bitch who likes results. And trust me, he'll find a way to take credit for your work down in the Keys. He'll probably say it was all his idea in the first place and he had to force it past the President and Attorney General.' Jeb gave a short laugh. 'You have no *idea* how much that man hates Jack and Bobby.'

Stella, looking out of her window at the outlying suburbs of Washington that were now beginning to appear, shrugged. 'I couldn't care less if this Hoover person wants to claim credit for anything I might have done. He sounds a repulsive man, from everything I've heard about him from Lee. He says he's a perfect bully, and obsessed with power. Lee told me that most of the FBI loathe him and politicians are terrified of him because he knows all their secrets.'

Dorothy had turned around, grinning. 'Jack's rightly wary of him but Bobby's not remotely afraid of the guy,' she said, 'still less his wife. Last year Ethel took her kids on the official tour of FBI headquarters and outside of the firing range she said there was a suggestions box, with a big sign above it saying: 'Tell us how to make the FBI a better place.' Ethel took out her red pen — *everyone* knows she always uses a red pen — and wrote: 'Get yourselves a new Director.' Good for Ethel!'

'Hmm . . . up to a point,' replied her husband. 'Jack's right to tread warily. You don't want to

252

make an enemy of that man, honey.'

'Oh Jeb, don't be so stuffy.'

★　★　★

Half an hour later the Lincoln was approaching its destination and the women insisted Jeb pull over so they could refresh their make-up.

'Are you nervous, Mummy?' Stella asked, as she passed Diana her powder compact and accepted a lipstick in return. 'I certainly am, and I've met them before, and on my own, too.'

'A little, I suppose,' her mother admitted, powdering her nose. 'Who wouldn't be? But from everything you told me about that day on the beach in Martha's Vineyard, I think it'll be fine after the first few minutes. Anyway, Jeb and Dorothy here know them pretty well, don't you?'

'Yup, and your mother's right, Stella,' Jeb replied, lighting a fresh cigarette and opening his window. 'I've seen folks who looked like they were gonna have kittens just before meeting the Kennedys, and a few minutes later it's like they're talking with the folks back home.'

He turned and gave Diana an unmistakable look of warning. 'But a word to the wise, Diana. And I'm being serious now, OK? Jack's a great guy but he's a player. He can't help it. You're a beautiful woman of around his own age and you're unattached, not that that makes much difference to Jack.' He glanced slyly at his wife. 'Remember when he suggested that you and he — '

Dorothy clamped her palm over her husband's

253

mouth. 'Shhh, Jeb. That can keep for another time.'

She turned to Diana. 'But he's right, dear. If Jack Kennedy can make a pass at an old stick insect like me — ' she ignored the loud protests that erupted all around her — 'he'll be enraptured when he sets eyes on you. So stay with the pack and don't accept any offers for a personal presidential tour round the Oval Office.'

Diana tried to suppress a smile as she snapped the compact shut.

'Don't worry, everyone,' she said drily. 'I can take care of myself, believe it or not. So . . . are we all ready?'

The Lincoln moved smoothly away from the kerb and towards 1600 Pennsylvania Avenue.

45

Lee reluctantly placed the long-distance call on the morning of his tenth day in Key West. He couldn't think of anything else to do, other than just waiting around like this.

Former FBI department head Ted Bradley picked up the kitchen extension on the seventh ring. He'd just come inside from his daily early morning swim in the garden pool of his house in Scottsdale, Arizona. He and his wife had moved there from Washington the year after his early retirement in 1959. Although barely in his sixties, Bradley had fallen prey to the arthritis which had plagued his own father three decades earlier, and his doctor had recommended he quit Washington — alternately damp or freezing in winter, hot and humid in summer — for the bone-dry heat in the deserts of America's south-west.

It seemed to have made a difference, as Bradley's wife had told him only the evening before. 'You're moving more easily than you were even two years before you retired, Ted,' she said over supper. 'At the very least it's not getting any worse.'

He grunted. His wife's optimism notwithstanding, it was nevertheless an undeniably gnarled and swollen hand that now reached for the receiver.

'Bradley.'

'Ted, it's Lee. How the heck are you?'

His old boss gave a dry chuckle. 'I'm just fine, Lee. Been waitin' for you to call. Still not got the cuffs on him, huh?'

'Nope. He's close by, Ted, I can feel it. I just can't seem to cut a break down here. Thought if I spoke with you, you might see something I'm missing.'

The older man nodded. 'Sure. Just let me have some coffee and eat those flapjacks I can see Helen starting to mix up, and then we'll talk. Call me back in an hour — say, eight-thirty?'

'That I will surely do. Thanks, Ted. Say hi to Helen for me.'

★　★　★

Bradley had been Lee's chief mentor and cheerleader at the FBI. Early on he'd spotted the young man's instinctive feel for how a case might be cracked, when the Mayor of Cincinnati's young son was abducted and a series of ransom notes received.

Local Feds suspected the kidnapping was the work of the city's mafia. The mayor had declared war on them in his election campaign the year before and the ransom messages, as well as demanding a huge sum in cash, appeared to contain coded warnings to the frantic father to back off in his crusade against organised crime.

But Lee was doubtful. The ransom notes somehow smelled wrong to him with their odd mix of the pecuniary and the political. He struck off on his own, delving into the mayor's chequered marital history. Seven years earlier he'd divorced his drunken, faithless first wife after her third affair; the missing child was the issue of his second, happier marriage.

Lee followed a hunch and tracked the first wife to a run-down apartment on the city's east side. He had her movements watched and within twenty-four hours she had unwittingly led detectives to an even seedier apartment nearby where her current boyfriend, a small-time hood, was holding the missing boy. The ransom notes' hints of mafia involvement had been a ruse to throw investigators off the scent.

Bradley had gone out on a limb to support his protégé's intuition so the successful outcome to such a high-profile case reflected well on both men. They formed a deepening friendship based on mutual trust and respect. Even when they were working on cases in different parts of the country, it wasn't unusual for one to call the other for advice.

Lee had been downcast two years earlier when his mentor told him he was planning on retiring early. 'Who'll I call for advice now?' he grumbled over farewell drinks in a Washington bar.

'Me, of course,' the older man answered, surprised. 'For Chrisakes, Lee, I'm not handing my brain in along with my badge.'

★   ★   ★

When he called Bradley back, Lee spoke more or less uninterrupted for almost ten minutes before pausing for breath, closing his long monologue with: 'So that's about the size of it, Ted. There's a chance, of course, that he's slipped away, but like I said I don't believe that for one second. I'm looking down Duval from my office window now and every bone in my body is telling me he's out there, maybe not two hundred yards from where I'm standing right this moment.'

'Yeah . . . reminds me of the Clevedon case, remember that one?' his old boss replied thoughtfully. 'Clevedon spent more'n a month pumping gas on a forecourt not one hundred yards from my headquarters. I felt just like you do now. You know, that not only was the murdering bastard lyin' low, he was within smelling distance of me too. Damnedest feeling I ever had.

'Your man Woods has gone to ground all right, that's obvious,' he continued, 'and let's assume that the old Foster instinct is playing you true and he's right there in Key West. So we need to kinda wander over the course here a little; establish some fundamentals. To be honest with you, Lee, I've been doing some thinking about the case anyway, based on what I've read in the papers and seen on Most Wanted. Like I said, I've been expecting your call. Just hold the line a second now — I'm gonna get my briar. Helps the old mental juices flow.'

After a moment Lee heard the rattling of drawers followed by the unmistakable strike and flare of a match. Then Bradley was back, coughing and clearing his throat. 'You still there, Lee?' he asked between hacks. 'Sorry about this racket. First pipe of the day. Always does this to me. Hang on . . . '

After more hawking and spluttering, he was able to continue.

'OK, so . . . let's see now . . . first off, Woods's night-run down there to Key West. I'm thinking it was pretty much opportunistic and unplanned. You say there's no evidence he'd been there in recent months so I very much doubt he'd established some sort of redoubt or hideaway there, stocked with provisions, that sorta thing. Anyway, he wasn't expecting the cops to get anywhere near him so early on in his beautiful new career, was he? The arrogance of the psychopath, huh? One of the weaknesses they all have in common, thank the Lord . . . anyway, he had to get out of Key Largo fast as soon as he realised you and this Arnold girl were breathing down his neck. I'd like to meet her, by the way, Lee.

'Second, he's not Superman. He needs to eat, drink, sleep, go to the bathroom. That means he *has* to be interacting with others. Getting their unwitting co-operation — unwitting, because who'd help an on-the-run homicidal maniac like Woods? No one in their right mind. So it's reasonable to infer they don't know who he really is. That being the case, we come to the all-important point three.'

'Oh, Christ. I know exactly what you're gonna say next, Ted.'

His old boss laughed. 'Of course you do. We used to call it the Sherlock mantra, didn't we? Go on, refresh my memory. How does it go?'

'As if you need reminding. OK . . . '*Once you*

eliminate the impossible, whatever remains, however improbable, must be the truth.''

'Well spoken, Agent Foster. Conan Doyle would be flattered by your power of recall. So what's our little nugget of truth here?'

Lee sighed. 'Christ, it's so goddamned obvious now I'm speaking with you . . . ' He sighed again. 'He's changed his appearance, hasn't he? He's in serious disguise, right? He's moving around right under everyone's nose. Why the hell didn't I — '

Bradley cut in quickly. 'Don't go beating yourself up. What else does Holmes says to Watson in that same story? *'Nothing clears up a case so much as stating it to another person.'* Everyone needs a sounding board from time to time to help them focus. And as far as I remember, you've never dealt with a disguise case before, have you? They're much more unusual than people like to think and as M.O. they tend not to jump out of the frame at you. I've only seen one and it took me a helluva long time to figure out what was going on.'

Lee had been profuse in his thanks but Bradley brushed them aside.

'You'd have got there yourself in the end. You know what to do now. Good luck, Lee. I don't think you'll be needing to call me again on this.'

★ ★ ★

Ten minutes later two of his best officers were standing before him scribbling down a string of orders.

260

'Get hold of a really good police artist. There'll be one in Miami — chopper him down here today. Have sketches done and wire them to the papers. If we work fast we can get them in tomorrow's editions, and on TV news tonight too. I'll call WCBA in a minute.'

'Sir?' one of the men interrupted. 'Why don't you go on the local TV station yourself with the drawings? Have more impact that way.' He coughed to cover his mild embarrassment. 'I, er, heard one of the girls in the Marshal's Office here say you'd look good on TV. I'm just sayin', sir.'

Lee laughed. 'I'll think about it. Now, about these sketches. If I'm not around when the artist gets here, tell him to base them on Woods's photograph, but to make several versions. He'll have dyed his hair, either lighter or darker. He may well have grown a moustache or beard — it won't be much of one, he's only been down here a few days, but even a light growth would help change the shape and nature of his face. I'd bet a ten-spot he's wearing glasses of some kind — maybe those fashionable coloured lenses to hide his eye pigment.

'We need to put some drawings out there based on all his options — blond, dark, hirsute, clean-shaven, bespectacled — every possible permutation. One of them will be him as he is now and we'll start getting calls. That means I'll want everyone in later, and I mean *everyone* — we have to be ready to send out a series of snatch squads to check out every possible sighting as soon as they're reported to us. I'm

261

not having the bastard doing another duck-dive. Not this time.'

The second man opposite him nodded and lit a cigarette. 'We'll get right on it. But pardon me, sir, no disrespect, why didn't we do this earlier?'

Now that's a damned good question, Lee thought to himself, and it deserves an answer. Because I've been eyeballing this case up close since the day I landed in Florida and I'm damned tired. Because I was tired even before I got here, straight from nailing that last one in California. Because I didn't have the guts to tell the Director I needed some furlough first; just a few days would have been enough. Because Stella's not here. Wise, clever, intuitive Stella. How many reasons do you want?

But all he said was: 'Because I didn't think of it until now. Which is what's known as a fuck-up, sergeant. My fuck-up and no one else's. Let's just hope we're not too late.'

'No one thought of it, sir. Don't beat yourself up.'

That's the second time someone's said that to me this morning, Lee thought gloomily.

'I already have,' he replied succinctly. 'Right, let's get those sketches taken care of and assuming they're ready this afternoon and I get a six o'clock slot on local TV tonight, I want everyone in here by four at the latest for a full briefing. We should get some responses after the telecast but if not, I'll want everyone back in by five in the morning ready for the papers. Also, I want as many copies of all Woods's potential new looks run off so we can post them in every bar

262

and on every telegraph pole in Key West first thing tomorrow.

'He's right here in Key West, guys. Let's go and get him.'

46

The four of them had been shown by a dark-suited flunkey into a sort of ante-room, a smallish lounge, where they had now been waiting for several minutes. Portraits of past presidents looked down on them benignly from the walls and an enormous vase of lilies adorned a polished cherrywood table in the centre of the room.

Jeb, deep in a chintz-covered armchair, glanced at his watch.

'This is a bit odd,' he said. 'The Kennedys are usually punctilious about meeting their guests personally as soon as they arrive. I wonder what's going on?'

As if on cue the door opened and Jackie Kennedy walked into the room.

Stella caught her breath. The casual Beach Jackie in slacks and sweater had vanished: in her place was the stunning fashion icon slavishly copied by women around the world. This evening the First Lady was dressed in a simple black shift worn to the knee, with three-quarter-length sleeves. She was in black low-heeled shoes and wore a single-strand necklace of pearls with matching drop earrings. Her hair, which sometimes looked black in photographs and on television, was in fact a rich, glowing chestnut. Tonight, it tumbled down to her shoulders and the front was swept up and back from her smooth, wide brow. Her make-up was minimal.

The simple-but-chic glamour may have been understated, but its impact was stunning. Stella glanced across at her mother. Diana appeared to be transfixed, her mouth very slightly open as she stared at the vision that stood smiling at them all from the doorway.

'Good evening, everyone, I'm so sorry about this delay,' their hostess said as she moved further into the room, and the spell was broken. Everyone stood up.

'It's a real pill and I think our plans for tonight might have to change,' she continued, crossing to shake hands with Diana, who was wearing a sleeveless dark-green dress and matching court shoes with heels at least two inches higher than the First Lady's. 'You must be Diana. I'm Jackie — welcome to the White House. Gracious, you're beautiful. Mind, Jeb did tell me you were.'

Diana murmured something that nobody could quite catch and Jackie turned to Stella and shook her hand too. 'Hello again, Stella. Last time we met we could hardly hear ourselves speak above the noise of Bobby and Ethel's children.'

Stella laughed. 'They're certainly quite a handful, Mrs Kennedy, I could see that.'

Jackie waved one hand quickly. 'It's Jackie, please . . . ' She turned to the Rockfairs. 'Dorothy, Jeb . . . you're both looking very spiffy tonight.'

'Sounds like we're all dressed up with maybe nowhere to go, except back to our hotel,' Jeb smiled. 'But you look fabulous, Jackie, as always.

Don't you ever have an off night?'

'As a matter of fact we're *all* having an off night tonight, or we're about to, I suspect,' Jackie replied. 'I can't go into details but something serious has just blown up, and I mean *very* serious. Bobby's juggling about seven phone calls at once and the President's going to be joining him shortly. Ah, but here he is now.'

Jack Kennedy had walked into the room. Stella had last seen him in swimming shorts and an old T-shirt; now he looked every inch a president in his beautifully tailored charcoal-grey suit, gleaming white cuffs shot an inch below the sleeves, and a narrow silver tie knotted beneath his button-down collar.

Afterwards, Stella and her mother would agree that the mere sight of him had delivered an almost physical jolt, a small electric shock to the senses.

He was smiling at them but there was tension beneath the smile; they could all see that.

'Jeb, Dorothy . . . Stella . . . and, ah, you must be Diana,' he said, unconsciously echoing his wife a few moments before. 'Welcome to the White House. Has Jackie explained how the land lies here this evening?'

'Sure,' said Jeb, speaking for all of them. 'Jackie says that there's a problem, and whatever it is, it's a biggie. Is it some kind of political knot, Mr President? Anything I can do to help unravel it?'

Jack Kennedy's smile tightened. 'Thanks, Jeb, but I, ah, think not, on this particular occasion. Even Bobby's beaten to the wide on this, though

266

he'll rally. He'll have to. No, it's not a political problem — not a domestic one, anyway. Let's just say we, ah, unexpectedly find ourselves in what I might call uncharted waters. It's not something one of your beautifully crafted speeches or press releases is going to fix, Jeb, I can tell you that.'

'Wow.' It was Dorothy. 'My imagination's running riot here. Is this something you're going to have to go public with, Jack?'

For some reason her use of his Christian name seemed to relax him a little. But he shook his head. 'No. Not yet at least. We're still assessing the situation. But if this is what we think it is then, yes, I can see myself having to go on TV with it in a day or so.'

Jackie slipped an arm around her husband's waist. 'It's all going to turn out fine, Jack. You and Bobby are smart guys. You'll settle this business between you, you know you will.'

Jeb looked at the others. 'Well, whatever it is it sounds like we should all get out of your hair, Mr President. We'll go back and eat at the Willard, once we've checked in. It's only a block away from here.'

The President nodded. 'I'm real sorry about this, especially for you, Stella.' He turned to her. 'I was very much looking forward to hearing how you pulled off such an, ah, extraordinary achievement down there in Florida. But it'll have to keep for another time.'

He looked directly at Diana. 'I hear you have to go home to England in a day or so, Diana. Perhaps next time you're in America you'll let us know so we can invite you back here with your daughter and these two, ah, good-for-nothings.'

What extraordinary eyes he's got, thought Diana as she thanked him, while Dorothy simultaneously blew the President a raspberry. A sort of greenish-grey. They seemed to look right into you.

The President held her gaze for a moment longer than was necessary, and Diana felt the beginnings of a flush rising from her throat.

Then he was addressing his wife.

'Jackie, I've got a couple of things to pick up from down the hall here, and then I'll be in with Bobby for the rest of the evening. Don't wait up for me, this is going to be a long night.'

He turned to their guests. 'Once again, I apologise. We'll do this again properly, I promise.'

And he was gone.

'Well . . . ' said Jeb. 'If someone could see us downstairs, Jackie, we'll go over to the Willard. Would you care to join us there for supper?'

The First Lady shook her head. 'No thanks, Jeb. I feel I should stay here tonight, but it's nice of you to offer.'

Diana, who was still feeling faintly unsettled by the President's unflinching gaze, raised one hand. 'I'm sorry, everyone, but I just need to powder my nose . . . Mrs Kennedy, where's the nearest bathroom?'

The First Lady smiled. 'Diana: I'm afraid our rescheduled dinner is entirely dependent on your agreeing to call me Jackie from this moment on.'

Diana returned her smile. 'Then I'd be

delighted to, Jackie.'

'And I'd be delighted to show you to the nearest bathroom. Come along with me.'

The two of them went out into the corridor. After a few moments, the others heard both women laughing.

'Crikey,' Stella said. 'I've never seen my mother like *that* before. She looked like she'd swallowed a horse-tablet or something. Sounds like she's getting back to normal now, though.'

'Oh, everyone freezes up a bit when they first set eyes on either of those two in the flesh, let alone both of them together,' Dorothy said matter-of-factly. 'You wouldn't be human if you didn't. I certainly did. Especially when JFK zaps you with those amazing eyes of his. The Germans have a word for it, don't they — *Führer-Kontakt*. There's something almost hypnotic about someone who wields enormous power, whether it's for evil or for good.'

She turned to her husband and lowered her voice. 'Did you see the way Jack looked at her just now, Jeb? I hope Jackie didn't notice.'

He shrugged. 'She probably did, but who knows what goes on in a marriage, Dottie? We've spoken about this before. Whatever his weaknesses, she loves him. She will do until the day he dies.'

⋆ ⋆ ⋆

Diana had not been using a polite euphemism, she really *did* need to powder her nose.

Jackie told her she'd see her back in the room

with the others and Diana spent a minute or two in the fragrant, thickly carpeted bathroom re-applying lipstick and powder in front of an enormous mirror in its gold-painted frame.

She felt slightly embarrassed that she'd been so tongue-tied with the Kennedys. Still, they were the most famous and gilded couple in the world. Next time — if there really was going to be a next time — she'd give herself a good talking-to in advance.

She snapped her compact shut, rinsed her powdery fingers in the sink beneath the mirror and opened the door.

President Kennedy was standing directly outside, holding a large black leather-bound notebook in his hand. He grinned at her, gesturing to the book. 'Found it,' he said obscurely. 'And I, ah, wanted to find you too, before you leave us.'

Diana stared at him in surprise. 'How did you know I was here, Mr President?'

'I was coming out of the room at the end there when I saw you go in, so I figured I'd wait here for you.'

He moved a little closer to her, still with that engaging smile on his face.

As an attractive woman, Diana was well used to men making passes at her and she had learned to see them coming, but this man, she thought, beat the lot. He had to be the fastest mover she'd ever encountered.

'The thing is, Diana . . . the thing is . . . '

The next second he was kissing her, the back of his free hand resting lightly on her cheek.

She almost began to respond — in fact, reviewing the extraordinary moment later, she had to admit to herself that she definitely *did* start to respond — but managed to pull sharply back, pushing him firmly away with both hands. Her undeniable thrill of excitement gave way to a sudden and powerful desire to laugh. This was *ridiculous*.

'Now look, Mr President,' she said as firmly as she could. 'This is NOT happening. I have just met your lovely wife and she's in that room just down there. Quite apart from anything else, what if she came out here and saw you kissing me? Now, I'm going back to my daughter and my friends and we will pretend that this never happened. All right?'

He was entirely unperturbed.

'On the contrary, Diana, the memory of kissing your lovely face will sustain me through what I have no doubt is going to be the most difficult evening of my presidency thus far. But you're right, of course. This is neither the time nor the place. The next time we meet I will be certain to, ah, arrange things differently. It would be my pleasure to spend some time alone with you.'

Now Diana couldn't stop herself from laughing aloud. 'Perhaps it would, but it's not ever going to happen! You can be completely certain about that, sir.'

His eyes crinkled as he laughed in his turn. 'We'll see about that, Diana. We'll just see about that. I always say — '

Diana never discovered what it was the 35th

President of the United States always said because at that moment Dorothy emerged from the room further down the corridor, calling: 'Diana? Are you lost? We're — ' She came to a full stop when she saw the two of them. Jack Kennedy gave her a friendly wave.

'Oh!' Instinctively, she waved back. 'Um . . . are you ready, Diana? We're off now.'

'Yes,' Diana called back. 'I'm just coming.'

She turned and put out her hand, which the President shook with an elaborate formality. He continued to grin at her in the most disarming way.

'Goodbye, Mr President. Good luck with whatever the matter is that's troubling you. I'm sure your wife is right and everything will turn out well in the end.'

His smile faded just a little.

'It has to, Diana. For all our sakes, it has to.'

47

He could see that his boss was in a bad mood. It was obvious from Tom's sulky expression and the set of his shoulders as he walked slowly back into the Springfield less than an hour after leaving for an afternoon in bed with his new — and very secret — boyfriend.

'I thought you left me in charge until happy hour,' he said as the owner stamped behind the bar and poured himself a generous scotch. 'You told me you wouldn't be back 'til six.'

'That was the plan,' Tom snapped. 'But Bruce got a phone call almost as soon as he'd taken his gun and uniform off. Afternoon leave cancelled. They're calling everyone back in to his headquarters because of this Keys Killer thing, you know, the manhunt. They still think he's hiding out in Key West, and there's been some kind of a breakthrough.'

He was careful to show no emotion and carried on methodically stacking the still-hot-to-the-touch tumblers he'd just taken from the automatic dishwasher — the first one he'd ever used — and asked in a voice as offhand as he could manage: 'His uniform? Headquarters? What, you're telling me your new boyfriend's a cop?'

'Yes, and he's gorgeous. Not that I got to do anything with that fantastic body of his this afternoon. And from what he told me I might

273

not get another chance for days, unless they get lucky. He said there's been some sort of development in the investigation. All hands on deck.'

He closed the door of the empty dishwasher and began wiping down the bar top. Steady now, he told himself. Don't look too interested. Let's not frighten the horses here, OK?

'Well good, actually.' *His voice could hardly sound more casual.* 'Because I'm sick of seeing that guy's face wherever I go around here. If they nail him then at least they can take all those frigging posters down. They give me the creeps.'

'Really? I think he looks cute myself, quite the regular piece of eye candy. But your wish might come true because from what Bruce said they may as well tear them all down right now for all the use they are. He's changed his appearance, apparently. Looks totally different now.'

OK. Stay cool.

'Wow . . . is that the breakthrough? What are they doing about it? Why are they calling everyone back to the ranch today?'

'Bruce didn't know at first — they just told him to get his sorry ass back there pronto. I stayed in bed when he'd gone, watching some mindless daytime game show and eating the chocolate cake I'd brought for him — Bruce loves chocolate cake — and finishing off the bottle of Chardonnay we'd started together.

'But just before I left, he called me from work. Of course, he has to be careful. If they find out he's . . . well, you know . . . he'll be kicked straight out of the force, maybe even sent to jail,

274

and it's much worse for cops on the inside, obviously. Anyway, he said they're getting one of those police artists to draw some of the different looks the killer might have adopted — you know, blond like you, or the total opposite. Maybe with glasses . . . hey, like you again, Den! Watch yourself — you could be pulled in on suspicion of being the famous Keys Killer!' He laughed.

'Jesus, don't joke about it, Tom. I skipped bail, remember? I'm a wanted man, for Chrisakes. I don't want to find myself dragged all the way back to Texas on some fucking framed-up soliciting charge.'

His boss looked uncomfortable.

'Of course not . . . jeez, Denny, I'm real sorry, I wasn't thinking. It was just a stupid joke . . . anyway, we'll get to see what they think this guy looks like now in a coupla hours — his mugshot's gonna be on the main news show out of Miami at six o'clock, you know, the one hosted by that Todd Rodgerson guy, who, by the way, isn't half as cute as he obviously thinks he is.

'But he's gonna show the drawings. That's why Bruce and everyone has been ordered back in — they're expecting a whole bunch of calls. He says the picture that attracts the biggest response is the one they'll check out first. Bruce thinks they might even make an arrest just a few minutes after the first broadcast — after all, this is Key West, not Miami. There ain't many places to run to. But if not, the sketches will make the morning papers, too. It's all quite exciting, don't you think? I always say I enjoy a good manhunt!'

Laughing at his own wit and with his spirits restored, Tom offered to hold the fort if Dennis wanted to take a late lunch.

'Thanks, Tom. I'll do that. I just need to go to my room for a coupla things. I'll be back to help out at happy hour, OK?'

Five minutes later, he slipped out through the rear fire exit, so his boss wouldn't see he was carrying the bag he'd arrived with the week before. It had briefly crossed his mind to kill Tom before leaving but too many other people, staff and customers, could testify that he'd been working in the Springfield and he could hardly kill them all.

When he got out to Duval he reached into the back pocket of his skin-tight cords for the coaster some sad old queen had insisted on giving him the night before, telling him: 'I'm always at the house, gorgeous, if I'm not in here. Come up and see me sometime. You could make an old man very happy.'

He squinted at the phone number, blurred by spilt beer, that the old guy had scribbled down in red ballpoint before tottering off home. Was that a three, or an eight? Fuck it, it didn't matter, he'd dial it both ways.

Without looking back at the bar that had been his sanctuary, he headed for the phone booth on the corner of Duval and West. He glanced at his watch as he went.

Four-thirty.

He didn't have much time.

★　★　★

The street was just a couple of hundred yards up from the old Pier House, built on land that had been reclaimed from the mangroves more than a century before. It was a near-forgotten corner of this last fragment of the United States, a single boulevard of shabby, paint-peeling clapboard houses that petered out where a long-silted-up channel that once connected to the Gulf now lay dank and stinking. Residents said half of Key West's mosquitoes bred here in summer and that the town should dig it out and then concrete the whole damn thing over. Make it a parking lot or something.

The old man had been delighted to receive his call. The jerk had a phoney English accent that sounded even more pronounced over the wires. But he had to admit the guy was pretty funny too, with his immediate invitation to 'come and have tea with the Queen, darling!'

He'd hung around for a while at the top of the street, checking that no one was around. But the place was quiet, just a couple of beaten-up cars sagging on old springs against the kerb, and nobody sitting out on any of the mostly half-ruined porches, their rotted rails in splinters and the planks that made up the private boardwalks that ran alongside the properties either badly split or missing completely.

When he was as satisfied as he could be that it was safe to move unobserved, he walked quickly to the address he'd been given. It was almost at the very end of the street and the house opposite was boarded up. Good.

He climbed the steps to the front door and

277

yanked at the cracked ceramic bell-pull. He heard a tinkle from somewhere inside and after a long pause, just as he was about to ring again, the shuffle of footsteps.

The front door opened and there he was, the old fuck, practically dancing from foot to foot with delight, powdered and rouged all to hell. Jesus. Mascara too. The guy looked like a decaying marionette.

'You darling boy, you came! When I returned home last night I decided I'd wasted my time and a very large tip on you.'

He grinned, said something meaningless about wine improving with age — where did he get crap like that from? — and a moment later he was standing in the hallway, the door closing behind him.

'I guess I thought . . . well, why not. I have a coupla hours off shift. Why the hell not?'

The old guy looked hurt.

'Oh well, if this is merely a pity visit . . . '

He reached out with his left hand and rested it gently on the old guy's shoulder, giving him a reassuring squeeze.

'Hey, don't be so goddamned sensitive. I came because you invited me over, OK? I assume it's just you and me here, by the way.'

'Of course, dear boy. I told you last night; I've lived alone here for years.'

'And you have a TV?'

'What? Yes, yes of course I do. Doesn't everybody these days?'

His hand, resting so casually on the bony old shoulder, instantly became a grip of iron. He whipped back through ninety degrees, right arm extending simultaneously behind him, and spiralled back round again, delivering a tremendous straight-armed punch to the old man's face.

The decrepit body flew more than a yard backwards and slammed down onto the floor, the head snapping back against the uncarpeted boards and bouncing up again towards the chest in a grotesque parody of a courtly bow, before falling all the way back to expose a sad, chicken neck.

He stepped across the unconscious man and stamped hard on his windpipe, continuing to press his foot against it, using all of his weight. After a few seconds the body shuddered and the heels drummed frantically against the floorboards. Then, sooner than he expected, he felt the instinctive, primal fight for life fade away. The body slackened and became perfectly still.

He calculated that it had taken the old fart less than thirty seconds to die.

48

'You cannot be serious. I really have to wear make-up for this?'

The girl sighed. She got this kind of crap from almost every guy who was booked to appear on *South Florida News Tonight*.

'Yes, Mr Foster, you do. Everyone does. Otherwise you'll end up looking as pale as a ghost, and after you've been under the studio lights for one minute you'll be perspiring so much you'll look like a ghost that's been splashed with cooking oil. I don't try to tell you how to do your job, sir, so will you please just let me do mine?'

'Holy smoke, after a telling-off like that? I can only apologise. I am putty in your hands.'

He was somewhat reassured to be told that President Kennedy always wore make-up for television. 'Don't you remember that pre-election TV debate he had with Nixon in '60?' the girl asked him. 'Nixon refused make-up and that's why he looked so sweaty and shiny and kinda untrustworthy. Did him no favours at all. JFK looked cool and composed because he wasn't embarrassed to have a little base and powder beforehand — and in the commercial breaks, too, I heard. So just relax, sir. If it's good enough for the President, it's good enough for you.'

Ten minutes later he was on set as the

programme counted down to transmission. The red light flashed once, twice, and then stayed on as the opening titles rolled. They showed pelicans gliding over a shining sea; a police helicopter taking off from the top of a Miami skyscraper; hot-rod cars blazing along an endless smooth sandy beach, all interspersed with shots of nubile young women wearing tiny bikinis frolicking in the sea.

The monitor in front of him cut to a wide studio shot showing both himself and the anchor — a household name in southern Florida — sitting on either side of a narrow wooden desk.

Lee was terrified.

The host, impeccably coiffed and improbably tanned even by Floridian standards, began talking to the camera. Lee couldn't believe how insouciant and relaxed the man appeared, considering that hundreds of thousands of people must be watching.

'Good evening, good people,' the anchor began in a crisp baritone. 'You're watching *SFNT* with me, Todd Rodgerson.'

The camera cut to Lee, who under the thick panstick could feel himself starting to perspire.

'And this is FBI agent Lee Foster. His agency believes the infamous Keys Killer is not only still at large in Key West, but is concealing his true identity' — the standard mug shot of Woods appeared onscreen — 'in a cunning disguise. Police artists, commissioned by this programme,' (Lee raised an eyebrow at that) 'have been working to give us some idea of how the fugitive,

John Henry Woods, may now appear. So, does he now look like *this* — '

A drawing of Woods with jet-black hair appeared on screen.

'Or this . . . ' Now the wanted man had dark stubble, too.

'Or *this* . . . ' Woods was blond now, first with a nascent beard, and then without.

'Or THIS?' The screen split into multiple images to show the wanted man in all the previous incarnations, but this time wearing tinted spectacles. The images began to slowly rotate with full-frame shots showing each possible permutation.

'Agent Foster . . . over to you, sir.'

Lee had been told by Todd's enthusiastic producer that their available audience stretched from Cape Canaveral to the north, Key West to the south, and Tampa and Naples to the west. There was nothing to the east, except the Bahamas, which broadcast a taped copy of *SFNT* six hours after transmission. Beyond those islands was the broad Atlantic stream that divided North America from Europe.

He didn't give a hoot about what the producer told him was the station's 'footprint'. All he cared about were the viewers watching in Key West.

'Thanks, Todd,' he said, trying to hide his jitters. 'As you say, we strongly suspect Woods to be in Key West, masquerading under some form of false identity. It's what we call hiding in plain sight. If any of the images your viewers are looking at right now remind them of someone they have seen in recent days, or even today, in Key West, we urge them to call us immediately.' He paused uncertainly. 'Er . . . do I give the number at this point, Todd?'

The host shook his head. 'No need, sir. It's right there on the bottom of the screen. As viewers can see, it's a toll-free number, so it won't cost anyone a red cent to dial it. How dangerous do you think Woods is right now, Agent Foster? It's been a while since he killed.'

Lee nodded. 'Yes, clearly he's been lying low. But he remains exceptionally dangerous, partly because he's backed into a corner now and that's bound to make him unpredictable. If any of your viewers think they may have seen someone similar to one of these pictures, they must on no account approach him. It's highly likely that he is armed and given the horrifying nature of his crimes thus far he won't hesitate to kill again if he thinks he has to.'

A studio floor manager standing beside Todd's dedicated camera began to give the anchor a sign to wind up the interview.

Todd riffled his script for visual punctuation and said: 'Thank you, Agent Foster, but I'm afraid that's all we have time for. Everyone here at *SFNT* wishes you and your men a speedy and successful conclusion to this operation.'

Lee held up one hand. 'Just one more thing, please.'

Todd looked faintly annoyed. 'Make it brief, sir. Time and commercials wait for no man.'

'Sure. It's just that if anyone *does* recognise one of these images, it'll be that of a new kid in

283

town. Coupla weeks at most.'

'Point taken, Agent Foster, and thanks again. After the break — the Miami Dolphins. Doomed, desperate and destined for defeat against Denver? That's when we come back.'

The programme's sting — a brief, stirring cacophony of French horns — cued the commercials. Todd slipped his earpiece out and proffered his hand to Lee.

'Nice going, Mr Foster, especially for a first-timer. You're a TV natural. Had me worried for my job a moment there.' He laughed.

Lee smiled back at him as they shook hands. 'You have to be kidding. My heart was going like a jackhammer. I was more nervous than when I got into my first shoot-out. Anyway, thanks for the spot.'

The make-up girl was back, dabbing at the presenter's nose with an enormous powder puff.

'Sure, no problem. By the way — d'you really think he's still in Key West?'

Lee stood to go.

'I damn well know he is. And now the bastard knows I know.'

49

He switched off the TV and took another of the old queen's cigarettes from the varnished bamboo box by the side of the bed, lighting it with the gold Ronson he'd found on the same elegant French-polished table.

Shit, shit, shit, shit, shit.

The artist's impression showing him clean-shaven with bleach-blond hair and tinted glasses might just as well have been a Polaroid of him that someone had taken that very afternoon.

Sliding off the bed, he went to the enormous Baroque mirror that was fixed at a suspicious angle on the wall opposite the end of the ornate four-poster bed, and stared at his reflection.

He was fucked. If Tom or anyone else who worked at the Springfield had been watching the broadcast, they'd almost certainly be on the phone to the cops right at this very moment. Every one of the bastards would be chasing that $10,000 reward, not to mention the bar's regulars, too. Everyone would recognise him from the picture; you'd have to be blind or stupid not to. Jesus, even the wrinkled old tart whose body he'd just dragged down into the fruit cellar would otherwise have probably been tottering down Duval to Key West's police headquarters to turn him in.

Then there was the small matter of tomorrow's papers. The eerily accurate sketch was going to be all over them. The Courier, the Herald, probably even the frigging Keys Shopper.

Jesus.

He drew hard on the cigarette. It was time to face reality. This whole thing was unravelling much, much more quickly than he would have believed possible at the start. Which was when, exactly? Christ, not even two months ago. He'd honestly believed it would be way past Thanksgiving or even Christmas before the cops or the Feds got so much as a sniff of him. When he sensed that, he would have been out of the state with a new off-the-shelf ID before they'd even got close.

Well, they were close now all right. And it was all thanks to his English rose. Boy, did that bitch have a poison thorn on her.

He turned away from the mirror and crossed the bedroom to a sideboard that stood underneath the bedroom window. He pulled the double doors open and grimaced. The top shelf was heaped with sex toys, mostly enormous and elaborate phalluses. But underneath was a circular rotating platform crammed with bottles of exotic drinks. He poked through the assorted crème de menthes, cherry brandies and Benedictines until he found some whisky, almost a full bottle, and yanked it out.

A couple of minutes later he was in the dead man's kitchen rooting through an ancient and filthy freezer in search of ice. He found a block in a drugstore-bought bag of ice cubes which had solidified. He smashed it repeatedly onto the floor until some usable chunks broke loose.

He couldn't find any clean glasses so he rinsed a crystal tumbler that was lying in a heap of unwashed crockery in the sink, and mixed himself an enormous scotch on the rocks with just a dash of water from the tap.

He took it back upstairs and lay down fully-clothed on the four-poster.

He had a lot of thinking to do, a lot of planning.

His run might be almost over, but he'd end it on his own terms.

'An English Rose for a Keys Killer'; that's what those headlines had said.

Yeah. Damn straight on that.

The time had come to take what was rightfully his.

50

Tom was surprised and slightly annoyed when Dennis didn't show up for happy hour. He had two other guys on duty, but a shift was a shift and he hated staff taking advantage of his easygoing nature.

He went upstairs to his apartment above the bar, making a mental note to pull his newest barman up short when he eventually deigned to show up for work. He wouldn't make too much of it, though — so far Dennis had been hard-working and reliable. That's why he was surprised by tonight's no-show.

Tom always changed for evenings in the Springfield and he expected his staff to smarten up a bit after sundown, too. His parents had always changed for dinner; he supposed he got it from them.

He switched on the portable TV in the lounge and carried it through to the bedroom, adjusting the aerial when he got there. The picture sharpened nicely but he kept the sound low for now. An ad for the latest Cadillac was airing and he glanced at his watch. Two before six. Good; he was in time for Todd Rodgerson, who he had a bit of a thing for, if he was honest. He'd never read anything in the *Miami Herald* gossip columns that indicated whether the unmarried anchor was or wasn't straight, but he had his suspicions which team the guy batted for.

Something told him that if the TV host came down here to Key West he'd be more comfortable drinking in the Springfield than in the Hog's Breath.

He opened his wardrobe and wondered whether he should wear the seersucker jacket he'd picked up on his last trip to New York, or his new captain's blazer with the brass buttons he'd bought from the menswear store next door a few days back.

He'd just decided on the seersucker and was picking out a shirt and tie when he heard Todd's distinctive voice coming from the portable. His show had started and he was saying something about Key West. Bruce had been right, then. Curious, Tom crossed the room and turned up the volume.

Todd was sitting opposite some guy — also very cute, Tom noted with appreciation — and talking about the Keys Killer and some sort of disguise. He turned up the sound a little more.

' . . . some idea of how the fugitive, John Henry Woods, may now appear. So, does he now look like *this* . . . '

Todd and his guest were replaced on screen by a montage of sketches of the wanted man. After the first two or three, Tom shrugged and went back to the wardrobe. He'd never seen anyone like that down here.

He slid a pale blue shirt from its hanger and turned back to look at the TV while he put it on.

His fingers froze in the act of buttoning down the collar.

'Holy fuck.'

Staring out at him from the little screen was the man he'd sent off on a late lunch break two hours earlier.

'Holy *fuck*.'

The series of sketches were now being repeated over and over, lazily succeeding each other on screen as the cop or G-man or whatever he was talked about the manhunt. Every time the version that had to be Dennis — *had* to be — appeared, Tom felt like he was being punched in the stomach.

Now the cop was saying something about not approaching the fugitive, how he was a ruthless killer, and to call the toll-free number on the bottom of the screen if you recognised him.

Tom half sat, half collapsed on to the end of his bed, his shirt still unbuttoned. This was unbelievable. This was totally unbelievable. Todd was wrapping the segment up but the cop interrupted him. He said the killer would be a new kid in town and would only have shown up in Key West in the past week or two.

Dennis had walked into the Springfield, what, ten days ago?

'Jesus, I hired a fucking psycho,' the bar owner whispered to himself. And then a sudden spasm of fear gripped him.

What if he's on his way back here now?

Chanting the police phone number aloud over and over to keep it in his memory, he raced down the stairs, shirt flapping open as he went.

He burst into the bar, running to the phone on the wall opposite.

'Pete, Harry — lock the doors,' he shouted. 'Do it now.'

The bartenders stared at him in astonishment.

'But we've got some customers in already,' one of them objected. 'We can't lock them in, they'll — '

'*I said lock the frigging doors! Now!*'

The next moment his trembling fingers were transferring the numbers in his head to the phone, forcing the dial back against its ratchet between each digit in an effort to speed it up.

Finally he was done and after a few moments he heard the ringtone.

'C'mon . . . *c'mon*,' he breathed. Behind him he could hear the bar doors slamming shut and bolts rattling into place. One customer was protesting but he could take a hike.

At last someone picked up the phone at the other end.

'Police — Keys Killer hotline. You have information for us?'

Tom took a deep breath.

'You can say that again.'

51

Lee had barely driven out of the TV station's parking lot in downtown Miami when the radio on his cruiser's dash crackled into life. It was the sergeant he'd left in charge of the phone room back in Key West.

He snatched the microphone from its holder. 'Talk to me, Ben. What kind of response are we getting?'

'Quantity — lowish,' the voice replied. 'Quality? Now there we're cooking.'

'Go on.'

'Almost no one so far responding to the sketches showing Woods in a beard or with black hair, sir. But that one of him as a blond bombshell with glasses? That's really hitting the spot. We've had five calls already from people who are certain they've seen him in Key West but here's the thing, sir — all the sightings are concentrated either on Duval or in that twinkie bar down past the Hog's Breath, the Springfield Tavern. Three calls placing him there so far. Two were anonymous, for obvious reasons, I guess, but hold on to yourself, sir — one guy identified himself as the Tavern's owner, one Thomas Bilson. He says he hired a barman answering the blond's description on the very evening that we know Woods came ashore on the island. He's been living in a room above the bar ever since. It's got to be him, sir.'

Lee silently punched the air in triumph, before saying as calmly as he could: 'I agree. How many men have you sent over there?'

'Six, sir. But I've told them to stay well back and keep the bar under observation.'

'*What?* Why? Why aren't they going straight in?'

'Bilson says he sent Woods — who's going under the name of Dennis Clancey, by the way — on a late lunch break at about four o'clock today and he's not back yet. He's surprised at that — says the guy's usually a good timekeeper.'

Lee's elation began to fade. 'How late is he?'

'Should have been back there before happy hour — half past five at the latest. He's almost an hour overdue now.'

Lee nodded to himself before saying in a voice that failed to conceal his disappointment: 'It's what I was worried might happen. He's seen the broadcast. Maybe he was in a bar somewhere with a TV. But it doesn't signify. It's only a matter of time, now.'

He paused, thinking hard before continuing: 'OK, here's what I want you to do. Stay back from the Springfield Tavern until seven o'clock and if he hasn't shown up by then, go in. Get a full statement from the owner and search Woods's room. Meanwhile set up a roadblock where Route 1 joins the Key. He may steal a car or even hijack one.

'If he takes a boat there aren't nearly as many embarkation points as there are in Key Largo so we can probably stop him this time. Get some of the guys down to the Marina. I don't want any boats leaving without us giving them the once-over first. Radio ALL departing boat registrations to the Coastguard cutter that's been standing outside the main channel out to sea since yesterday. Send a couple of back-up launches to join them. Any boats we haven't told them about are to be stopped, boarded and searched. Finally, get everyone else out on the streets, checking out likely spots. I'd start with the churches. They're pretty quiet this time of night. But use your initiative. All clear on the above, Ben?'

'Crystal. I'm on it, sir. What time d'you think you'll get back?'

'Close to ten tonight. But I'm on the radio. So much as a fly farts down there, I want to be told. Out.'

It was still an hour before sunset but high cirrus clouds had moved in from the west, and Lee found himself driving under what his grandfather used to call a mackerel sky. He wondered if it might presage rain later.

He went over the orders he'd just given. Had he missed anything? If so, he couldn't think what it might be.

Assuming Woods was still at large when he rolled back into Key West, he knew *exactly* the first person he was going to call.

Stella. If he was missing something, she'd be the one to spot it.

Of course, he *was* missing something, he reflected as he drove twenty-five over the limit through Islamorada.

He missed Stella like hell.

52

The five customers who'd been locked inside the Springfield Tavern for the last forty-five minutes stopped complaining when Tom explained that all drinks were on the house until the police arrived and he felt it was safe to unbolt the doors.

They'd all taken full advantage of his offer and were now mostly drunk or very drunk, so it was a relief when he heard a loud banging coming from outside and the shouted command: 'Police! Open up!'

The drunks were politely led out on to Duval and left to make their own way home.

Back in the bar, Tom was now sweating profusely as the sergeant questioned him. He was always nervous around policemen — excepting his new boyfriend, of course; he'd had some pretty bad experiences in the past, always entirely down to his sexuality. Key West was the first place in his life where he felt mostly hassle-free from local law enforcement.

He was dreading one question in particular and when it inevitably came, he could feel himself turning a beetroot red. That always happened when he prevaricated or lied, and he was about to do both now.

'You say this man was a good worker and timekeeper,' the sergeant was saying. 'Why d'you think he makes an exception like this and disappears? Where might he have gone? Any ideas?'

Oh God, this was awful, just awful. Denny — no, he must stop thinking of him as that — had disappeared because he, Tom, had passed on inside information. He might even go to jail because of it, and what about his poor boyfriend? Neither of them had meant any harm but what on earth was he supposed to say to this policeman, who was beginning to give him an increasingly puzzled look as the silence lengthened.

'Why hasn't he come back?' he managed, with a pretence at an airiness he did not feel. 'I'm sure I don't know, sergeant ... perhaps he was watching the TV news in some bar or other and saw those pictures of himself. That must be it.'

Sergeant Ben Moss stared at the bar owner. He'd been a cop for more than twenty years and he knew evasion when he heard it. He'd learned that the blunt approach usually worked best.

'OK, I'm gonna ask the question again, Mr Bilson, because I don't think that was the straightest answer you have in you. Remember this is a multiple murder investigation and we can do this down at headquarters just as well as in your bar here, OK?'

Tom trembled. 'I'm sure there's no need for — '

'There's no need for *anything*, sir, other than for you to answer my questions with the straight dope. So let's try again ... are you aware of any reason why the man we know as John Henry

296

Woods didn't return from his meal break this afternoon?'

It was no good, he simply wasn't built for this kind of thing. His head dropped forward as he answered dully: 'Well ... yes, yes, I suppose there is, now I come to think of it. You see, sergeant, I have a ... a friend ... a friend who I was with this afternoon enjoying a, er, private conversation in his apartment, and we were interrupted by a telephone call ordering him to return to ... to return to ... the building you've just threatened to take me to.'

Moss raised his eyebrows. 'Say what? The guy you were with is a cop?'

'Er ... yes, but please don't ask me his name because that's one thing I'm NOT going to tell you.' Tom raised his head and looked defiantly at the other man. 'I mean it. It's a private friendship.'

The sergeant stared evenly at the sweating man opposite. He could come back to the question of the cop's identity later; it was what he might have said that mattered most right now.

'OK, Tom, we can park that point if you like. What did the officer say to you about why he had to come back in? Take your time. Just tell me the truth.'

The bar owner wiped the sweat from his eyes and forehead with the back of his hand before continuing.

'Well, he said it had something to do with the hunt for this guy it now turns out I've been harbouring here all this time ... he didn't know exactly what, though. But about an hour later he phoned me to apologise again for spoiling our, er, lunch, and said he was going to be busy this evening too. That's when he told me about the artist's sketches and the TV and the newspapers and all.'

The sergeant nodded.

'And you told Woods when you got back here. Did you also tell him what the sketches would look like?'

Tom hung his head again. 'Yes,' he said miserably. 'I'm sorry. I even teased him that one of the pictures was apparently going to show the killer with blond hair and glasses, just like he had. But how was I to know who he really was? And I must say he didn't seem all that interested. He only asked a couple of questions and then wandered off for lunch. If he was alarmed, he certainly didn't show it.'

Ben Moss sighed. 'Look, it's OK. You're right; you weren't to know. But it's a damn shame all the same. If you hadn't said anything, we'd have him in the cells right now.'

'I know . . . as I say, I'm sorry. Sergeant . . . do you think he'll come back here?'

The officer gave a short laugh as he stood up. 'Are you kidding? Would you? Relax, Mr Bilson. The next time you see John Henry Woods he'll be on TV being taken into the courthouse in cuffs and leg-irons. Stay here, please, I haven't finished with you. I just have to radio my boss.'

* * *

Lee pounded the steering column in frustration when Moss finished his account.

'This is so *frigging* annoying! So he knew in *advance* he was going to be on the TV news tonight, did he? No wonder he disappeared in a puff of smoke. *Jesus*, Ben! When is this bastard's luck going to run out? It's like he has some fucked-up guardian angel over his shoulder, whispering in his ear every time we get close.'

He drummed his fingers against the steering wheel a moment, then clicked the mic on again.

'Have you made all those dispositions I ordered earlier?'

'Yes, sir.'

'OK then, carry on questioning this Bilson guy and I'll see you back at headquarters. I'm about an hour away now. Should've taken the chopper. But look, Ben, things just got a lot more complicated. If Woods had a coupla hours' heads-up, he had just enough time to make some kind of plan. He won't be skulking in the back of some dark bar or in the side-room of a church. He'll have come up with something. He's a clever bastard.

'But I'm a clever bastard too. And I know someone who's even cleverer than Woods and me put together. I'm gonna call them the second I get back.'

53

He glanced at the pretty blue china ashtray, its contents now overflowing onto the bedside table, and counted the number of butts.

Seventeen. Almost a whole pack. What you might call a seventeen-fag plan. Eighteen, if you included the body in the cellar. He laughed inwardly at his own joke. He could be a pretty funny guy sometimes, not that people would know; he hadn't told anyone a joke in his entire life. He'd never seen the point in trying to make another person laugh.

Calmly he reviewed the strategy he'd worked out; a strategy he was reasonably confident would get his English rose down here to Key West. He knew from an interview this Foster guy had given to the Courier last week that she'd gone back to Massachusetts now that what they called 'the killer's profile' had been established.

And he had to give the kid credit for working out so much about him with so little to go on. She was smart as a whip. He ought to be angry with her but he wasn't. In fact he was looking forward to spending time with her, and not just because of the way he'd decided he was going to kill her. They'd have a nice fireside chat first.

He grinned when he remembered that dumb newspaper interview with the Fed; how he'd been so goddamned confident he'd have his man in days, if not hours. What a prick. He'd only got as close as he had because of the girl, although to be fair, he had admitted that to the reporter.

Well, he'd see to it that this Foster guy would be asking for her help again soon. He couldn't guarantee this new plan would work, that it would see the kid jumping on the next plane to Miami and coming down here to Key West, but he thought it had a better than even chance. And if at first you didn't succeed . . . he'd only have to do this thing once more, he reckoned, for it to have the desired effect.

And once she was down here? He'd already worked that out, in general terms at least. It would mean thinking on his feet a bit, but he'd always been good at that, hadn't he? Remember that village in Korea . . . What the papers hadn't reported the other day, because there was no way they could have known, was that he'd come up with the whole mercy-killing thing only after he'd walked into the place. He'd made a good case for it with the guys and led by example, blowing the brains out of an old peasant woman who genuinely was dying in agony, fun though that had been to watch. Later, he'd been surprised to discover that killing could be contagious. Some of the others had enjoyed it almost as much as he had.

He dragged his thoughts back to the present. He accepted that this was it; that kidnapping and torturing the girl would be his final flourish. He still hadn't decided whether he wanted to be arrested so he could gloat over his successes in a courtroom — he was pretty sure the finer details

301

of what he'd accomplished would have some of the more lily-livered jurors throwing up or fainting, and lawyers bleating for adjournments and smelling-salts — but on the other hand he quite liked the idea of making a grand exit once he'd finished with the girl. He'd be going to the chair anyway so blowing his own brains out here in this house meant he'd stay in full control right up to the end.

He'd have to think about it. No need to decide right now.

He looked at the antique clock, ticking softly on a shelf next to the window that looked out at the condemned house across the street. The building was more or less invisible on this moonless night. Good. The darker the better for what he had planned later.

Nearly eleven o'clock. It wouldn't be safe for him to go outside for a while longer, even if he was in a fresh disguise, courtesy of the old fart's wardrobe. The guy had obviously been into cross-dressing in a big way; there was a small but high-quality selection of dresses and wigs neatly stashed away next to his regular clothes, the ones he'd worn on his regular visits to the Springfield, where the sad-sack had invariably tried to make a clumsy pass at him. He'd always given him the brush-off but thank God he'd kept that phone number. He must have known somewhere in the back of his mind that he might need it.

He yawned. He wanted to go to sleep, but he had work to do.

He slid off the bed and stretched. Hopefully his dead host had some sort of toolkit somewhere. He didn't need much stuff — a saw, a hammer and some nails would do.

He pushed both hands under the mattress and heaved it up and away. Excellent. There were about twenty horizontal wooden slats that formed the base of the bed. He'd probably need about six of them.

He dropped the mattress back and headed downstairs to the kitchen; he'd start the search for tools in there. With any luck he should have knocked up something pretty special for his English rose by the time he was ready to go outside into the darkness and roll out the first part of his plan.

He yawned again. It was going to be a busy night.

54

By the time Lee had reached Key West and de-briefed his sergeant it was past midnight and too late to call Stella up at the Rockfairs'.

There had, of course, been no sightings of Woods, or the slightest indication of where he might be. Lee was as certain as he could be that his man was still in Key West — although a person-to-person call from J. Edgar Hoover, the gist of which was: 'Let him get away a second time and you can mail me your letter of resignation along with your badge', had hardly done wonders for his confidence. The old bastard. When did *he* last close a case?

Sergeant Moss was in the next room writing up his report. Lee found the click-clack of the typewriter strangely comforting at this time of night: a reminder that he was not alone here in the small hours.

For the hundredth time since first arriving in Key West, he wandered over to the window and looked down along Duval. It was still pretty busy, but the hookers had mainly taken over from the beggars and buskers now. Lee wondered if they had an informal arrangement over shift patterns.

He thought about what Moss had told him the bar owner had said. Woods, by the sound of it, had played the part of the persecuted homosexual on the lam to perfection. But how, Lee wanted to know, had he had dealt with the inevitable come-ons from other guys?

'He's a fly one, judging by what Bilson said,' the sergeant replied. 'When one of the other barmen made a move on him, Woods let him down easy. Explained that he he'd been pretty traumatised by the whole police sting operation on him up in Dallas and he'd currently lost his appetite for that kind of thing. He told all the guys working in the bar that he was in a sort of purdah. Bilson told me he had to look the word up. To be honest, sir, I'd never heard of it either. But Bilson said he thought the man he knew as Dennis Clancey punched above his weight, brains-wise.'

'Meaning?'

'He says he had the impression he was unusually quick on the uptake. Well read, too. Has a copy of Milton's *Paradise Lost* with him. Bilson said Woods used to take it with him on his meal breaks. He also came back once from the Hemingway Museum over on Whitehead Street with a bunch of the guy's books he bought from the store there. Offered to lend Bilson one of them. *A Farewell to Arms*, I think he said.'

Lee raised an eyebrow. 'My favourite Hemingway, as it happens. Read any of his stuff, Ben?'

'No, sir.'

Lee sighed. 'I'm not sure that knowing Woods's literary tastes helps us any. We already know he's a clever bastard, don't we? Maybe he quotes poetry to them while he's killing them . . . sorry, Ben, that wasn't remotely funny. It's been a long day. But to get back to this other thing: we're as sure as we can be that Woods didn't form any kind of opportunistic relationship with another man to add to his cover? Maybe give him a bolthole to go to when the crap hit the fan? It's possible he's hiding out in some guy's home somewhere, maybe killed him there and is sitting pretty while he works out his next move.'

Moss shook his head. 'That's a smart theory but we don't have a shred of evidence for it, sir. Bilson says Woods kept himself to himself. Worked his shifts, was polite with the customers but never responded to any of their chat-up lines; slept alone in his room, went out now and again to the nearest diner or burger bar. Exactly what you'd expect from a guy who's jumped bail and wants to lie low for a while.'

'Hmm . . . I still think we're missing something, Ben. I reckon I'll go talk to this Bilson guy myself in the morning. No offence, sergeant.'

'None taken, sir. He was pretty much in shock when I spoke to him. Maybe he'll remember something after he's had a stiff drink or three and a good night's sleep. I'll set you up a meet at his bar at ten o'clock. That do?'

'Fine. Type up your report and then we can both get to bed. I'll see you back here at eight in the morning and we'll give the guys a pep talk. Then I'll go see Bilson and by lunchtime we can decide what our next move should be. I know the roadblock's working on the top line because I came through it on the way back here and watched things there for a while. Not so much as a mouse could get past those guys. What about the boats?'

Moss laughed. 'Nothing gets off or on the Key without us knowing about it. It's not making us the world's most popular with the boat owners and one rich bastard really lost it when the boys insisted on taking a look round his yacht before he left for the Dry Tortugas. Not surprising really; he had two underage Mexican hookers below decks and a nice big bag of cocaine to go with. I'd say he's looking at ten years.'

Lee grinned at him. 'Well, it's nice to know we're getting some side-orders while we wait for the main course,' he said. 'One more thing — I'm gonna call Stella Arnold up in Massachusetts tomorrow morning. I'd like to run all of this past her. She'll have a fresh take on things and it might give us a steer on what to do next.'

Moss cocked his head to one side. 'Is it true what I heard — you two are more than just friends? That's pretty fast work there, sir.'

Lee nodded. 'Yeah, it's true. God knows when I'll get to see her again, though.'

'I've only seen her picture in the papers,' the other man went on. 'But she's quite a looker, if you don't me saying so. So, she's back in Massachusetts now?'

Lee nodded. 'Yup, and having a fine old time by the sound of it. Her last letter was quite something — she'd just come back from Washington with her mother over from England. They'd been invited to the White House, met the President and Jackie there, were gonna have dinner and all — it was a thank-you to Stella for what she did down here — but right before the soup the whole thing got called off. Some big political crisis of some kind, apparently. Stella said that the President reckoned he might have to go on TV with it, but he hasn't, not yet, anyway. Maybe whatever the problem was blew over.'

'Wow. I'm impressed at all this inside information. D'you think we'll get an invite to the White House too after we've nailed Woods to the wall?'

Both men laughed. 'I reckon not, don't you?' Lee said. 'You're pretty cute, Ben, but not as cute as Stella, or her mother, come to that. Stella sent me a photograph of them both. Either one of them would have Elizabeth Taylor running to the powder-room for a freshen-up if they walked into the same room as her . . . Anyway, like I say, I'll talk to Stella first thing, see what she comes up with.'

But he wouldn't be talking to her until much later the following day, still less interviewing the owner of the Springfield Tavern.

There were going to be rather more pressing concerns to deal with first.

55

He threw the hammer down and stepped back to look at his handiwork.

Not bad. Not bad at all — pretty crude, but then the originals had been, hadn't they? They weren't supposed to be objects of beauty, for Chrisakes. The reflection made him smile. Jesus, he could be a witty guy sometimes.

He wasn't sure whether to leave the thing lying there on the bedroom floor or prop it up against the wall. In the end he decided on the latter, but it looked a bit unstable like that so he sawed up another of the planks from the bed to make a couple of wedges for the base, and took the largest nail he could see from the tin of mixed screws and nails he'd found with the tools, and hammered it through the very top part of the contraption so it was anchored firmly against the wall. He gave it a good hard shake, but it barely moved. Good. She'd never see it like he was seeing it now; she'd have what you might describe as a different perspective.

The last thing left to do was to cut up some lengths of rope from the coil he'd found in the same cupboard as the other stuff, and toss them into a corner. That was pretty much it. He pushed the cannibalised bed all the way across the room to give him some space for manoeuvre when the time came, and looked at his watch. It was a quarter before two in the morning.

Just time for another scotch on the rocks. Then he needed to get changed.

* * *

The hooker standing on the corner of Smith and Coral promised herself she'd quit for home after her next trick. She was getting tired. The last john, a fat little guy with seriously bad breath, had turned out to be a royal pain in the ass. He hadn't been able to get it up and said that meant he didn't have to pay her anything. It had been a long night so she didn't bother arguing with him, just kneed him in the balls and took his wallet as he lay gasping for breath on the sidewalk. The tight-fisted, limp-dicked jerk had ended up parting with four or five times as much as he would have if he'd played her straight. Serve him right.

Annoyingly she'd lost her watch in a particularly frenzied encounter earlier with a madly excited kid she reckoned was on his first time, so she didn't know what o'clock it was, but it must be close on three. Everything was starting to go quiet now.

After a few more minutes she made up her mind to call it a night and was just about to head back to her apartment where her sister was minding her kid for her — Lucy always stepped into the breach like this when she was let down by her flaky babysitter — when a soft voice behind her said: 'Ma'am? Excuse me?'

She jumped — she hadn't heard anyone approach — and spun around.

'Jesus, you scared me . . . um . . . sir?'

It was a freakin' tranny. She could see that, even though the streetlights on this particular junction were unusually dim — they were pre-war and long overdue for replacement. What a way to close the night.

She'd only had a couple of transvestites before and she never quite knew how they liked to be addressed, as a man or a woman, so she just waited. The guy would spell out exactly what he wanted soon enough.

His make-up was awful — lipstick smeared clumsily across his mouth and deep into the corners; rouge painted with a heavy hand on both cheeks, and powder way too thick and hopelessly unevenly applied. It was hard to tell the colour of his wig in the bad light but she thought it might be a brassy red. He was dressed in a long plaid skirt and a creased cream blouse with a pale shawl thrown over his shoulders.

He looked like a circus clown's comedy sidekick.

'C'mon, hon,' she said when he remained silent, staring at her. 'You're my last of the night. I wanna be tucked up in bed in half an hour at most. What do you want to do, sugar?' Sugar, she thought, should cover it both ways.

When he spoke, it was in the same soft voice that he'd first addressed her.

'I want to do it to you from behind,' he said simply. 'I know the way I look but I can only do it when I'm . . . when I'm dressed like this. My wife won't accommodate me, so that's why I'm . . . that's why I'm . . . ' he tailed off a moment,

311

before continuing: 'Where can we go? How much will you want?'

'Fifty dollars, hon,' she said flatly. 'Sorry, it's double rate for the weird stuff. I've had a coupla experiences this evening that have pissed me off so if you don't mind I'll ask for the money up front. Want to go ahead or shall we both just go home?'

His answer was to fish somewhere inside the skirt and hand over three crumpled bills. 'I only have twenties,' he explained.

'Sorry, sugar, this store don't give change. Still want to play?'

'Of course. Where do we go?'

'Over here.'

She took his hand and led him around the corner to a scrap of empty ground next to a disused gas station.

'See that wall over there? We'll do it behind that, OK? Do you want me standing up or lying down?'

'Standing up, please.'

'OK, let's go. Jeez, what's that smell on you? Reminds me of the dentist's. You're not a dentist, are you?'

He nodded. 'As a matter of fact, I am.'

She laughed. 'Takes all sorts, I guess. Now, when you come, keep the noise down. We don't want the neighbours complaining.'

She went behind the wall first with him following close behind, and faced towards the brickwork, placing her hands against it and setting her legs apart.

'I'm not wearing panties, hon, so you just have

to lift my skirt. Knock yourself out.'

They were the last words she would ever say. Next moment the chloroform-soaked pad was forced against her mouth and nose and after a moment's desperate struggle, she collapsed backwards into his arms, twitching slightly.

He took out his knife, carefully cut off all her clothes, and got to work.

56

It was Diana's last day in the house on Bancroft Road. She was due to fly back to London that afternoon, and after her morning shower she decided to finish packing before joining the others for a late breakfast.

As she crossed the downstairs hall a couple of minutes after snapping shut the latches of her suitcase, the telephone on the table near the front door began to ring. She could hear the muffled voices of Stella and the family coming from the breakfast room, so Diana picked up the receiver.

'Rockfair residence. Who's calling?'

There was a distinct pause at the other end before she heard a chuckle followed by the words: 'Judging by that wonderful accent I'm either talking to the Queen of England or Stella's mother.'

Diana laughed in her turn. 'Diana Arnold speaking, without a speck of blue blood in her veins. Who is this?'

'Agent Lee Foster. Good morning to you, Mrs Arnold.'

Diana laughed again. 'As my hosts here would say, 'right back-atcha', Lee . . . I may call you Lee? You must certainly call me Diana. No more Mrs Arnold, please. That's strictly for my bank manager.'

'Agreed,' he said. 'I thought you'd left for England, Diana?'

'I go later today, more's the pity — it's such a shame we couldn't meet before I went back. But Stella's told me so much about you. It's obvious to me that she thinks the world of you.'

'As I do her. In fact I've never met anyone quite like Stella. She's very, very special. Look . . . please don't think I'm being rude, but I haven't much time to talk right now. Something real bad happened down here in the Keys last night to do with the investigation. I need to talk to Stella, not as my girlfriend but as a special advisor to the FBI. It's pretty urgent; in fact I may ask her to fly down here today, so maybe you'll be sharing a ride to Logan Airport later. Would you put her on to me, please?'

Diana raised her eyebrows. 'Hold the line, Lee, I'll go and get her. And goodbye for now.'

'Goodbye, Diana. We'll meet soon, I'm sure.'

In the breakfast room Stella was laughing with Sylvia over a cartoon on the front page of the *Boston Globe*.

'Come and look at this, Mummy,' she called as Diana entered the room. 'It's *so* funny. Sylvia says — '

'I'm sorry to interrupt, dear, but Lee is on the phone for you from Key West. He says something bad happened down there last night.'

Stella got up from the table and hurried into the hall, snatching the receiver from the table.

'Lee? What's happened?'

He told her.

★　★　★

315

Three hours later, as Lee had predicted to Diana, mother and daughter found themselves in a car together, headed for Boston's Logan Airport. It wasn't a cab; the shiny black Chrysler that had pulled up outside the Rockfairs' house was an FBI cruiser. Its driver sported the inevitable crew-cut: Stella wondered if Lee was in breach of some agency regulation by wearing his hair in a short-back-and-sides and that floppy fringe.

Stella had provided the rest of them with the latest headlines from Key West before running to her room to pack again for Florida. As she folded her clothes into the same bag that she'd so recently emptied, she could hear Jeb on the phone downstairs making excuses on her behalf to the head of her college. Today was meant to be her induction day and she'd been looking forward to exploring the campus and meeting her tutors. All that had been torpedoed by events taking place over a thousand miles away. She began to wonder if she'd ever get around to studying for her doctorate.

As Stella was now explaining to her mother, the latest body had been found shortly after six o'clock that morning. Lee said that a woman hotel cleaner taking a short-cut to work across a patch of waste ground had seen the blood first; a great pool of it that had flowed out from behind a wall before congealing into a waxy puddle already half-covered in a black swarm of flies.

When she had timidly poked her head around the brickwork and seen what lay on the other side, the cleaner had promptly vomited her breakfast all over the crime scene, much to the later annoyance of the forensics examiner who had been flown by helicopter down from Miami.

'Same M.O. as the others?' Stella had asked Lee over the phone.

'Yes and no. It's definitely him: the torture wounds are typical — long slashes and puncture wounds in all the usual places, the knife buried up to the hilt in the left eye. The handle's already tested positive for his fingerprints.'

'So what's different about this one?' she asked him.

She could practically hear him thinking during the pause before he answered her.

'Well, for a start . . . I used the word torture — but I don't think this woman felt a thing. There were no signs that her hands and feet had been bound; none of the usual burn-marks from struggling against the ropes.'

'That *is* odd. So she was killed *before* he did his stuff?'

'No — there was far too much blood on the ground. The pathologist reckons the body may have only had a couple of pints left in it by the time he did his party trick with the knife to the eye. As a working hypothesis, I'm thinking he drugged her in the usual way with chloroform — we found traces of it on her — and cut her in the usual way while she was unconscious. I don't believe she ever woke up again.'

Stella was deep in thought for so long after hearing this that eventually Lee said: 'Honey? You still there?'

'Mmm? Yes, sorry . . . just thinking . . . Did

you say there are other aspects here that vary from the norm?'

'Yup. The victim herself, for a start. We know he likes them young — late teens, early twenties, good girls. This was a 43-year-old prostitute, name of Mary Strimmer, string of convictions for soliciting and a couple for assault with a deadly weapon — if clients didn't pay her for services rendered, she was quite capable of sticking a switchblade into them.

'The other aberration is that there was no prior interception and abduction. He took Mary just a few yards around the corner from her usual pitch and butchered her. We have one witness who saw her alive and touting at about two o'clock this morning. Body temperature and rigor mortis indicate she died sometime between three and four. So this was a totally uncharacteristic, opportunistic, even rushed hit. He must have crept out of wherever he's holed up — in disguise, one assumes — and grabbed the first woman he came across. No real preparation. High-risk stuff, with the sadistic element entirely missing. It doesn't make sense.'

Stella nodded to herself. 'It certainly doesn't. I was going to say that maybe he's become sexually frustrated since going into hiding and he couldn't resist the urge to kill again . . . but the whole point of these attacks for him was always to inflict unimaginable pain on women, and listen to their suffering. Why go through the motions while she was comatose?'

She paused again, and this time Lee allowed her thought process to go uninterrupted.

After almost a full minute's silence, she spoke again. 'As I say, we know he likes to listen to them, that's why in the past he's taken them right out into the mangroves where no one else can hear. So I can see he might have been worried last night that people living nearby might have heard screaming and come running or called the police . . . so why not just gag her or stick some tape over her mouth? There's a totally different motive here, Lee. He's up to something.'

She heard him sigh deeply before saying: 'Could it be he's just taunting us? Showing he can pretty much do what he likes, right under our noses? You know, 'I'm the king of the hill, you can't catch me', kinda thing?'

'Possibly. But he probably thinks he's already shown that, merely by staying one step ahead of the investigation. Look, Lee, I'm going to have to give this a lot more thought. Would you like me to fly down there? He might do this again before you find him, you know. I can be there by this evening. Shall I come?'

'My sweetest, dearest Stella. I thought you'd never ask.'

* * *

When she'd finished her account of the conversation with Lee, Diana smiled at her.

'Doesn't it a feel a little odd to be working on a murder case alongside a man you say you're in love with?' she asked.

Her daughter shook her head vigorously. 'No,

319

not at all. Of course I know what you mean — it *is* a bit of a rum way to meet a boyfriend. But somehow it feels perfectly natural and almost *meant*. Anyway, I suppose we both know something like this is highly unlikely to happen again, working on the same case, I mean.'

Diana looked surprised. 'I wouldn't be too sure about that. Assuming things work out between you, Lee is bound to discuss future cases with you, isn't he? And you said this isn't his first involving a psychopath. The more you study the phenomenon, and the more cases he's assigned to, the more you're bound to exchange ideas and theories, whether it's officially or unofficially.'

'Gosh, I hadn't quite thought of it like that. I suppose you're right. I can be Watson to his Holmes. Or maybe it's the other way round . . . '

Stella grinned suddenly at her mother.

'But it's all rather exciting, isn't it? And speaking of exciting, Mummy, what *did* happen between you and President Kennedy in that corridor? Every time I ask you, you change the subject.'

Diana turned to look out of the car window. 'Oh look,' she said, craning her neck towards the sky. 'The geese are flying south for the winter.'

57

The latest murder was all over the radio breakfast shows and lunchtime phone-ins. By that evening he was headlining every broadcast outlet in the state and was impressively high up on the running-order of networked news bulletins.

He'd brought the radio from the kitchen to the spare bedroom — the master bedroom was unusable for sleeping now that he'd pretty much demolished the four-poster — and he'd dragged the upstairs TV on its castors across the landing and to the foot of his bed.

The State Governor, C. Farris Bryant, had been taped for the early-evening news, pledging the recall of FBI special advisor Stella Arnold to the case.

He sipped his scotch as he watched the interview play out. 'Miss Arnold, to whom we already owe a substantial debt of gratitude, is on her way down here as I speak,' the Governor informed his interviewer in reverent, sonorous tones, as if a mere touch of the hem of the English woman's garment would lead investigators to make an immediate arrest.

His plan had worked. It had fucking worked! She was coming, and the fact that she was coming meant that no one — not even her — had figured out the real reason he'd killed the hooker. Because if they had . . . well, she

321

would've been kept safe and sound back up in Massachusetts. But he'd set his snare and she, with the connivance and encouragement of the police, the FBI, even the frigging State Governor, was walking right into it.

He was still unsure exactly how to spring the trap closed — until he switched channels to Todd Rodgerson's nightly news show. It was good old Todd who unwittingly supplied the break he was looking for.

The anchor informed his viewers that the police and the FBI had called a news conference for three o'clock the next afternoon in Key West. Stella Arnold was expected to attend and make a brief statement in response to overwhelming press interest about her role in the case.

He stared at the TV screen for a moment before slowly toasting it with what remained of his scotch. He genuinely could not believe this.

They were serving her up to him on a plate.

58

Stella's FBI helicopter landed in Key West shortly after five that evening. She looked out of the cockpit's Perspex bubble and almost immediately saw Lee standing outside the special arrivals hut reserved for helicopter passengers and crew. He was waving at her, a huge smile on his face.

The earphones the pilot had given her before they took off from Miami an hour earlier, so they could talk to each other on the way down, crackled into life.

'That yer fella, the one you been tellin' me about?'

She nodded happily.

'Yes, that's my Lee.'

'He sure looks crazy to see ya again.'

When the blades above them had stopped turning, the pilot leant across her and opened the passenger door, reaching behind them for her bag. 'I'll bring this over to ya. Looks like yer gonna need both hands free.'

A few moments later Stella had run across the strip of tarmac that separated her from Lee and was in his arms.

'Oh Lee . . . I've missed you *so much*,' she whispered, holding him tight. 'I just want this *stupid* case over with so we can spend some proper time together. Let me look at you.'

She pulled away from him slightly and stared at him.

'Lee, you look exhausted,' she said, genuinely concerned. 'You've lost weight and you're much too pale and there are dark rings around your eyes.'

'Thanks,' he said ironically. 'You, by comparison, look fabulous next to this wreck of a man.'

'Don't be silly!' she retorted. 'I'm just worried about you. You've been under a colossal strain.'

He smiled down at her. 'Nothing a proper kiss won't put right.'

A minute or so later they pulled slowly apart.

'You *do* look a bit better now, actually,' she said dreamily. 'Really, you've got some colour back in your cheeks.'

'Well, the love of a good woman, as they say . . . c'mon, I've got lots to tell you on the drive back to your hotel.'

'*My* hotel?' she said as they walked to the car. 'Don't you mean *our* hotel?'

'Not tonight, Josephine,' he said drily, tossing her bag onto the back seat and opening the passenger door for her. 'I'm sleeping on a cot at headquarters. Given what went down last night I have to be on constant call. And speaking of being on call . . . ' He went round to the driver's side and climbed in, starting the engine.

'Go on,' she said. 'What about being on call? And why do you suddenly look all shifty?'

He glanced guiltily across at her as he drove towards the airfield's perimeter gates.

'Because . . . well, there's something happening in the afternoon, Stella, that everyone wants you to be involved in.'

324

She looked at him with increasing suspicion.

'Going by the expression on your face, I don't think I'm going to like it.'

'Like it? I think you're going to hate it.'

59

He turned the volume all the way down so he could figure out exactly how to exploit the press conference he'd just learned about, courtesy of Todd Rodgerson. Now he could see good old Todd mouthing his goodnights and then the screen cut to President Kennedy, sitting behind a desk yacking away to the camera. It looked like he was speaking from the White House. Another my-fellow-Americans piece of horseshit propaganda, no doubt. He switched the TV off.

This news about the press conference fitted pretty well damn perfectly into the general plan he'd been formulating. He was still playing the odds, of course — there was a lot that could go wrong, he realised that — but those odds had definitely just shortened in his favour.

The first thing to do was to establish if the old queen owned a car. If not, he'd have to go out and steal one. Risky, as would driving the thing be, even for the short round-trip involved. If the theft was reported, some on-the-ball cop might spot the licence plate and pull him over. He'd probably end up dying in the inevitable shoot-out that would follow.

But last night when he returned from killing the hooker as bait, he'd noticed there was a single garage tacked on to the side of the house.

He went downstairs, opened the front door a

little way, and peered out cautiously. It was dark and the street lighting was poor. No one seemed to be around. In fact he was beginning to wonder if the dark, silent homes on each side of him had been condemned and abandoned like the boarded-up house opposite.

He stood there, taking his time. He heard a car door slam much further down the street, towards the town, and a few moments later the sound of the engine starting up before the car was driven away. Then all was silence again.

He decided it was safe for him to move. He slipped outside and turned left to the garage. The double doors were padlocked so he had to go back into the house to look for the key. It took him a while to find it, hidden in a large coffee mug on a shelf in the kitchen. A set of car ignition keys was there too. His hopes began to rise.

He unlocked the garage and tried to open the doors, which were stiff on their hinges and creaked loudly. He cursed under his breath. Dead leaves and dirt scrunched back with them as he hauled on the handles. He figured the garage couldn't have been opened for weeks, months even.

Eventually he dragged both doors open barely wide enough to squeeze through. In the darkness he could just make out the outline of a car and the faint, dull gleam of chrome.

So far, so good.

He felt around on the wall for the light switch. When he found it he carefully noted its position before going to the doors and yanking them closed again. Then he groped his way back in the pitch dark to the switch and flicked it up.

There was a feeble glow from the ceiling, accompanied by a humming noise, and after a moment a pair of fluorescent strips reluctantly came on, filling the garage with a flickering, sickly light.

He was looking at a Ford Country Sedan, probably a late '50s edition. It was covered in dust and grime, and the roof was encrusted with gecko shit from the little bastards that lived in the roof tiles above.

He figured the car hadn't been driven for at least a year.

But beneath all the dirt the Ford looked in good condition. He walked slowly around it. There were no dints or scrapes on the side panels, green and cream in colour, he thought — it was hard to tell under all the filth — and the white-walled tyres seemed OK when he kicked them in turn. Maybe one of the back ones was a little squishy, but it would do.

The car's doors were unlocked and he slid behind the steering wheel and put the keys in the ignition. He wasn't expecting anything to happen when he turned them, and it didn't. The battery was flatter than a witch's teat.

He climbed out again and walked to a pile of assorted junk heaped against the garage's back wall, hoping against hope that he'd find a trickle-charger for the battery.

There wasn't one.

OK, he'd just have to crank-start the bitch.

The handle was missing from where it was supposed to be stored along with the spare wheel.

'Shit.' He realised he'd cursed aloud.

Refusing to give up hope, he went back to the mountain of junk and rooted through it.

The handle was lying on top of a box of old newspapers.

Slightly giddy with relief, he went back to the car, switched on the ignition, pumped the gas pedal a couple of times and pulled the choke all the way out.

Then he moved around to the front where the hole for the crank-handle should be. He found it and pushed the open hexagonal end of the handle inside, feeling it engage smoothly with a satisfying metallic click.

He removed his jacket — crank-starting a car that hadn't been fired up for a year was going to be the very bastard, bugger and bitch of a job — and swung the handle.

It took him ten minutes and all the strength he had, but at last the engine coughed, stuttered, and burst into life with a throaty roar that settled back immediately into a satisfying, steady tick-over.

Drenched in sweat, he staggered round to the driver's door and peered at the dashboard to see how much gas was in the tank. The needle was still rising slowly from the empty position, and as he watched it settled a little way above the red warning zone. That was fine. There must be about four gallons in the tank. He'd use less than half a gallon running the engine to charge up the battery, and that would leave more than enough for his needs.

He detached the crank handle and snapped out the light. The space was beginning to fill with exhaust fumes and he wasted no time pushing the doors back open far enough for him to slip out. He walked down to the sidewalk and turned back towards the garage.

The set-up wasn't perfect — an alert passer-by would notice the doors were ajar, and would probably just be able to hear the quiet purr of the engine, but fuck it. There was nothing suspicious in that, and anyway, this end of the street remained deserted. In any case, the battery would be charged up in twenty minutes or so and then he could switch off the engine and close the doors.

He went back inside the house. Crank-starting the Ford had not only exhausted him because of the effort involved: he was famished, too. He realised he hadn't eaten all day.

In the kitchen larder he found some tins of corned beef and beans in ketchup. He put a pan on the stove to heat up while he opened the tins and chopped up an old onion he'd found languishing in the refrigerator.

He'd make corned beef hash, get his strength back, and then go through the hotel section of the Yellow Pages and make a few calls. He had already mentally written his script for that part.

Operation English Rose, he thought to himself when he sat down to eat, was going like clockwork. All he had to do now was remember

330

the name of that Courier reporter who'd written most of the stories about him when he was up in Key Largo. What was he called? It would come to him. He never forgot a name.

60

'It wasn't my idea, Stella, I swear. This has come from the State Governor and Hoover's rubber-stamped it. I tried to make excuses to get you out of it but no one wanted to listen. You won't have to say much, I promise, and I'll be sitting right next to you all the time.'

Lee looked unhappily at her. She had taken the news about tomorrow afternoon's press conference every bit as badly as he'd feared. They had just sat down to dinner at her hotel, La Concha, but they hadn't stopped arguing since he had reluctantly given her the news in the car on the way there.

'But I don't *want* to talk to a whole roomful of reporters, Lee,' Stella said stubbornly for what must have been the fourth time. 'One journalist on their own, I wouldn't mind so much. But this is going to be a complete circus, by the sound of it. And what good will it do? We should be trying to find Woods, not waste time talking to the newspapers.'

He grimaced. 'Er . . . not just the newspapers, honey. Radio and TV will be there too.'

'Oh God, this gets worse and worse. What am I supposed to *say* to them all? And, I repeat — what's the bloody point?'

He reached across the table and took both her hands in his.

'Listen to me, Stella. You haven't let me

explain properly. Every time I try, you cut me off. Will you just give me one shot at this? If when I'm done you still feel the same way, I'll tell everyone and you can forget the whole thing. I'm not going to let anyone, be it C. Farris Bryant, J. Edgar Hoover or your new best friend JFK, make you do anything you don't want. OK?'

She looked at him, a little mollified.

'OK. Sorry, Lee, but I can't help being stubborn. I always have been, ever since I was a child. I loathe being told what to do.'

He took his cue from her slightly softened tone. 'Then let me try and *persuade* you. Here goes . . . Now, this is — '

He was interrupted by the waiter, who arrived to take their order. But the atmosphere further lightened when, as seemed to be becoming something of a habit, they opted for exactly the same starters and main courses.

When the man was gone, Lee took her hands in his once more and began again.

'I was going to say, this is *America*, Stella. The press are hugely powerful here. They assume the right to know just about everything that's going on, and if I'm honest, I don't think that's a bad thing. It means we live in a very open, accountable society.

'Whether you like it or not, you've become a huge story, and not just here — back home in England too. But our papers *love you* — how smart you are, how you managed to stop the slaughter up in Key Largo by practically giving us the killer's name, date of birth and eye colour and forcing him to go on the run.'

'That's a bit of an exaggeration,' Stella objected. 'All I did was — '

'All you did was break the case wide open, Stella. But since I came down here and you went back to Massachusetts, things have stalled. *I've* stalled.'

She impulsively squeezed his hands. 'That's not your fault, Lee.'

'Maybe it is and maybe it isn't, but now Woods has started killing again and the agency has its back against the wall. If I don't get the cuffs on the guy PDQ I'm gonna have J. Edgar shooting at me from one side and the newspapers from the other. And I'll be totally straight with you, Stella. You appearing at the press conference tomorrow will buy me a little more time. You'll wow the press boys, you'll look great on the TV cameras . . . in short, my dear, *you* will become the story for a while. Most importantly of all, you'll put a positive shine on things. And then you and I can get on with the job of working out where the S.O.B. is holed up.'

He paused for breath. 'That's it. I've said my piece.'

He realised she was smiling at him.

'Lee,' she said gently, 'if you'd told me in the first place that by doing this I'd be helping *you*, I'd have said yes straight away and we'd be talking about something else now.'

He looked at her with a slightly stunned expression. 'As simple as that?' he asked her.

'As simple as that. I'd kiss you to . . . how is it you Yanks put it? Oh yes, 'seal the deal', but look, our waiter's coming back and he seems to be in something of a flap.'

'He certainly does,' he agreed, noting the approaching man's distracted expression and rapid walk.

'Agent Foster,' he said to Lee, 'I'm sorry to disturb your evening but the manager has asked if you would care to join him in his office immediately, given your position with the FBI.' He nodded politely to Stella. 'You too, ma'am, of course. He has a TV in there and he thinks you should be watching it. Apparently it concerns a matter of vital national importance.'

They both stared at the waiter.

'What do you mean?' Lee asked him. 'What's going on?'

'I have no idea,' the man shrugged. 'The TV networks are telling everyone to stand by for a live personal statement from President Kennedy at seven o'clock tonight.' He looked at his watch. 'That's in less than two minutes. The manager's office is next to check-in. Shall I tell him to expect you?'

★ ★ ★

The hotel manager was staring at a blank television screen when they arrived in his office.

'Hi,' he said, turning round to them. 'Don't worry, this thing ain't bust — the last show just finished and the network's waiting to be patched through to the White House. Ah, here we go.'

A full-frame photograph of the domed building Stella had visited days earlier appeared, to be replaced after a few moments by a mid-shot of President Kennedy. He was sitting absolutely still and staring blankly at them from behind a desk.

'Waiting for his cue,' Lee said quietly.

Someone must have delivered it, because the next moment the leader of the western world began to speak. His tone was calm, measured, matter-of-fact.

But as the meaning of his words became clear, the millions of people across the country watching him felt the blood in their veins run cold.

'Good evening, my fellow citizens. This government, as promised, has maintained the closest surveillance of the Soviet military build-up upon the island of Cuba.

Within the past week, unmistakable evidence has established the fact that a series of offensive missile sites is now in preparation on that imprisoned island.

The purpose of these bases can be none other than to provide a nuclear strike capability against the western hemisphere.'

Lee turned to Stella. 'Holy Christ, Stella. He's talking about nuclear war. And we're right on the fucking front line down here.'

Stella had gone pale. 'No wonder he spoke about being in uncharted waters. No wonder he said Bobby was beaten to the wide and — '

'Shhh!' It was the manager. 'I'm trying to hear this, for Chrisakes!'

They turned back to the screen. The President was saying something about a blockade of Cuba, and continued:

'It shall be the policy of this nation to regard any nuclear missile launched from Cuba against any nation in the western hemisphere as an attack by the Soviet Union on the United States, requiring a full retaliatory response upon the Soviet Union . . . '

When he had finished, the screen faded to black again and all three of them looked at each other in silence.

It was the manager who broke it, with an attempt at gallows humour.

'You guys ordered dinner yet?'

Stella, astonished by the irrelevance of the question, nevertheless managed to croak: 'Yes . . . we have.'

'Then considering the next stop down from here is Havana, I'd suggest you both to go back to the restaurant and enjoy a nice meal while you still can. The way things are looking, it could be your last supper.'

61

Henry Stewart. THAT was the Courier guy's by-line. He knew it'd come back to him eventually.

He scribbled the name on a scrap of paper. He'd already jotted down the phone numbers of the hotels he thought she was most likely to be staying in — the Casa Marina, the Marquesa, and La Concha. Upmarket, but not expensively so. They were all what were known as 'historic' hotels, well-established places in the quiet Old Town area of Key West. He figured they'd be exactly the sort of places the FBI would park its more senior agents and contacts.

And if he drew a blank, he'd simply try some others until he found her. There weren't that many candidates to pick from in a place as small as this.

He took a slug of scotch before dialling the first one. He'd already sunk two glasses of the stuff since supper but it wouldn't matter if he sounded a little drunk. All reporters were lushes, everyone knew that.

After a couple of rings, the receptionist picked up.

'Casa Marina. How may I direct your call?'

He affected a bored tone.

'Yeah . . . this is Henry Stewart of the Courier calling for one of your guests. She would've checked in a coupla hours ago. A Miss Stella Arnold.'

'One moment please.' *He could hear her riffling through the hotel register, humming some dumb tune to herself, before she spoke again.*

'A Miss Arnold, did you say? I'm afraid we have no one of that name staying with us.'

He rang off without bothering to say anything else and called the Marquesa.

No dice there either. 'No English rose at the marvellous Marquesa,' *he sang as he rang off.*

He caught himself. Shit, he was a little drunk, wasn't he? Too much whisky and too little food. He crossed the hall to the kitchen and ate what was left of the still-warm hash straight from the pan, before going upstairs to the bathroom to relieve himself and splash his face and neck with cold water in the sink. Then he took the old man's toothbrush and toothpaste and spent a couple of minutes cleaning his teeth.

Refreshed and sobering up some, he went back down to the phone and dialled a third time.

'You've reached La Concha,' *the receptionist said brightly.* 'How can we help you this evening?'

He repeated the mantra he'd spouted twice before, but this time his heart leapt when she replied: 'Yes, she's here. She was in with the manager earlier but I think she's in the dining room now finishing her supper with her companion. Is this urgent? Should I interrupt her?'

He thought fast. The 'companion' was probably that FBI jerk Foster. But he could be useful. He could draw him in to the deception if

339

he was clever, give it some spurious authenticity.

As usual, he followed his instincts.

'No, no, please don't disturb her meal,' *he said as urbanely as he could.* 'If she could just call me back on — ' *he read the old queen's phone number off the dial* — 'before she goes to bed I'd be most grateful. Tell her it's pretty important, though.'

He rang off. What was it his old platoon commander in Korea used to say?

'Slowly, slowly, catchee monkee.'

Sometimes, even when you were in a corner as tight as this one, it still paid to be patient.

62

'I can't even begin to see what Khrushchev and Castro think they're doing,' Lee said yet again as they ate their steaks. 'Fidel letting that Russian maniac put nuclear warheads on Cuba, ninety frigging miles from American soil! Which, by the way, is ninety miles from you and me at this precise moment. It's a gun to our heads. Do they *want* to reduce the planet to a gently-smoking cinder? Jesus.'

The colour had returned to Stella's cheeks, now she'd had time to think.

'It won't come to that, Lee,' she said calmly. 'Really, it won't. What do they call this ridiculous nuclear arms race? Oh yes — M.A.D. Mutually Assured Destruction. No one's going to press the button, not now, not ever. This will all turn out to be some stupid power-game and the whole thing will fizzle out. I don't know the first thing about international politics but I do know about human nature. You Americans have an expression that covers this situation perfectly, actually.'

'We do?' Great Scott, he thought, Armageddon is staring us in the face and she's making me feel better about it already. I love this woman.

'Of course. Dorothy told me it just the other day. 'Turkeys don't vote for Christmas.' Kennedy and Khrushchev will have to find a way to settle this, believe me, otherwise they both know they're going to hell in a handcart and taking rest of the world with them. That is NOT an option that's open to either of them.'

Stella popped the last piece of her steak into her mouth and groaned as she swallowed it.

'Oh no . . . that damn waiter's scurrying over again. What now? The Martians have landed?'

But it was only a scribbled message from reception. He handed it to Stella, bowed, and left.

'What is it?' Lee asked, still lost in admiration for his new girlfriend's chutzpah.

'Oh.' She frowned. 'The journalist from the *Courier*, Henry Stewart, wants me to call him. He says it's urgent.'

'Let me see.' He took the note and quickly scanned it. 'Well, at least he had the manners not to drag you to the phone while you're eating. Stewart's OK, actually. I've read most of what he's written about this case and it's been pretty accurate and not as sensationalised as you'd expect for the *Courier*. Still, you could hardly exaggerate this story, could you? It's pretty much off the scale as it is. Why don't you call him while I order dessert for us both? You know we'll want the same thing.'

'Oh, do I, Mr Clever-Clogs?'

'Pardon me?'

'Smart-ass, in your debased language. All right. I'll go and call him. And I'll have the cheesecake, please.'

'I knew that already.'

She stuck her tongue out at him and went to reception.

'Can I use this phone?' she asked the girl behind the desk.

'No problem. Long distance?'

'I don't know.' She showed the receptionist the number.

'Oh, that's fine, ma'am, that's a Key West number. Local calls are free. Go ahead.'

Stella dialled and waited. The fourth ring was interrupted by a pleasant voice: 'Hello?'

'Hello, this is Stella Arnold. Is that Mr Stewart? You asked me to call you.'

'Yes, I did, Miss Arnold. Thanks for getting back to me so quickly. My paper's sent me down here for the press conference tomorrow. I've just learned it's scheduled for three o'clock, which is a bit later than we were expecting.'

'That's right. I'm not looking forward to it, to be honest with you, Mr Stewart. I've never done anything like this before.'

'Ah . . . well then, you might be willing to help me out here. The *Courier* is a morning paper but we're running a special, one-off evening edition tomorrow because of you. We — '

'You mean because of Kennedy's speech tonight about the Cuban missiles,' she said drily. 'There's no need to flatter me, Mr Stewart.'

There was a brief silence at the other end.

'Yes . . . Kennedy,' he said at last, non-committally. 'Kennedy, yes, of course. You saw him on TV earlier?'

'I did,' she said. 'It's a huge story, especially for you down here in the Keys, so close to Cuba.'

He seemed to be struggling for words.

'Well yes, of course,' he managed at last. 'But the Keys Killer story and your part in it is important too, and we . . . we want to include it

343

in tomorrow's special edition.' He sounded back on track again. Stella decided that even a hard-nosed journalist could be thrown by something as big as a nuclear stand-off.

'But here's the thing, Miss Arnold,' he continued. 'We go to press at three-thirty. There's just no way I can file my piece in time for that, so I wanted to ask you a *huge* favour. Would you give me a short interview, one-to-one, at, say, two-thirty? That way I can just about meet my deadline.'

Stella considered a moment before replying: 'I'd like to help you, Mr Stewart, but I'll probably be on my way to the press conference at the town hall by then. And I'll be busy earlier in the day working on the case.'

'That's exactly what I thought you'd say. So here's my idea: I'll pick you up in the *Courier* car from La Concha and drive you to the town hall myself. I have a miniature reel-to-reel tape recorder which I can prop up on the dashboard to record our interview. I know it's only a five-minute journey but it'll give me just about enough to file a story, and, if you don't mind me saying so, allow you a chance to rehearse for the press conference. I won't be asking anything anyone else won't ask. It'll be a sort of dry run for you and if you make any mistakes, I give you my word I shan't report them. In fact I can put you straight on them, as just between you and me. What do you say?'

'Will you hold on, Mr Stewart? I need to go and consult someone on this.'

'Of course. Take all the time you want. I'll be here.'

Back at their table Stella quickly summarised her conversation with the journalist to Lee. When she'd finished he said: 'Sounds like a good idea to me. Like I say, the *Courier* has played it pretty straight with us so far, especially this Stewart guy. Anyway, what with tonight's news we may find the numbers are way down at the press conference tomorrow; everyone's gonna be chasing the end-of-the-world angle. I was worrying about that, to be honest. So yeah, a bird in the hand, and all that. Go for it.'

Thirty seconds later Stella was back in reception.

'Mr Stewart? Are you still there?'

'I'm here, Stella.'

'The answer's yes. Where will I see you?'

There was a hiatus at the other end; it sounded like the reporter had been seized by a fit of coughing. Eventually he spoke.

'Sorry about that, I have a touch of the grippe. I'll be right outside La Concha in my car, ready to go so we don't waste a second of your precious time — or mine, come to that. It's a green and white Ford Country Sedan . . . a sort of station wagon. I'll keep the indicators flashing; you won't be able to miss me.'

'Green-and-white . . . got it. All right, Mr Stewart, I'll see you there. Two-thirty?'

'Two-thirty.'

Stella put the phone down.

Maybe she'd been wrong about journalists.

This one seemed rather nice.

63

He replaced the receiver and slumped back in the little wicker chair next to the telephone table. He was exhausted. The phone conversation had been as demanding, mentally, as crank-starting the Ford earlier had been physically.

What was all that stuff she was saying about Kennedy and Cuba? He'd had to tap-dance for his life there. He hadn't the slightest idea what she was talking about. Thank Christ at least he'd seen Kennedy on TV earlier, even with the sound down. He supposed he'd just about bluffed his way out of it. Whatever 'it' was. He'd better watch the late news tonight; something big was obviously going down and as a reporter he'd be expected to know all about it.

Christ, he was tired. That was partly the reason he'd almost cracked up laughing when she'd come back to the phone to tell him she'd meet with him tomorrow. Relief mixed with triumph and a kind of hysteria brought on by fatigue. Korea again. When they'd wiped out that village they'd all laughed fit to bust.

Nothing ever really changed, did it?

The lust within him for killing was stronger than ever. And now it was focused completely on the girl. When he thought of what he was going to do to her, alone together upstairs in that room, his chest grew tight and his throat constricted with hunger and desire.

But he was ready to die, too.

When it was done.

He stood up and went slowly into the kitchen, where he filled a bucket of water and added some liquid soap.

He just about had enough time to wash the car before the late TV news.

As he passed the cellar door on the way to the garage, a familiar odour caught his nostrils.

He smiled, nostalgically.

Korea.

64

Next morning there was not even a paragraph about the Keys Killer and his latest victim in any of the newspapers. It was Cuba, Cuba, Cuba. Photographs of Castro, Khrushchev and Kennedy dominated the front pages and for all Stella's optimism of the evening before, the consensus amongst editorial writers was that the world was teetering on the brink.

She and Lee had to make a pact to stop talking about the crisis. Stella had come down here to help find Woods and there was nothing to be gained by speculating who would make the next move in this terrifying game of nuclear chess.

'I still think it'll be all right in the end,' Stella said stubbornly, by way of having the last word on the subject. 'As Jackie said, her husband and Bobby are smart guys. They'll find a way through this.'

The pair of them had met up at Lee's makeshift headquarters in the boarding house on Duval. It was within walking distance of Stella's hotel. 'I could have stayed with you last night,' he grumbled after kissing her thoroughly. 'Zip happened here. You OK about the news conference later?'

'I suppose so,' she said, reluctantly pulling away from him and sitting down on the other side of his desk, which was strewn with notes and photocopies of Woods's last known disguise. 'Henry Stewart was very kind — he's offered me a sort of crash course from the reporter's perspective on how to handle myself in front of the press pack.'

Lee nodded. 'Yeah, it was the right call to do that interview beforehand. It'll warm you up. Now . . . you've had all of twenty-four hours to reflect on where the case stands now' — he smiled to show her he was being ironic — 'so anything jumping out at you? I'm all ears!'

She frowned and shook her head slightly. 'Not really, I'm afraid. Well, nothing that you haven't already come up with.'

He spread his hands. 'That's OK. I'd still like to hear you go over it. As an old colleague of mine says, 'nothing clears up a case so much as stating it to another person'.'

'Oh, so you worked with Sir Arthur Conan Doyle, did you, Lee? You're older than you look.'

He laughed. 'You've read Sherlock Holmes too?'

'Every single story. *The Speckled Band* is my favourite. You?'

'*The Devil's Foot*. Creepiest damn tale I ever read.'

She sighed. 'We could do with Holmes right now, couldn't we? Anyway, back to our own mystery . . .'

Stella spoke carefully and lucidly for several minutes. Lee listened intently, making the occasional note on the pad in front of him. When she'd finished, he nodded slowly.

'So you think wherever he is, it's tied up

somehow with this whole homosexual act of his.'

'I do. These men, through no fault of their own, are in a completely criminalised society, Lee. I know the police down here in Key West turn a blind eye, but most of these chaps have spent their whole lives ducking and diving from the law. It's the same in England. Just before I left, two men seen kissing in a pub in London were arrested and ended up getting six months in prison for outraging public decency, or some ridiculous charge like that. There was quite a fuss about it but no one expects the law to change for years.'

'One state's repealed it here — Illinois,' he told her. 'That's why the bar Woods worked in is called the Springfield — it's named in honour of the state capital.'

'Ah, I see . . . anyway, my point is that it's very much an underground society, secretive and defensive and quite hostile to police and law enforcement generally. It's what's known as a group conditioned response.'

'Wow. Quite the expert.'

She shook her head. 'Not really. I did a first-year paper on sexual repression in society when I was at Cambridge. But Woods has manipulated this repression of homosexuals to his own benefit. He came up with a convincing story about being set up by police in Texas and won everyone's sympathy and support because a lot of them will have experienced a similar injustice, or know someone who has. If the story had been true and the police *had* arrived with a warrant for his arrest, his new friends would have done everything they could to protect him — lie, obfuscate, get a warning to him if he wasn't there at the time.'

She took a deep breath.

'SO . . . ' she continued, 'I think that just before he was unmasked — which he had advance warning of, we now know — he conned someone, almost certainly a customer because all the bar staff are accounted for, into letting him stay at their house or apartment. He'll be there now, when he's not prowling the streets murdering prostitutes.'

He nodded. 'I'm with you there. But let's not get on to the last killing just yet. Tell me more, if you can, about his hiding place.'

She pushed a stray strand of hair from her eyes and despite the subject under discussion, Lee's heart lurched. God, she was lovely. The hell with being on call in this dump, tonight he'd hold her in his arms, even if he did have to park his two-way radio under the bed.

She was frowning, entirely unaware of his thoughts.

'Well . . . as I said, whether it's an apartment or a house, it's got to be the home of one of the men who drink at the Springfield Tavern. I can't see it being anyone else. Do the police here keep a record of known homosexuals and where they live? They do in a lot of places in America.'

He sighed. 'They used to have one, but not any more. They dropped the practice around the mid- to late 1940s, apparently. Someone's gone down to records to see if they can find the last list that was put together. Don't hold your breath, Stella — I've seen the records department here. To say it's chaotic would be a compliment.'

'OK.' She rooted through her bag. 'Damn. I left my cigarettes at the hotel. May I have one of yours, Lee?'

'Sure.' He lit two; one for her. 'So, where were we?'

She inhaled deeply and the smoke exited from her mouth and nose as she replied.

'I think you have to go back to the Springfield and ask the owner for any names and addresses he can give you of men who drink there. But you'll have your work cut out. As I said, by necessity it's pretty much a secret society.'

He smoked thoughtfully for a while before asking: 'Assuming you're right — about him talking his way into a customer's home, and I think you are — what'll have happened to that guy?'

'Oh come on, Lee, it's obvious. He'll have killed him on the spot. He won't have bothered to tie him up and keep him prisoner or anything like that. The trouble is it's still only forty-eight hours since Woods's cover was blown. That's probably a bit too soon to ask if any regulars at the Springfield have stopped showing up.'

'It's worth a try,' he said crisply. 'This is all good stuff, Stella. You're concentrating my mind here. Straight after the press conference I'm going to the Springfield to talk to the owner, this — ' he consulted the notes in front of him — 'yeah, this Tom Bilson guy. Ben Moss said he was pretty co-operative, actually. More scared of

Woods showing up there again than he is of us.'

'Well, that's a help,' she said. 'Shall I come with you? He might feel a bit less intimidated with a woman there.'

'Good idea.' Lee stood up. 'Right, I've got some men to marshal and I need to see that the roadblock and boat checks are still working on the top line. What are you going to do?'

'I'll go back to the hotel, have an early lunch and freshen up for this blasted news conference.'

He winced. 'Sorry.'

'The *Courier* man is picking me up at two-thirty so I'll probably be at the town hall a bit before you.'

He shook his head. 'Oh no, I'm not leaving you unsupported for a second — as soon as those waiting pressmen see you they'll all be pestering you for exclusives like bees swarming round a honeypot. I'll be there prompt at half past two and I'll wait on the steps for you so we can both go in together.'

'Thank you,' she said gratefully, moving forward to hug him. 'Now, what kind of car did he say we'll be in . . . a Ford something or other. Green and white, I think he said. A sort of station wagon, what we call estate cars at home.'

'Sounds like a Country Sedan to me,' he said. 'I'll keep an eye out for it.'

He kissed her. 'Gotta go. See you at two-thirty. Good luck with the interview.'

'Do you know,' she told him over her shoulder as she left for her hotel, 'I think I'm actually beginning to look forward to that part of it.'

65

He lunched on tinned soup but ate it upstairs. The smell coming from the cellar was getting worse and was pretty noticeable in the kitchen now. It didn't bother him that much, but when it came to eating he preferred to do it in untainted air.

The car looked good as new. He was right, it was a '57 but had only been driven a couple of thousand miles since leaving the dealership forecourt. The thing was barely run in.

He'd wiped a damp cloth over the seats and the insides of the windows, which he'd then rolled down to air the cabin. It smelled pretty musty after all those months sealed up in the garage.

It was a little after two o'clock and soon it would be time to leave for La Concha and what he'd begun thinking of as his 'rendezvous with a rose'. He liked words, and playing with them. Sometimes he wondered what it would have been like to be a writer.

He went into the living room and gathered up an armful of books from the shelves — dog-eared paperbacks, hardbacks, a few big coffee-table books of coloured photos of the Florida Keys — and staggered with them to the car, where he piled them on to the front passenger seat. He didn't want her sitting alongside him and maybe recognising him. From behind he

354

would look anonymous enough, especially wearing the yachting cap he'd found in a drawer and the pair of tortoiseshell Ray-Bans he'd taken from the guy's dressing table.

He was wearing a loose-fitting cream linen suit — about the only non-flamboyant item in the dead man's entire wardrobe — and an open-necked cotton shirt. He checked himself in the full-length mirror in the hall, before which his victim had doubtless preened and twirled on countless occasions.

Actually, he now decided, he probably could have risked her using the passenger seat after all. The hat and sunglasses and emerging stubble after two days without shaving made a pretty big difference to his appearance. Never mind. Better safe than sorry.

He remembered to bring the carrier bag with the pad and chloroform in it, and checked that the coast was clear before leaving the house and going to the garage. The car started first time and he pulled out onto the street. He glanced at his watch as he headed towards the junction with the main road a couple of hundred yards up ahead.

Twenty past the hour. He'd be there in five minutes. If she was on time, they'd be back at the house in fifteen.

This was going to be the best thing he had ever done in his life, better than that day in Korea, better than the peaches up in Key Largo.

He shivered with excitement.

66

Lee checked his watch for the seventh time.

Almost three o'clock. Where the heck was she? There'd been no sign of the car she described to him. He took one last look down Duval before going into the hall to announce to the assembled journalists (he'd been right earlier — there weren't nearly as many as they'd expected) that the conference would have to be delayed by half an hour. They'd grumbled a bit but he knew they'd be fine when Stella got here. *If* she got here.

He'd been back out on the steps for a good ten minutes getting increasingly worried when a voice behind him said: 'Any news, boss? The natives are gettin' restless.'

It was his sergeant.

'Hi, Ben. No, nothing. Maybe this Stewart guy's abducted her so he can get the scoop and . . .'

Abducted. Why had he said that?

The uneasiness he had been feeling threatened to mushroom into something else entirely. The expression on his face must have given him away because Moss looked at him with concern. 'You OK, sir? You look like you just saw a ghost.'

Lee stood stock-still for a few moments, thinking furiously and trying to keep his rising panic in check.

Finally he spoke.

'You stay here, Ben, in case she shows up. I'm going to make a phone call.'

He ran into the town hall and headed for the administration office. When he got there he flashed his badge at the woman behind reception: 'I need you to call the *Courier*'s Key Largo office right now, please, ma'am. When you get through ask for the news editor and then give me the phone. This is *real* urgent.'

'Sure, hon,' the woman said in a tone that implied she'd seen and heard it all before.

A minute later she was handing him the phone. 'There you go.'

He tried not to snatch it from her hand.

'This is Agent Lee Foster, FBI down in Key West. Am I speaking with the news editor?'

'Yup. What can I do you for, Mr Foster?'

'Have you sent one of your reporters down here for the Keys Killer press conference today?'

'No. I was going to, but this missile thing's kinda messed up my schedule for the day, maybe everyone's for all eternity. We'll be taking the conference copy from the wire service.'

Lee's world began to fold in on him.

'I want to be absolutely clear on this. Have you sent one of your men, Henry Stewart, down to Key West for any other reason, maybe on a story? I believe he's driving a cream and green Ford Country Sedan.'

The news editor laughed.

'Sir, I can state with absolute certainty that Henry Stewart is nowhere near Key West today. In fact, he's sitting right here behind this desk. I'm Henry Stewart. And furthermore, I drive a

Dodge. I happen to think Fords are a pile of crap.'

With infinite slowness, Lee handed the receiver back to the receptionist.

'Oh dear God,' he asked her, in a voice so quiet she could barely hear him, 'what have I done?'

67

Stella saw the car approaching the steps leading up to the hotel lobby and waved at its driver. He flashed his headlights in response and pulled up a few yards past her at the kerb.

The windows were down — the car didn't look expensive enough to have air-conditioning — and as she walked towards it he twisted around in his seat, craning his head low in the gap between the front seats so he could see her. It was dark inside the car in contrast to the sunshine that drenched the street, and all she could really see of him was a peaked cap that made him look more like a taxi driver than a journalist.

'You'll have to ride in the back, Stella,' he said loudly as she drew close. 'I stopped by the second-hand bookstore this morning and as usual I got carried away. The seat next to me's piled high with books that I'll probably regret buying by this time tomorrow.'

'That's OK,' she said, opening the back door and climbing in. 'You sound like me — I have more books than I know what to do with. Even so, I'm arranging to have a trunk-load of them shipped over from England. Must be mad.'

She closed the door with her left hand and stuck out her right. 'Stella Arnold.'

He was checking his mirror before pulling out into traffic and put his own hand over his shoulder without turning around.

'Henry Stewart. Pleased to meet you, and thanks for doing this.'

'It's a pleasure. I only hope I can give you something you can use.'

He suddenly coughed. When he'd recovered, he apologised. 'It's the grippe. Hope I don't pass it on to you.'

'Oh, I had my summer cold a month ago,' she said. 'What do you make of this Cuba thing?'

She saw him shake his head. 'It's just blind panic. Soon as I've done this with you my paper wants me to interview the Mayor of Key West. People here are freaking out, lots of crazy talk about being invaded — Christ knows who by — or the air base here being nuked. Personally, I think it'll all blow over just fine.'

'Me too,' Stella agreed. 'Anyway, we haven't much time. I suppose you'd better start asking me some questions. What do you want to know?'

'I'll tell you what,' he told her. 'This ain't much of a way to do an interview. There's a quiet street just up here. I'll park up and get in the back with my reel-to-reel so we can talk face to face.'

'Fine, but remember I only have a few minutes.'

'Sure.'

He turned into the street. It was the same one in which he'd murdered the hooker. He drove to the same patch of deserted waste ground and stopped the car.

'Hold on, Stella, I'll just get my stuff.'

'OK.'

He climbed out with his bag and looked around. There were a couple of people walking up the street about fifty yards from the car but they were headed away from him. With his back to Stella's window, he removed the chloroform and cotton pad and drenched it in the chemical.

'Sorry,' he called to her. 'Just threading up the tape. All done now.'

He walked around to the other side of the car and climbed in the back next to her.

'So,' he said pleasantly. 'Let's get started. Question one. Ever been chloroformed?'

He yanked her head back by the hair and crammed the soaking pad over the lower half of her face.

Stella's eyes widened above it as she stared at him in shock and terror.

'John Henry Woods at your service, Stella. Have a nice sleep. I'll see you when you wake up.'

Her eyes rolled back to the whites.

68

Lee pelted back to the steps of the town hall as fast as he could run.

Ben was still there. The big man was staring up Duval Street and shielding his eyes against a sun that was beginning to drop noticeably lower in the sky as the afternoon wore on.

'Ben! Ben! He's taken her!'

The sergeant wheeled around. 'What? Come again, sir?'

'Woods has abducted Stella Arnold. He impersonated a newspaper reporter, set up a fake interview, and he's got her. God knows where, but he's got her. I'm certain of it. And I agreed the interview, Ben! This is all my fault!'

The sergeant stared at him for a moment. He was even taller than Lee, a reassuringly substantial figure, in his mid-forties and with a kindly face that nevertheless managed to communicate an inner toughness. He looked like the kind of cop who'd probably seen it all before. Now he placed large hands gently on the younger — and senior — man's shoulders.

'Right. Now calm down, Lee, and let's take it from the top. You're on the edge of panic and that's not going to solve anything. When was this interview arranged and how do you know it was a set-up?'

With an almost superhuman effort, Lee managed to force back the waves of icy dread that were threatening to engulf him and freeze his mind.

'Stella got a phone call at her hotel last night. I was with her — we were having dinner together. It was about eight o'clock, an hour or so after JFK's TV address . . . '

By the time he'd finished, Ben had taken out his pad and was scribbling notes.

'And you're sure this Henry Stewart you just spoke to was the real deal? No chance of a mix-up?'

'None. I'm telling you, Ben — Woods has her.'

'OK . . . assuming the pick-up took place at two-thirty, she's only been with him for approximately forty-five minutes. I'm going to radio an immediate stop-on-sight for the car.' He checked his notes. 'A green and cream Ford Country Sedan, right?'

'Right.'

Without wasting another second, Ben put out the call to all units. When he'd finished, he turned to his boss.

'That's done. Now, sir, I suggest you take five to just — '

'It's OK, Ben, I'm back on the horse — thanks to you. I know what I need to do. One of the last things Stella said to me this morning was that she thought the key to where Woods is hiding lies in his pretence at being homosexual. She and I were going to go to the Springfield Tavern after the press conference to re-interview the owner, see if he was holding anything back, or if he's remembered something that he doesn't think is all that important. Do you have a spare radio?'

Ben reached behind his back and unclipped a walkie-talkie from his belt.

'There you go.'

'Thanks. If I get anything out of him, I'll call you right away. If we find the car, radio me immediately. In the meantime get every man we've got out looking for that car or any sign of Stella.'

'Yes, sir. And the news conference?'

'Cancel it. All they really want to write about is Cuba anyway.'

Lee turned to leave for the Springfield, barely two hundred yards up the street. He intended to run every step of the way.

'Sir?'

'Yeah?'

'I'm real sorry about this, sir.'

'Not as sorry as that piece of shit's going to be when I get my hands on him.'

Lee started running.

69

He drove straight into the garage and switched off the engine.

She was still completely knocked out in the back, but he knew from experience that it wouldn't be much longer before she started to come round. Five minutes, ten at most.

He got out of the car and walked down to the sidewalk, looking up and down the street. Deserted, as usual. There'd be more life in a cemetery.

Even so, he wasted no time going back to the car and pulling her out by her arms. As her body began to slide off the back seat he squatted down and caught her under the armpits, lifting her as he stood up again and throwing her over his shoulder in one smooth movement.

Even though he knew there was no one around, he moved as quickly as he could across the splintered, sun-bleached boardwalk to the front door, and kicked it open with one foot. He'd deliberately left it slightly ajar when he'd left the house barely twenty minutes ago. He didn't want to be fiddling around with keys with an unconscious girl draped over his shoulder.

He slipped inside and back-heeled the door shut. She moaned faintly.

'You'll be making a lot more noise than that an hour from now, I promise you,' he told her as he climbed the stairs. A lot more.

70

There was only one barman on duty in the Springfield when Lee ran into the Tavern, and no customers at all. It was low tide, between lunchtime and happy hour.

Lee's heart faltered. He needed to talk to Tom Bilson right now, not in an hour, not even in ten minutes. Now.

He flashed his badge to the kid, a trainee, whose bored expression turned immediately to one of fear and suspicion.

'It's OK, you've got nothing to worry about,' Lee reassured him, trying to control his rapid breathing after the 200-yard dash. 'This isn't a raid or a set-up. I'm just here to see your boss. Where is he?'

The boy pointed to the ceiling. 'He's up in his apartment. He's taking a nap.'

'Which is his apartment?'

The boy blinked, confused. 'What? I can't just — '

'*Which is his fucking apartment!*'

The boy flinched. 'OK, OK. It's second door on the right once you're up there. But you can't just — '

Lee was already on the stairs. He took them two at a time.

Tom Bilson was asleep on his couch. He was dreaming of a thunderstorm, one of those huge ones that terrified visitors to the Keys but which locals knew were all sound and fury and not especially dangerous. Then the dream changed. A gun was being fired, bang bang bang bang —

He jerked awake. Someone was pounding on his locked bedroom door. He planned to keep it locked until the maniac who'd been sheltering under his roof was caught.

'Who is it?' he asked tremulously.

'FBI. Open up, please, Mr Bilson.'

'I want to see some ID first.'

After a moment a slim wallet was pushed under the door. Bilson looked at it, and fumbled with the door key. 'OK, come in, Mr Foster.'

Lee stepped into the room, still breathing heavily. 'Thank you. I'm sorry to disturb your rest but something extremely serious is happening right now. You know that the man who worked here killed again, the night before last?'

'Of course. Some poor wretched hooker, wasn't it? But how can I help, Mr Foster?'

Lee wiped the perspiration from his face with the sleeve of his jacket. 'This afternoon — within the last hour — we believe the man you knew as Dennis Clancey abducted a young woman from her hotel here on Key West.'

Thomas Bilson blanched. 'That's awful. But why have you come here? What could I possibly know about that?'

Lee took a beat. He remembered how Stella had warned him about frightening the man off. That was why she had offered to come with him here.

He came to a sudden decision.

'Mr Bilson, I'm going to take you completely

into my confidence. The young woman in question is my girlfriend. She's an expert on psychopaths like Woods and she's been helping our investigations. We've — we've — '

He ground to a halt. He was dangerously close to tears, and that wouldn't do at all.

But Bilson stood and swiftly crossed the space between them, taking one of Lee's hands into both his own.

'I'm so sorry. She's that beautiful English girl I read about in the papers, isn't she? Susan . . . Sharon . . . '

'Stella. Stella Arnold. She was going to come with me to see you this afternoon. She's a very, very smart person, and she was — *is* — convinced that Woods is taking refuge in the home of one of your customers. A man he may have formed some sort of relationship with before his cover was blown.'

Bilson dropped Lee's hand and shook his head in genuine regret.

'Sincerely, there's nothing I can tell you about that — not because I won't, but because I can't. I made it clear to your colleague that Dennis — I mean Woods — always kept himself completely to himself, so much so that, to be honest with you, I wondered if he was becoming confused about his preferences and leaning toward the idea of . . . well, being with a woman. He never flirted with my customers or asked for anyone's phone number. That's the truth.'

Lee tried to fight back the despair that began to swirl around him again.

'Of course, I can see that . . . but have any of

your regulars stopped showing up here in the last couple of days?'

Tom shrugged helplessly. 'Not so I'd notice. As you say, it's only been two days, hasn't it? It's simply too soon to tell.'

Lee stood up to leave, utterly defeated.

'All right. If you think of anything — *anything* — call me or Sergeant Moss immediately.'

'Of course. I have your phone numbers. I'm so sorry I can't help you. I'll say a prayer for her.'

Lee looked wearily at him. 'You're a religious man?'

'Yes. Why? You think my sort aren't allowed to believe in God?'

'Of course not, I didn't mean to . . . Anyway, thank you for your prayers, Tom. I'll see myself out.'

Lee was almost at the head of the stairs when a voice behind him called out: 'Wait!'

He spun round to see the bar owner hurrying after him.

'I've remembered something. It's probably irrelevant, but . . . '

Lee felt the faintest flicker of hope. 'I'll be the judge of that. Go on, Tom.'

'I told you that Woods never responded to anyone's advances, and most people got the message and left him alone. But there was one customer, one of our regulars going back years before my time here, who simply wouldn't give up. He's a sweet old thing, must be well into his seventies now. I think he used to be bit-part actor. Goes by the name of Charlie Booker.'

'Go on.'

'Well, he was always flirting outrageously with Denn — *dammit* — Woods, buying him drinks, leaving ludicrous tips. I don't think Charlie seriously thought he stood a chance — and neither did we. There must have been over four decades between them — he was just fooling around, having a bit of fun. That's why it never occurred to me to mention it.

'Anyway, the other night — the night before Woods disappeared, now I think of it — I saw Charlie trying to give what looked like a coaster to him. I'd seen him — Charlie, that is — scribbling something on it a minute or two before as he sat alone at his usual table.

'At the time I thought it must be some sort of naughty message or a rude joke or something — Charlie was pretty canned by then — but it could have been his phone number. I wouldn't put it past the old queen. Anyway he tottered off into the night and, as I say, I forgot all about it.'

Lee didn't move.

'What did Woods do with the coaster?'

'That's the strange thing. I think I saw him put it into his back pocket. I can't be sure, but it certainly wasn't on the bar a minute or so later.'

'Have you seen Charlie since?'

'No. He's not been in. But there's nothing unusual about that. He's not in here every night, like some of them.'

Lee felt the flicker of hope begin to burn a little brighter.

'I don't suppose you have Charlie's address?'

Tom Bilson nodded.

'I do. We run a tab for him and he settles up at

370

the end of each month. But last Christmas he was laid up and didn't show up again until March. He insisted I send him his account in the post every month from then on, so that he didn't fall behind. I've got the address downstairs in a drawer somewhere. Come with me.'

Less than two minutes later, Lee was standing outside on the street with a scrap of paper in one hand and the borrowed walkie-talkie in the other. He pressed the transmit button. 'Ben, come in. It's Foster.'

After a couple of seconds the radio squawked and Ben's voice crackled out of the ether.

'Boss? You got something?'

'I think I may know where Woods has been hiding out. It's about three minutes on foot from where I am now. The address is . . . ' He looked at the piece of paper he was holding. 'It's 28 Wilson Street. But listen, Ben, if he's there he'll have Stella with him. We can't just raid the place. If by the grace of God he hasn't killed her already he surely will if we barge in. I want you to assemble a tactical unit at the end of the street and await my orders. I'm going there to assess the situation. Out.'

Lee checked his weapon.

Then he started running again.

71

He hadn't used the nails yet. They'd do for later. For now he'd just tied her hands and feet. The only items of clothing he'd removed were her shoes; that made it easier to secure her by her ankles. He would cut her clothes off when the time came, as he did with all of them.

She was coming round fast now so he went downstairs to make himself a scotch on the rocks that he could sip while he chatted to her. He might as well be comfortable. As an afterthought he filled a glass of water for her. The chloroform would have left her mouth dry and although that wouldn't interfere with the screaming he did want to be able to hear what she had to say beforehand.

When he got back upstairs with the slopping glasses her eyes were open and she was licking her lips the way they all did after they regained consciousness.

'Hello, Stella. How you feeling?'

Because of the way he had arranged her on the home-made crucifix — those bed boards had been perfect for the task — her head was about eighteen inches higher than his so that she was looking down on him. When her eyes had been shut it didn't matter, but now it made him feel uncomfortable.

He decided to ignore it. If it hadn't bothered

the Roman centurions, he wouldn't let it bother him.

She didn't answer his question so he tried again.

'Want some water?' He held up her glass while he simultaneously took a belt of scotch from his own.

She stared dully at him. He grinned at her.

'Cat got your tongue? C'mon, take a sip.'

He held the glass up to her lips but it was awkward trying to give someone a drink from below and the water slopped down her chin and onto her blouse.

'Shit, I'm sorry. Hang on.'

He went into the bathroom and soaked a none-too-clean bath sponge under the cold tap. Then he went back to her and held it to her lips.

'Try it this way.'

She sucked a little of the moisture up.

'There you go. Better?'

She spat the whole lot into his face.

He cursed and stepped backwards, spilling half his drink and almost tripping up over what was left of the coil of rope he'd used to bind her. He cursed again as he steadied himself, then put what was left of his drink carefully on the floor and crossed the room to the ruined four-poster. He dried his dripping face on one of the pillows before turning to face her. He was smiling.

'I'm not gonna tell you that you'll be sorry you did that, Stella, because before very long you'll be regretting much more important things, like that you were ever born at all. But I'm gonna cut you some slack before I start cutting you. I guess you must feel pretty strange. I mean, there you were, thinking you were my nemesis — that's the right word, isn't it, college girl? — and here we are. Turns out I'm actually *yours!*'

He roared with laughter before going back for his drink. He sipped it, considering her awhile.

'Did you see me on the beach that evening in Key Largo? I think you did, Stella. That's why you went down to the water, isn't it? I spooked you some. You know why that was? Because we're kinda the same, you and me. Creatures of instinct.'

She continued to stare at him. Jesus, she was starting to seriously annoy him.

'Stella, I can *make* you talk, you know that. Look.'

He went to the bag in the corner that held the things he'd need later, and pulled out the knife, holding it towards her so she could see its slimness and length and glittering sharpness.

'I bought this, just for you. You know what I do with these special knives, don't you? Of course you do, you've seen the photographs. And I'm going to use this one to make you scream, you know that too. But I'd rather you spoke to me first without any . . . *encouragement.* Won't you parlay with me a little before we get started? It'll be your last chance to make any kind of noise that anyone could understand.'

Her eyes remained fixed on his, and he sighed.

'I have to tell you that this is *real* disappointing, Stella. You a psychologist and all. I thought we could discuss stuff. I thought we could discuss *me.* I'd really like to know what you think about me, what I am, what I do. I've read so much *crap* in the newspapers about me. No one gets it *at all.*'

He put his head on one side.

'You ever read *Paradise Lost*, Stella? Lucifer's cast out of Heaven but he doesn't give a shit, he just sets up in Hell as the Antichrist with all the other guys who've been cast down with him. I keep it by my bed. I read it most nights. My God, it's beautiful. Most beautiful fucking poem ever written.

'I don't think I'm the Antichrist, Stella — I'm not crazy, though I know you think I am — but I really dig him. He's so brave and perfect and *powerful.* He can change anything he wants — he arranges it so that Adam and Eve are kicked out of the Garden of Eden, for Chrisakes. And look at us two now. Me down here, you up there . . . you with the whole world on your side, and me all alone. Yet I've prevailed, haven't I, Stella? I've fucking prevailed.'

He swilled the scotch in his glass and then drained it off in a single swallow.

'I'm gonna die soon, Stella, but the Antichrist will be waiting for me. He'll be pleased with me, and everything I've achieved. He might make me one of his fallen angels. He might even — '

He stopped. He could see he was wasting his breath on her. He tried another tack.

'Aw c'mon, Stella. *You* explain how you worked me out so fast, and *I'll* tell you why I do it. Or why I *think* I do it. Jesus, I know I'm a psychopath. It's how I'm wired. But like I said, I'm not mad. I was hoping you'd explain me to

375

me, before I give you a practical demonstration of my methods. Talk to me, my English rose! To put it crudely, you'll buy yourself some time if you do. Hell, you might even cure me! Think of that! Then I'd cut you down from the cross and we'd go praise the Lord in some church and afterwards see a movie together! How does that sound?'

Just that fucking stare. OK, OK . . .

'All right, I see how it is. So here's what we're gonna do. I'm going back downstairs to replenish the drink you made me spill. I'll probably make myself a snack too because I'm getting hungry, and I don't like to work on an empty stomach. When I'm done I'll come back up here and give you one more chance to shoot the breeze. If you're still not interested, then we'll move on to the main feature. And remember, Stella, I've seen it before. I know the soundtrack. And I know how it ends.'

72

Lee reached Wilson Street in just over ninety seconds. He jogged down its crumbling sidewalk, looking for number 28. He quickly worked out it was going to be on his left, and probably near the very end of the road.

No wonder Woods had been able to hide out here so successfully. The whole street was practically derelict. Charlie Booker must have been one of the last people still living there.

He reached number 26 and stopped. He had to get his wind back: if he went into 28 heaving like this he might as well announce his arrival through a bullhorn.

When he was breathing normally again, he walked as casually as he could past the house, all the way to where the road ended in some kind of stinking, fetid bog. He turned around and strolled back, more slowly this time, stopping in the shade of a tree that stood in the front yard of number 30.

He could see a wooden lean-to garage built on the side of Booker's house. He scanned the windows of the building for movement and when he was satisfied that there was no one looking down onto the street, he walked quickly to the garage doors. They were slightly ajar. He pulled one open as gently as he could, wincing as it squealed on its hinges. Then he peered through the gap he'd made.

Parked inside was a green and cream Ford Country Sedan.

Lee pulled the radio out of his back pocket.

'Foster here,' he said quietly. 'Ben, where are you?'

The response came immediately.

'Sir, twelve of us are about to leave headquarters. We're in three cruisers. ETA Wilson Street two minutes. Where are you?'

'Outside number 28. Woods is definitely here — his car's in the garage. I'm about to make an entry into the house. Stand by. Remain at the end of the road until I order otherwise. Do not, repeat not, initiate radio contact.'

'Understood.'

Lee slipped the radio back in his pocket and drew his automatic pistol, clicking the safety off as he did so.

He had no intention of going in through the front door. It was probably locked and could be alarmed or even booby-trapped.

He returned to the garage. Sometimes there was an inner door that connected to the house. He slipped inside, found the light switch, and turned it on.

No door.

He crept around to the back of the house, stepping on the planks of the ruined boardwalk as close to the walls as he could so they wouldn't creak and groan. Even so, he made more noise than he would have liked.

He approached a filthy window, half-drawn tattered curtains hanging on either side, and dropped into a crouch so he could peer through one of the dirty panes of glass at the bottom.

He was looking at Woods. The man was standing profile to him, digging into a can of baked beans with a spoon and cramming them into his mouth.

Lee's mind raced. He could carry on trying to find a way in, or he could . . .

Fuck it. He'd shoot the bastard where he stood and argue the toss later.

One, two, three . . . he stood upright and swung into the firing position.

Woods had left the kitchen.

Lee swore under his breath. Then he told himself to get a grip. He still held the element of surprise. He knew Woods was inside. Woods did not know that he, Foster, was outside.

He *had* to find a way in, and fast. God willing, Stella might still be alive and unharmed.

He sidled along the back of the house. Reaching the corner, he looked down at a manhole cover with a raised handle. It was half-buried under dead leaves but when he swept them clear away he decided it wasn't actually bolted down.

Bracing his feet either side, he tugged at it as hard as he could with both hands. After a few moments it suddenly broke away from its seating, almost sending him toppling backwards.

He was looking at a wide metal chute that sloped diagonally down into what he assumed was a cellar. A moment later a dreadful smell wafted out and he fought back the instinct to retch. He'd encountered the smell of death before and in all likelihood Charlie Booker had to be the source of this appalling stench.

But he had found his way in, and Lee's hopes lifted. Holstering his gun, he lowered himself into the stinking chute.

He slithered, bounced and crashed down and landed, bruised and half-winded, on his side. After a few moments he was able to look around him. Enough light was coming through the shaft above to make things out reasonably well. There were a few empty apple boxes scattered around and some old sacks piled up at the foot of a precarious-looking wooden staircase in the far corner.

Lee crossed to the stairs and kicked the sacks to one side. The stench intensified tenfold as he exposed the upper torso of a man. The face was black with blood — it looked to Lee as if the guy's teeth had been knocked out — and the throat was livid with bruises.

Charlie Booker's last role. Murder victim.

Lee climbed the stairs as quietly and as quickly as he could, praying the door at the top wasn't locked. He eased back the handle and the door opened a fraction. Lee put his ear to the crack. He could hear nothing.

He drew his gun again and moved silently into what turned out to be the hall. The kitchen where he'd seen Woods was to his left, and there were two rooms ahead of him to the left and right of the stairs.

Lee crept forward, gun extended, and cleared both rooms in turn.

The bastard must be up on the first floor. With Stella.

He began to climb the stairs, carefully keeping to the sides of the treads as he had outside on the boardwalk. This time he made absolutely no noise and as he passed the halfway point he could hear the sound of a voice talking in a steady drone. It had to be Woods. And if he was talking, it could only be to Stella. She was still alive.

He had to pause for a moment to allow a wave of sheer relief to pass through him. Then he was moving again. When he reached the landing, Woods's voice was a little more distinct and he could make out what someone was saying.

' . . . you won't, you won't. Just don't say I didn't give you the chance for some friendly conversation, Stella.'

Lee heard him laugh.

The voice was coming from his right, a double doorway leading into what he assumed was the master bedroom. He edged along the passage towards it.

Now, Woods was clearly audible.

'Well, of course you *can't* say I didn't give you the chance because you won't speak to me, will you? At least, not until now. Although you won't be forming what you and I and most people would recognise as actual words, Stella. Far more primitive noises than that. Oh, and on that point, feel free to make as much racket as you like when I get started. The houses opposite and on both sides of this one are abandoned, so there's no one to complain. Nobody to hear you but me. And as you figured out a long time ago, the more noise you make, the more I like it. So, if you're ready, we'll begin. We'll start with the nails.'

Lee stepped into the doorway and simultaneously cocked the hammer back on his pistol. Woods was ten feet in front of him, a mallet in one hand. He heard the metallic double-click of the gun and spun round.

Directly behind him, Stella was hanging grotesquely from the wooden cross he'd tethered her to. She was still fully dressed, but at her feet Lee could see a box cutter, which he instantly realised was intended to slice the clothes from her body.

Woods was staring at him in disbelief, his mouth opening and closing like a fish. He had dropped the mallet.

Lee moved into the room and took a step to his right. He didn't want the bullet he was about to put through this animal's head passing through and hitting Stella.

'It's time to die, you piece of shit.'

Without a shred of compunction he squeezed the trigger.

There was the faintest of clicks, but nothing else. Both men stared at each other in disbelief.

Fuck! The safety got knocked back on when I fell into the cellar!

Lee thumbed the catch down but he was too late. Woods was on him like a panther, knocking the gun out of his hand and delivering a vicious karate chop to his Adam's apple.

Lee went down hard and the killer delivered a tremendous kick to his solar plexus. Lee thought his heart might explode. He almost passed out.

Next moment Woods was dragging him across the floor and propping him up against the wall next to Stella. Then he picked up Lee's gun from where it had skittered all the way across the room.

He checked that the safety was off before pointing the barrel at Lee's right leg, and without hesitating put a bullet through his shin. Lee bucked and writhed in agony and for the first time Stella spoke. 'Leave him alone, you bastard!'

'Piece of shit, am I?' Woods sneered at Lee. He turned to Stella. 'Found our voice, have we? A bit late in the day for that, my sweet fucking English rose.'

He grinned at them both. 'Well, I couldn't have counted on my day ending like this. A lovely rose to prune to pieces and an audience to watch me do it.'

Lee somehow managed to stand up. Incredibly, he seemed to be bracing himself for an attack on Woods.

The killer laughed. 'Oh, please. You think I'm gonna let you die a hero? Not a chance, Agent Foster.'

He raised the gun again, this time pointing it at Lee's stomach.

'I'm gonna gutshoot you. I saw plenty of guys gutshot in Korea. Did a little of it on my own account, as it happens. It takes about twenty agonising minutes to die. Roughly the same time the lovely Stella will hold out for. You might even live long enough to see me stick my knife in her eye.'

He took a step back from Lee, steadied his aim, and thumbed back the hammer.

'Party time.'

The explosion was louder than Stella's despairing scream, but not much.

Woods stood still for a moment, a puzzled expression on his face. Then he toppled forward, arms outstretched towards Stella as if in an act of worship. Or abasement.

Ben Moss stepped into the room, breathing heavily, his smoking gun still in the firing position. He moved swiftly to the body, hauling it roughly over onto its back. The gaping exit wound spoke for itself.

He turned to the others. 'Jesus H Christ. You guys OK?'

'No,' said Lee, still propping himself up against the wall. 'I'm shot and Stella needs cutting down from that fucking monstrosity, now. Use the knife on the floor there.'

Ben moved swiftly into the room and began releasing Stella while Lee called up an ambulance on the radio.

As soon as Stella was free she hobbled over to him as best she could. Her legs were stiff, while her arms, from which she had been suspended for so long, had almost entirely lost all feeling.

'Lee . . . your leg . . . Ben, you need to tourniquet this right away!'

The sergeant was ripping up a sheet from the bed.

'I'm on it, ma'am.'

Lee, trying to ignore the pain that blazed like fire, pulled Stella tightly to him.

'I'll never forgive myself for this. How could I have let you fall into that maniac's hands?'

She tried and failed to hug him; her arms simply would not respond to the messages from her brain.

Instead she kissed his throat, red and swollen from Woods's brutal blow, and rubbed her head on his shoulder.

'Lee, you saved me. You found me, and you saved me.'

'I didn't. My gun — '

'Lee, you did just enough. You bought me just enough time. You would have died for me.'

'He *will* die for you if you don't let me get this tourniquet on him,' said Ben grimly, striding across the room with his improvised bandage and firmly moving her to one side. 'Sir, I need you to lie down for me.'

As Ben expertly tightened the ligature around his boss's shattered leg, Lee considered his sergeant-turned-doctor.

'I thought I told you to stay back until further orders, sergeant.'

Ben Moss looked up at him and, for the first time since he had entered the room, he smiled.

'And I figured that was the most goddamned stupid command I'd ever been given, so it coming from you and all, I reckoned I'd plain misheard it. I was just comin' over here to check with you, sir.'

'Good job you did,' said Stella unsteadily, suddenly sliding down the wall into a sitting position. 'I was beginning to think we might be getting into difficulties.'

Ben squinted up at her as he tied Lee's tourniquet off.

'Is that the famous British stiff upper lip I've heard so much about, ma'am?'

Lee shook his head.

'No, Ben. That's just Stella.'

Epilogue

Three months later, Stella thought she might finally be getting over the worst of it.

She'd had to miss the entire autumn term, of course, although as she wryly told Lee more than once, she'd probably learned more about psychopaths in a single afternoon in Key West than she might in an entire year at Smith.

But even after Christmas she was not ready to begin her doctorate and reluctantly postponed her studies to the start of the next academic year.

Lee had been wonderful. He was owed weeks of furlough, plus sick leave to recover from his gunshot wound, and he had insisted on flying with Stella to England so that she could be with her mother and grandparents at the Dower House in Kent. The Arnolds quickly took him to their hearts.

They had been horrified to learn of her ordeal. Diana, in particular, was completely against her daughter ever returning to America.

But Stella was determined. 'I can't let that creature change my life,' she said defiantly. 'It's bad enough that he's managed to interrupt my plans to this extent. If I don't go back to Smith, he'll have won.'

Lee was supportive. 'You have to let her do this her way,' he gently told her mother and grandparents one evening after Stella had gone to bed. 'It's vital to her that she gets back to where she was, before any of this happened.'

Stella took Lee on long recuperating walks in the Kent countryside that surrounded her grandparents' home. The FBI agent was bewitched by the English orchards, meadows and hedgerows. One afternoon, as they stood on the high Weald looking down at the garden of England, he had a sudden change of heart; almost an epiphany.

'You know, honey . . . you don't have to go back to America. You have nothing to prove to anyone. We could stay here. I'd leave the FBI . . . get some kind of job in England while you do your doctorate at Cambridge.'

But Stella shook her head. 'No, Lee, that's not what I want,' she said firmly. 'I had lots of reasons for going to Smith in the first place and they haven't gone away. I have to go back, I don't have any choice. It's the only way I'll exorcise him.'

★ ★ ★

When Stella fully regained consciousness, Woods had been downstairs. As the terrifying reality of her situation dawned on her, she found herself fighting a fierce, choking panic.

She repeatedly told herself that she was an expert on psychopaths, she could get inside their minds. She must observe this one, as dispassionately and professionally as she could.

When she heard Woods coming up the stairs she tried to imagine that she was part of an experiment; she must make a mental note of

388

everything that took place as scrupulously as she could. That meant not interfering with the proceedings in any way, if she could possibly help it. It would take every ounce of her courage and strength, strength that was draining away by the second as she endured the physical agony of being tied to the makeshift, splintered crucifix. Her wrists and hands were already numb and dreadful cramps were beginning to spread across her shoulders.

When she spat in Woods's face, she regarded it as a professional lapse and silently reprimanded herself.

Managing to maintain a steady, neutral stare as he tried to bait her was another way for her to keep a tiny element of control. She could tell that her silence was infuriating him, but he seemed determined to break her down with words rather than admitting failure and torturing her to get her to speak to him. He clearly saw himself as her intellectual equal, if not superior. When he started talking about Milton she hoped he'd read out some of the interminable verses from *Paradise Lost*. Anything to buy more time.

Strangely, she hadn't been all that surprised when Lee appeared at the door with his gun drawn. She'd trusted instinctively that he would somehow find her in time.

But the violent events rapidly unfolded, culminating in Woods being shot dead right in front of her — she saw his heart explode out of his chest — triggered the beginning of a swift mental collapse.

She'd just managed to keep it together until

she and Lee were in the ambulance. Then the world beneath her had fallen away and she'd wept helplessly for hours.

It was impossible to remember with any clarity now, but she must have been under heavy sedation in the hospital for at least two weeks. Lee was constantly by her side.

★ ★ ★

'Stella! Lee! What are you doing up there? We're going to miss our flight to Washington! Dinner with the Kennedys waits for no man.'

Dorothy turned to Diana and Jeb, who were standing next to her in the hall of the house on Bancroft Road. 'Honestly, those two have been behaving so strangely today. All whispers and giggles. Diana, do you have any idea what's going on?'

Diana shook her head. 'Not a clue, but if Stella is still behaving like this when she starts at Smith next week, they'll probably suggest she forgets all about her doctorate and goes back to kindergarten. And Lee's not much better. Something must have happened when they were out at lunch today.'

Another burst of laughter floated down from above and then the couple appeared at the top of the stairs. They saw the others staring up at them, and began laughing again.

'What *is* going on with you guys?' Jeb demanded, hands on hips. 'At this rate Jackie's gonna send you straight to the White House rumpus room to play with her kids.'

'We'll have to tell them, honey,' Lee whispered to Stella as they came downstairs hand in hand. 'I know you wanted to keep it a secret until after the dinner tomorrow, but this lot are onto us.'

Stella nodded. The two of them turned to her mother and the Rockfairs. Sylvia had drifted out of the lounge. 'What's going on?' she demanded.

'What's going on,' Lee replied, slipping his arm around Stella's waist and holding her close, 'is that I subjected my chief suspect, Miss Stella Arnold here, to intense interrogation at lunchtime today and would not desist from questioning her until I got the answer I wanted. Which was, I am pleased to report, an unequivocal 'yes'.'

Diana's hand flew to her mouth. 'You don't mean . . . '

Stella nodded happily.

'Oh, but we do.'

Acknowledgements

Novelist Stephen King advises aspiring writers to trust their editor. Indeed he goes further, bluntly stating: 'Your editor is always right.' Living proof of this declaration is my own editor, Suzanne Baboneau. My thanks to her for her unfailing guidance and wisdom, and to my literary agent, Luigi Bonomi, for his endless enthusiasm and advice.

I should also like to thank Rory Kennedy, youngest daughter of Bobby Kennedy who was assassinated months before she was born. I have never met her, but her affectionate and riveting documentary tribute to her parents was a fascinating source of material. The private family footage of the Kennedys at play were powerful influences on the scenes in Martha's Vineyard in Part One of this book.

And finally the Florida Keys, where my wife and I have spent many happy, sunny days. It was great fun to revisit them, if only on these pages.

Other titles published by Ulverscroft:

SOME DAY I'LL FIND YOU

Richard Madeley

Diana Arnold marries the handsome and mysterious James Blackwell in haste, one summer morning in 1940 — and she is still wearing her wedding dress when her new husband is summoned back to base to fly his next, terrifying, mission. Then fate delivers what is the first of its cruel twists: James, that very day, is shot down over northern France. Diana is left a widow, and pregnant with their child. More than ten years later, living in the south of France with her daughter and new husband, Diana is flourishing in the Provencal sunshine — until one morning, when she hears something that makes her blood run cold: the voice of someone who will set out to torment and blackmail her, and from whom there can be only one means of escape . . .

FATHERS & SONS

Richard Madeley

Seven years before the Great War, ten-year-old Geoffrey Madeley was travelling to Liverpool with his family to take the ship to Canada to start a new life. But after their overnight stop on his uncle's farm, Geoffrey woke up to find that his mother, father and siblings had gone. In a heartbreaking betrayal, he'd been left behind. This child was Richard Madeley's grandfather. Shock waves would reverberate through the generations of Madeley boys, each struggling to cope with a tangled emotional inheritance. Starved of paternal affection, Christopher, Geoffrey's son, swore that for his son things would be different. But were they? And what kind of father did Richard become? *Fathers And Sons* is a journey into fatherhood in the most rapidly changing centuries in history.

THE HOMESMAN

Glendon Swarthout

In the American West in the 1850s, pioneer women are struggling with broken hearts and minds as they face bitter hardships. A 'homesman' must be found to escort a handful of these women back east to a sanatorium. Not exactly a job people are lining up for, it falls to Mary Bee Cuddy, an ex-teacher and spinster who is indomitable, resourceful, and 'plain as an old tin pail'. Mary Bee knows she can't make it alone, so she takes along her only available companion: the lowlife claim-jumper George Briggs. Thus begins a trek east against the tide of colonization, Indian attacks, ice storms, loneliness, and the unceasing aggravation of a disparate group of mad women. This is the tale of their journey, and a tribute to the men and women who homesteaded the frontier.

WITH OR WITHOUT YOU

Helen Warner

Martha Lamont has it all: a passionate marriage, two well-adjusted children, a lovely home, and a high-profile job as a showbiz interviewer for a major national newspaper. Her gorgeous husband, Jamie, is happy being a stay-at-home-dad while she pursues her career. But appearances are often deceiving. One day, Martha makes a discovery that rocks the very foundation of her world, and she begins to question everything she thought she wanted. Then, during an interview with a famous actor, Charlie Simmons, Martha finds herself pouring her heart out. And soon their friendship turns into an intense relationship . . . Now, Martha must make the toughest decision of her life. Does she fight to keep what she loves? Or are some betrayals just too big to forgive?

THE ITALIAN WIFE

Kate Furnivall

Italy, 1932: Mussolini's Italy is growing from strength to strength, but at what cost? One bright autumn morning, architect Isabella sits in a café in the vibrant centre of Bellina, when a woman she's never met asks her to watch her young daughter, just for a moment. Reluctantly, Isabella agrees — and then watches in horror as the woman climbs to the top of the town's clock tower and steps over the edge. This tragic encounter draws vivid memories to the surface, forcing Isabella to probe further into the secrets of her own past as she tries to protect the young girl from the authorities. Together with charismatic photographer Roberto Falco, Isabella is about to discover that some secrets run deeper, and are more dangerous, than either of them could possibly have imagined . . .